Caribbean Fire

By
RICK MURCER

PUBLISHED BY:

Murcer Press, LLC

Edited by
Janet Fix, www.thewordverve.com

Interior book design by
Bob Houston eBook Formatting

Caribbean Fire © 2014 Rick Murcer
All rights reserved
www.rickmurcer.com

ISBN: 0692271163

For JC, who loves me and keeps me on the path, eternally.

For Lily. You are a special girl.

For the late, great, Big Max. Thank you for helping me travel this road.

Caribbean Fire

A Novel

By
RICK MURCER

CHAPTER-1

Gazing at the list, his *special* list, he was hard pressed not to appreciate his own effort. It had taken time to compile, more than he would have guessed. Yet, there it was, jumping from his computer monitor like a gaudy Las Vegas billboard.

The list.

Had he done anything of more significance in his life? He believed not.

Shifting in the seat of his car, he moved the laptop away from the reflecting rays of the rising Mexican sun to get a more pointed look at the second name on the list, running his finger ever so gently back and forth. He truly had no need to read it again. He had it memorized. More important than memorizing the names on the list was the time he devoured to understand and observe the habits, and the families, of the proposed major players.

His unintentional mentors would be proud of him.

The exhaustive research to locate the perfect co-stars in his upcoming play had been daunting, but one can rarely evaluate another's motivation or, as the old saying suggests, walk a mile in someone else's shoes. If that were possible, another soul might grasp the full gamut of emotions that coursed through his mind and body. Then again, why speculate on such a thing?

In his line of work, he'd endeavored to be the best. To find ways to accomplish his assignments and goals and become an example. He'd been taught by parents who knew a thing or two about working hard. Added to that, he'd been warned when he took this job to make sure he excelled. An American living in Cozumel had enough problems fitting in without adding "overpaid slacker" to the equation. He'd taken that advice to heart and done well. They both had. The two of them only wanted to live in paradise, raise a family, and live the "exotic-dream" lifestyle. Hard work didn't seem too much to ask in return.

Yet others thought differently.

Clenching his hands together, he felt the heat rise in his face and the thunder boom in his chest. Unquenchable anger and unfathomable frustration bound together to motivate him to take his calling to the next level. The odd thing was, however, that he recognized the taboo emotions for what they were and embraced them anyway. He'd read that people could go through an event that altered one's sense of reality, of right and wrong.

No shit.

Gripping the wheel tighter, he watched the blood trickle to his bare knee. The red blot resembled something he'd seen on a Rorschach test card.

Dead people. I see dead people in this card.

He laughed. Then grew silent.

Perhaps everyone is just one circumstance away from altering whatever moral fiber they once held close. But should beliefs be transformed so easily?

Another dichotomy his world had embraced since . . . since . . . then.

So be it.

The sun rose a bit further and reflected off of the green palms and lush underbrush near the backside of the ruins. It was beautiful, mesmerizing even, and signaled the beginning of the new life he'd chosen.

Now was the time for the birth of that self-realized evolution. He loved how that felt.

Opening the door, he stood outside his vehicle, taking in the fresh ocean air as it mingled with the natural scent of the jungle. He wasn't sure he'd ever felt more alive, except with her.

A philosophical quote suddenly draped his thoughts. Sometimes, they weren't relevant, those random thoughts, but this one, well, it reeked of truth.

You are the master of your own destiny . . .

Indeed he was. From this moment on, that would be true for him. Not like his life before. Not like that at all.

Exhaling, he walked to the ancient rock slab that served as an altar in the year 1300 and stood over the man lying there. His acquaintance was bound and gagged properly. Yet the man seemed to not appreciate the effort expended. The dark, wide-eyed fear in the man's green eyes was apparent. He suspected this man was experiencing what all people did when facing the unknown.

He leaned down. "Do not fear. You are far more than this physical body suggests. We all are."

The man tried to talk, then did his best to free himself. His thrashing only bound him tighter.

Slowly, he reached for the Mayan headdress and carefully placed it on his own head. He then reached into the waistband of the ornate, golden loincloth and withdrew the silver-and-diamond-studded dagger. It dazzled against the sun's rays.

His companion's eyes grew wider.

Staring at the purple and orange horizon, he raised the dagger to the sky and began chanting an ancient ritual prayer, encouraging the gods he had chosen to hear his words and honor his actions. It was the way of the ancestors, he knew that now.

He uttered one more prayer and turned toward his sacrifice.

"It is time. I want you to know that you are performing an irreplaceable task and the gods are appreciative. Your family will be proud as well. You were born for this very purpose."

The man on the altar tried to yell but nothing came out, his eyes turning from fear to anger.

He frowned at his bound guest and felt his own emotion escalate. It would have been easy to give in to the anger, but not now, not this time.

Grabbing the man by the hair, taking in the fragrance of his perspiring body, he bowed closer. "Anger is unbecoming. I should think you'd want to leave this world in a more placid state of mind. It will bode better for you."

With that, he raised the dagger and quickly drew the incredibly sharp edge deeply across the man's ribcage just below his heart, making a seven-inch incision. The blood from the wound spurted once and then began to flow like a lazy river.

Another muffled scream reached his ears. This time, the man's eyes were filled with a different reality. He was pleading to be spared his fate, to live.

But it was no longer *his* life. It now belonged to a higher purpose.

Searching the heavens, he raised his arms toward the cloudless sky again. "I do this for you and beg your blessing."

With one swift move, he reached deep into the gushing wound. The hot blood and the warmth of visceral organs encased his hand as he searched. A moment later, he found what he sought and closed his hand around it, the heat of the object growing ever so intense.

The victim's body jerked as he gasped, seeking a breath that would never come.

He smiled. It was as it should be.

Gripping harder, he pulled with all of his strength and felt the man's heart join with his hand. He guided it through the cavity and stood still, looking at it. So small, yet so vital. Wasn't that the way with all forms of the heart real or imagined?

The feeling of power and elation was life changing. He'd done it. He'd completed his task, as it had been mandated.

Glancing at the man who'd just left this world, he nodded his appreciation. The man's blank, lifeless eyes told him that he hadn't seen the final gesture of gratitude. But there were far more ways to see than with one's eyes.

Perhaps in the next life, he and the man would have a conversation regarding this instant and what the moment had truly meant. He looked forward to that when the appropriate time arrived.

Lifting the crimson heart toward the north, he closed his eyes and reveled in his accomplishment. Not so much in the idea of the sacrifice, but in the *reality* of his change from one life to the next. It had been a requirement for him to continue.

Bringing the organ to his nose, he inhaled. The aroma of blood was overwhelming. Not simply with the coppery fragrance, but with the mystique surrounding life—and death.

Thirty seconds later, he placed the heart into the wide and ageless bronze bowl, reached for the small jar of gasoline he'd set on the opposite side of the altar, and doused the heart with the petrol, the bittersweet fumes finding his nose. He then reached into his waistband and pulled out a book of matches. Without hesitation, he struck one and tossed it onto the heart.

The organ was engulfed in flames instantly. He watched it burn and discovered a sense of poetic justice. His heart had been on fire these last six months, and the sight of flaming flesh helped ease his pain, for now.

Reaching into the other side of the loincloth, he removed another dagger wrapped in a small cloth. This one possessed an ancient emerald handle and was two inches shorter than the other. It had been used hundreds of years prior in ceremonies such as this.

Still watching the burning heart, he ran the blade over his index finger. He barely felt it, his eyes fixated on the last remnants of the once-beating heart.

Finally, he looked down at the blood slowly dripping from his finger, swabbed it with the knife's cloth, and then placed the cloth over the dead man's eyes.

Stepping back, he bowed toward the altar. His sense of elation had dissipated somewhat but would never leave entirely. How could it?

Turning back to his vehicle, he removed the feathered headdress, opened the trunk, and placed it carefully on the left side.

Away from the dark-haired woman with the large, dark eyes.

It wouldn't do to have his sacred dress touched by the less important.

It wouldn't do at all.

He stroked her hair. "Tomorrow, my flower, it will be your turn to appease the gods of right and wrong. I can hardly wait."

He laughed as he closed the trunk, got into the front seat, and drove toward his home.

CHAPTER-2

"Come on Williams, ya need to finish getting your arse packed. I'll hate being alone, but I'm not missing this trip, even for you."

FBI Special Agent Manny Williams glanced up from the bundle in his arms and grinned at Chloe, his wife. He hadn't seen her this excited since she set eyes on their new son five months ago.

"I'm packed. Some of us don't need two suitcases, a carry-on, and a pack mule to haul them."

Smiling that smile that always made his pulse quicken, she walked over to him. She was as beautiful as ever. Her red hair had grown a bit longer, her green eyes had grown a bit brighter, and her curves had grown a bit more pronounced. And her apprehension regarding motherhood had become a distant memory.

Becoming a mother suited her in ways he'd never quite understand.

He'd read that most women feel more complete, more grounded, after giving birth. It seemed their sense of purpose changed and provided a more practical approach to living.

Good God, had it ever. Furthermore, he loved Chloe's take on this new life.

His first child, Jen, had been born to his now-deceased first wife, Louise, almost eighteen years prior, and he'd thought nothing could match that experience. In many ways, he was right. But he suspected that, at age forty, he had learned a thing or two about family and fatherhood—making this child a special gift. Not to mention, what man didn't want a son to carry on after he'd checked out?

Chloe kissed him on the cheek. "Do you have a clue how hot it makes me to see you holdin' Ian like that?"

"Maybe, but you can show me when we get to Cozumel . . . or on the plane. Something about that mile-high club sounds kind of cool," he said, winking.

"Careful, Manny. It could happen, and it might be embarrassing, don't ya know."

Ian laughed, right on cue. The boy's big blue eyes danced, causing Manny's pride to swell as he was reminded how much Ian resembled his old man. A shock of blond hair helped, but Ian's hair also held a red tint resembling his mother's.

"Oh, what do you know?" he asked softly.

Ian laughed again.

Was there anything better than the sound of a baby's laughter?

"Okay, you two. You'd better get going. Your flight takes off in three hours. Wouldn't want you to miss it."

In the living room entranceway, Haley Rose Franson, Chloe's mother, who had been staying with them since she moved from Galway, Ireland, stood shoulder to shoulder with his eighteen-year-old daughter Jen. Both wore their special versions of *get your butt moving* looks. The two of them had become as thick as thieves over the last year. They spoke the same, walked the same, and even spouted the same sense of pleasant sarcasm that he'd learned to appreciate, if not enjoy. If there was such a thing as family in a long-past life, those two could make a case for the theory.

"Yeah, you're probably right," Chloe murmured.

Manny walked over and handed Ian to his daughter. "We'll only be gone five days. Take good care of him."

"We promise not to leave him at the casino when we leave," said Jen, grinning.

"We'd appreciate that." Manny kissed his daughter and son one more time.

Chloe watched his every move. He, in turn, noticed as she shifted her feet then kissed Haley Rose, Jen, and Ian. His wife hesitated, looking at her feet, before she stood beside him. Her excitement for the trip was fading as reality began to set in; she was going to leave her son for five full days.

He took Chloe's hand.

His time as a profiler for the FBI's Behavioral Analysis Unit had honed his natural ability to get into people's minds and motivations, which were both a curse and a blessing. He could feel the conflict raging inside of Chloe at leaving her son for a few days. He felt some of that conflict himself, but he also knew nothing most men experienced in that line would compare to the mysterious maternal instinct women possessed. Nothing.

It had been tough enough for Chloe going back to work part-time as a detective for the Lansing Police Department. Five days away, even in the Caribbean, was a different story.

"We can still cancel, Chloe. He's in great hands with his Nana and big sister, but if you're not ready, I get it."

She gazed at Ian and made eye contact with Jen and then her mother. Haley Rose gave her a subtle nod.

"No, I'm good," she said quietly, determination filtering into her voice. "We've never had a honeymoon, and we both need one. Besides, we can use Skype six or seven times a day to see him, right?"

"He'll be fine. He's as healthy as a horse, and getting about that size. He'll have two of the most protective women on the planet watching over him. Only God could do it better. And, in case you don't recall, girl, I've done this before," said Haley Rose, grinning.

"Yeah. And we promise only to take him clubbing just a couple of times," added Jen, straight-faced.

Chloe's look went momentarily blank, then she laughed out loud.

"Okay, I get it. The healthcare cards are on the microwave, just in case. There's more formula in the pantry if the breast milk runs out, and—"

"Okay. That's it, we got this covered. Get your arses out the door," said Haley Rose, shooing them away with both hands.

After kissing each family member one last time and giving his huge black Lab a quick ear rub, Manny picked up two suitcases. Chloe grabbed the other. He reached for the doorknob, but had to step back. Sophie Lee, his ex-partner at the Lansing Police Department and current member of the BAU, burst through the door. She was followed by Dean Mikus, one of the BAU's forensic experts and Sophie's new husband. Dean looked nervous as he adjusted his purple-paisley driver's cap. Nervous wasn't normal for the bearded CSI.

Sophie, a Lucy Liu lookalike, wore a mischievous grin.

"Hey, Sophie, sorry to be rude, but we're heading to the airport and can't chat," said Manny.

"Damn, Williams. You always think shit is about you? We're here to see my boy—sort of—and then to tell you something."

"Sophie. I don't think—"

"Relax. It'll only take a minute. I'm not leaving until I give Ian a kiss, then I'll be ready to go," she answered with far too much enthusiasm.

"Go where?" asked Manny, his suspicion rising.

Ignoring him, Sophie marched over, swept Ian from Jen's arms, and rained butterfly kisses on his son's face. Manny shook his head and grinned. This woman, who never before harbored a true thought of motherhood, was sure acting like one.

"Okay, boy. Take care of the womenfolk while we're gone." She kissed Ian one more time, handed him back to Jen, and strolled to the door, pulling it open. "Come on, we'll be late."

"Late for what? Where are 'we' going?" asked Manny.

"Damn. For a profiler, you ain't too bright. You *do* need a vacation."

"Answer the question, Lee."

She exhaled. "We're going to Cozumel with you and Chloe. We haven't had a honeymoon either, not that old Dean here hasn't had the time of his life the last few months, but I'm not waiting to get as old as you. So, we got reservations at the same resort. Cheaper than you, by the way. So did Dough Boy and Barb."

"Dough Boy" was Alex Downs, the chunky, balding, bespectacled Senior CSI assigned to the BAU, who doubled as his long-time friend.

"How did you know where we were going? We didn't tell anyone. And I thought Alex was going through testing this week on his new prosthetic hand." Manny tried to decide how he felt about most of the BAU accompanying him and Chloe on a romantic getaway.

"Didn't you know I'm close with the tech department? I got to see a couple of your emails. Buzzy Dancer and I are tighter than white on rice, and besides, women talk," Sophie said.

Manny quickly looked at his wife.

Chloe shrugged. "I didn't really say that much. I was just, you know, sort of excited."

"I'll deal with you later." He turned to Sophie.

She stepped back, but the spark never left her eyes. "Whoa, Williams. I don't want to know about you dealing with Chloe, get me? I mean that's just wrong to talk about your sex life in front of people. For crying out loud, your daughter's standing right there.

"To answer your other question, Josh got Alex's appointment changed. Josh also said he'd stay and hold down the psycho-killer fort, as long as we realize that we're on call. You know, in the event a case pops up. Besides, you know damn well Josh has a backup BAU crew if he needs to put one together fast."

Moving quickly, Manny grabbed Sophie with both arms, lifted his diminutive friend from the floor, and brought her face next to his.

"Let me get this right. You manipulated my wife, busted into my emails, got our boss to change Alex's testing and approve your vacations, talked Alex and his wife into tagging along, and then reserved your honeymoon in the same resort as Chloe and me? And I'm sure, booked the same flight?"

Sophie kissed him on the cheek. "Yep. That covers it. See, you're already getting back that cognitive trance stuff you do. I was glad to help. We're a team, ya know? You can thank me later. But right now, we've really got to get our fannies in motion."

Manny set her down and glanced at Dean, who shrugged, wearing a tiny grin. Chloe, his daughter, and his mother-in-law were grinning in various degrees. Even Ian let loose with another energized coo.

Having the whole crew on the same island wasn't what he'd imagined as a nice quiet time away with his wife, but there weren't many people on the planet with whom he'd rather spend time. Besides, apparently he had no choice.

Know which battles to pick, Williams.

Sophie was gazing at him like a child who'd just submitted a well-thought-out Christmas list for parental review.

Manny sighed. "Okay. You can come with us under one condition. You don't know our room number, got it? If you break that sacred rule, I'll file your missing-person report myself. And I hear the Mexican authorities are very busy these days. You'll never be found."

It was her turn to grab him. "It's a deal. I can live with that." Sophie tilted her head. "Seriously, Manny. Are you mad?"

"No. I don't get mad, I get even."

"I know. Listen, we can get a refund and sit here in this Michigan spring weather and become even more depressed. If that's what you want. No pressure to save us from committing suicide or anything, just saying."

He rolled his eyes. "Come on, let's go. I suppose you've got the FBI SUV loaded, and Alex and Barb are waiting in the driveway, right?"

"Damn. You *are* good. You know, that chicken shit Dough Boy wouldn't come into the house. Dean and I had to do this alone."

"He's a smart man," said Manny.

They hurried out the door, and Manny suddenly felt more at ease. He and vacations hadn't exactly been on friendly terms since the horrifying *Ocean Duchess* cruise three years before. Obviously, two serial killers on the same ship was hardly a typical Caribbean vacation.

He was due for a good one.

After all, what could go wrong on the sleepy little paradise island of Cozumel?

CHAPTER-3

Spinning slowly in his leather chair, Samuel Rozen gazed through the glass of his full-sized bay window. The eastern side of his expansive office possessed a view that most would consider incredible. They'd be correct.

The teal, iridescent Caribbean Ocean worked its way to the beach in slow, rhythmic waves that served not only as scenic eye candy, but as calm for the most despairing of souls.

He appreciated these moments. Nothing soothed his internal conflicts, of which he had many, like the sounds, smells, and pulse of the ocean.

He never really tired of the view. Familiarity might breed contempt, but that wasn't the case for him, at least in the beauty of Cozumel's white sand beaches and, of course, the ocean. Coming here as a young man and then making a way for himself had been a challenge, but like everything else in his life, determination had taken him where he wanted to go.

The island tour excursion business had done well, particularly after he partnered with three different cruise lines to offer his services to the never-ending stream of cruisers who wanted to taste the exotic flavors of Cozumel, if only for a day. For a nominal fee, guests could tour the Mayan ruins, snorkel, scuba dive, ride a Segway, or simply visit beaches like the one outside his window. He'd provided a means to that end. In fact, no one on this island did it better.

Standing, he moved his large frame closer to the window and caught a reflection of his shaved head and tanned face.

"One must look the part too, yes?" he said out loud.

Something else reflected in his peripheral vision: a translucent view of the antique cabinet that displayed his affinity for Mayan culture and artifacts.

The ambiance of Cozumel and successful business opportunities hadn't been the only promises that brought him to the island. Yes, he'd followed a dream, but in the course of that action, he had discovered something else, something far more valuable than all that he possessed. More than he'd aspired to be. More than mere words could describe.

He had found purpose. He wasn't sure about divine interventions or destiny or even how his heritage played into his future. But he was sure of one concept. No single thing, event, or person would get in the way of what was promised to him.

Turning back to his desk, he leaned over and shut down his computer, making sure certain files were password protected, changing each one for a second time today. He would call it a day in this world and begin another when he reached his home.

Glancing at his Rolex, he was a bit surprised to see it was after six. His staff would have been gone for over an hour—except for Rico. His driver and self-proclaimed bodyguard would be waiting for him in the outer office. There was comfort in that. While kidnappings of affluent citizens had slowed, and he had some extra vigilance from the local police, one couldn't be too careful these days.

Lifting his locked briefcase, he stopped to enjoy his personal collection of Mayan jade, gold, and silver again, then continued to the door. As he left his office, he turned to key the lock and was interrupted by a loud thump that echoed from the hallway.

"Rico? Is that you, compadre?"

No reply.

"Rico."

No answer. Frowning, he walked boldly around the hallway corner.

He stopped in his tracks, his mouth dropping open at the scene.

Big Rico was on the floor, blood rushing from his throat, his head resting at an unnatural angle. His friend and protector had been almost decapitated.

He wished that were all. A man wearing face paint and full traditional sacrificial clothing of a Mayan priest was standing over Rico, arms folded, staring directly at him.

Fear had entered his life a time or two, especially given his hobby, yet he'd never felt such an intense skip of his heart and out-of-body sensation.

"Wha-what have you done?" he managed.

The Mayan priest was on him before he could take a step, pinning him to the floor with a strength he didn't believe possible. His struggle against his attacker was rendered completely useless.

The attacker bowed low, his warm breath kneading his face. "What have I done?" he asked. "What have I done? I've simply torn a page from the book of life, as I've learned it. And you have been a teacher, Samuel Rozen. A very good teacher."

In the next instant, Sam felt the moist cloth cover his mouth and nose. A sickening-sweet aroma filled his senses. As his struggle slowed and stopped, it occurred to him as he faded into the comfort of darkness that he recognized his attacker's voice.

CHAPTER-4

The 767 bounced ever so slightly on the tarmac of a Cozumel International Airport runway and settled into a smooth, powerful slowdown. Manny had a clear view of Sophie's alabaster face as she quickly pulled out the white barf bag and snapped it open. Dean was rubbing the back of her neck, trying to help ease her nausea. The low whine that escaped Sophie's lips told him her new husband wasn't having any luck.

He shook his head. They'd hit two pockets of turbulence, both just as the jet had begun its descent. That was all that was required to put Sophie virtually under her seat. The woman simply couldn't catch a break. No wonder she hated to fly. Her motion sickness was bad enough, but invariably, her flights ran into stomach-wrenching air pockets or the turbulence from hell.

Dramamine, for some reason, had little or no effect on Sophie. She'd even tried a couple shots of spiced rum after they'd taken off. That had seemed to help for a while, but reality had the trump card.

"It's not nice to enjoy someone else's misery, Manny," said Chloe, trying to stifle a grin of her own and not quite pulling it off.

"True. I'm not really enjoying her sickness as I am the irony. She can be tough as nails but can't handle a flight on a plane as big as three or four busses. It's fifty-fifty whether she fills that bag or not . . . and I saw that grin, Irish woman."

"I wasn't grinning at her, but at . . . well, ah, your smile. You have that effect on me, don't ya know."

"Nice try, but it was a good answer," he said, kissing her and experiencing a certain awe at the feel of her lips. The jet slowed more, approaching the terminal and the unloading door. His excitement rose. Hot weather, white beaches, pina coladas, and his wife sporting a small pink bikini were going to be hard to beat.

It was going to be a hell of a five days.

He turned Sophie's way again.

She locked eyes with him. "What the hell are you staring at?" she moaned.

"Some things just never grow old."

Sophie put her hand over her mouth, closed her eyes, and then swiped at the perspiration on her forehead. "Yeah? Well, when I can stand without the thought of falling on my dizzy ass and puking all over this damn contraption, we'll see just how old you get to be."

"Why Agent Lee, was that a threat?" he asked, grinning.

"A fact, Williams, a fact."

"I'll watch my back then."

"What about me? Do I have to watch my back?" chided Alex from two seats behind Sophie and Dean.

"I'd need a wide lens for that, Dough Boy. And if you say another word . . ."

"You'll what? Hey, want a fat, greasy bacon burger?"

She started to speak again, stopped, quickly opened the bag, and stuffed half of her face inside. Manny expected that the next moment would find passengers and staff alike groaning at the sound of Sophie's lurching ejection.

It didn't happen. His partner somehow controlled the rising of her gorge. That was probably a good thing for both Alex and him. If she'd purged her stomach, she might have been ready to dole out a little pain. No one wanted a pink throwing star imbedded in a butt cheek.

Fifteen minutes later, Manny, Chloe, Alex, and Barb stood in front of the luggage carousel waiting for their bags to show. Sophie had made her usual run to the women's lounge, while Dean, as faithful as always, waited outside the restroom for her to emerge.

"I know you three go back forever, but that wasn't very nice, ragging on her like that," said Barb, flipping aside her long, platinum blond hair, trying to mask her grin with a compassionate, deplorable tone.

Manny thought it impossible for Barb to climb on Alex's case with any real conviction. She loved him with all of her heart. After twelve years, Manny still wondered exactly how the two of them had ever hooked up.

Alex was shorter than Barb, balding, a bit heavy, and not a partier by any stretch. Barb Downs was almost a prototypical Los Angeles model—tall, piercing blue eyes, and in great shape.

Love is what love is, and these two were poster children for that fact.

"Sophie *needs* me to do that," said Alex. "That's how she knows I care."

"Care, huh?"

"Well, in a loose, brotherly sort of way," he answered, his smirk growing wider.

"And what about you Manny? That was a bit heartless," said Chloe.

"Hey, I get my punches in with her when I can. Don't worry. She has the memory of an elephant. I just hope one of us doesn't end up in the emergency room."

"Good thinking, you jerks, 'cause this ain't over."

Turning, Manny saw Sophie holding hands with Dean. The color had returned to her face, and the *get even* glint in her eye danced like a fine gem.

Yep. Fur was going to fly.

"Wow. What a transformation. You look almost normal," said Manny.

"I've never been normal and don't start with the friendly shit. I'll let you know when that's an option."

Alex saluted. "Yes, ma'am."

Just then the red indicator light began to blink on top of the carousel to announce the arrival of luggage. The wide, black belt began to turn, and Manny felt his excitement rise once again. Picking up the luggage was a sure-fire sign that this vacation was ready to kick in.

Good God, he loved how that felt.

Nine suitcases later, the six friends went through the double doors to board the Caribbean Resort's shuttle bus to their exotic home away from home.

The humid heat and eye-squinting light was both immediate and welcome. Michigan in April possessed no such ambiance.

Cozumel. The Caribbean. The recipe for paradise. They were here, finally.

As they waited for the bus, he noticed three men and three women adorned in full, traditional Mayan dress on the wide sidewalk to his right, stepping in sync to the rhythm of beating drums— an ancient ritual dance perhaps. Bright greens, teals, yellows, and reds covered the dancers from head to toe, making the show a mesmerizing form of entertainment.

Manny had taken the time to do a little research on the Mayan influence in Cozumel, as was his geeky custom, according to Sophie, whenever he traveled.

He was looking forward to seeing firsthand much of what the Mayans had left behind. Providing he could pry any of his friends away from the beach and ocean for more than three minutes.

The Mayan dance group finished in a flourish that prompted scattered applause and the usual passing of the tip hat.

"Good start to this vacation," said Dean, clapping his hands. "This is what I'm talking about."

The group moved farther down the outside of the terminal and began their show once again as the resort's green and blue diesel bus arrived.

"Well, this resort is what I'm talking about," answered Sophie, kissing Dean like she meant it.

"Yeah, that works too," he answered.

"Damn, get a room," said Alex, shaking his head.

The driver emerged from the bus and began loading the suitcases. His and Chloe's bags were last. Manny tipped the driver and then walked around the bus to the join the others. He stopped. He raised his head and listened. He stretched his hands toward the sky, then ran his right one through his hair.

After a few more seconds, he searched his cluttered mind—the mind that was always in full work-mode. He did his best to turn the switch to off. It worked. He felt relaxed, almost. A true miracle for any workaholic, let alone an FBI profiler.

There were no open cases. No dead bodies to examine. No people murdered in such a way as to add to his already-full dance card of nightmare material. No bizarre crime scenes to process or psycho-ass killer to profile. No threat to him, his family, or to his friends, or to his precarious sanity.

Could it be true? There was simply nothing for the Guardian of the Universe—his daughter's nickname for him—to contemplate? No single thing?

Gratitude is one of those overlooked states of mind, but not for Manny. Not this time.

Reaching for the amber sunglasses in the pocket of his red-flowered shirt, he climbed in the bus behind Chloe, taking her hand.

She smiled and squeezed. He returned her gesture.

A hell of a week indeed.

CHAPTER-5

"Come on, Harry, I want to be the first one to that part of the ruins. You're slower than that fat lady we just passed. That old, fat lady, Harry. Move it out, or I'm going to leave your skinny behind in my dust."

Harry Sleep looked at his wife Gloria and shook his balding head.

What in God's name did she think they were? Young? He just celebrated his seventy-fifth birthday on the cruise ship last night, and today, after a few adult beverages and listening to his wife bitch about how tight the slots were in the casino, he was feeling most of those years. He simply didn't understand where the woman got her energy. She was a few pounds overweight and sagging in all of the wrong places, but she moved her seventy-plus body just fine. Especially when she was as excited as she was to do this excursion to San Gervasio. She was obsessed with seeing the place where the Mayans supposedly performed human sacrifices.

He wondered if she was thinking of regaining some of her youth by stretching *him* out on one of those altars and giving his heart to that Mayan goddess.

He smiled. Not that bad of an idea, if it worked.

"I'm coming you old bat. These damn knees don't work so good, you know that. And we should be waiting for the guide. They told us not to wander off."

"Don't care about no guide. I paid my money, and I can go wherever I want. And I hear that all of the time from you. I got arthritis too, you old coot, and I ain't dragging myself as bad as you. And by the God who made us, I told you to stop drinking last night. You can't handle it anymore. It makes you pee too much, and those farts are worse than anything coming from the damn dog. I can still smell 'em."

Waving his boney hand, he looked down, took another unsteady step on the archaic, uneven stone path leading to the back of the site, and stopped in frustration.

"Just go, Gloria. I'll get there, and be careful of them green and blue iguanas. Some get as big as lions and can eat you whole, I hear."

His wife of fifty years stopped and bent his way, pulling at her straw sun hat, an unsure look on her round face.

She was still a bit of looker, if you asked him. Those green eyes looked the same as when they got married. Her hair was still pretty much auburn, with a little help from Lady Clairol, but it worked for her. If she'd only stop talking.

"Are you messing with me, Harrison Markus Sleep? As big as lions?"

"Just telling you what I read. Maybe they was talking about those Komodo dragon lizards. I get mixed up sometimes."

"Look over there," he said, pointing about fifty feet toward the lush jungle.

A three-foot iguana stood like a statue, the morning sun reflecting from its teal skin.

She looked then put her hands on her hips, and gave him that infamous evil eye of hers. "Big as a lion? Hell, we got cats bigger than that in Georgia."

"Told you I might be wrong about that, but—"

"Never mind. You're just losing it, Harry. I'm going back there. It's about a quarter mile on that dirt trail over there, according to the map. See you when you get there."

With that, Gloria hurried, if one could call her lopsided gait hurrying, and then vanished around the thick line of palm and cebia trees.

He had to give her credit for determination, if nothing else.

Taking his time, Harry glanced down frequently to ensure a protruding stone or a hidden crack didn't send him on his ass, or worse, his hip. Everyone his age knew how things could go if you broke a hip.

Reaching the sandy, level-footed trail, he picked up the pace. He just might catch her before she stole some rock or remnant of a hand print that would send them both deep into the Mexican jail system. Sometimes, she didn't think the rules pertained to her, and God knew he was getting too old to have a boyfriend. A foreigner at that.

A few more steps and Harry felt like he was in top gear. He'd catch her in no time. He took another deep breath, walking faster.

The air was full of that undefinable island aroma. A mixture of ocean and jungle flowers that even an old geezer like himself could still smell. One more thing to help define the Caribbean travel life Gloria, and he supposed himself, was hooked on. He had to admit, once they got on the ship, this cruising thing was a pretty good way to go. It was a great way to see places like th—.

"AHHHHHHHH."

The blood-curdling scream stopped him in his tracks. He clutched his chest as his heart skipped a beat.

In the next moment, his feet began to move at a pace he thought he'd abandoned years ago. Realization that the scream belonged to his wife caused Harry to forget any physical ailment. Pure adrenaline coursed through his body at the thought of something happening to her. She was an old biddy from time to time, but she was *his* old biddy.

A second scream, closer than the first, told him he was almost there. He reached the end of the tree line, banked right, and saw her some thirty yards ahead. Gloria was standing in front of an old, uneven stone structure staring down at what looked like an archaic elevated platform with steps leading from two sides. He recognized it from some of the pictures he'd seen online. It was the altar where the Mayan priests had supposedly performed their religious human sacrifices.

He slowed down, shaking his head, breathing harder than his doctor would approve. She must have had a close encounter with an iguana or some other critter.

"Damn Gloria. You 'bout gave me a heart attack. I should leave you—"

If his wife had heard him, she gave no indication. She was still staring at that particular section of the ruins, mumbling. He got a few feet closer and heard what she was saying.

". . . help us, Jesus. Help us, Jesus," she repeated softly.

His uneasiness came back.

"What is wrong with you, woman?"

She raised her arm and pointed.

Harry glanced at whatever was mesmerizing his wife.

He wished he hadn't.

The body of the man was stretched out the full length of the jagged altar—his heart obviously torn from his chest. But that wasn't all.

Harry swallowed hard. He'd been in 'Nam and wasn't squeamish by nature. But this wasn't the sixties, and he wasn't in some dumbass Asian war that had gone too far.

Several sections of the man's flesh had been torn away by sharp teeth, obviously feasted upon by the local scavengers, leaving pale bone and graying muscle on display. The one eye he still possessed had turned a pale blue, but nevertheless seemed to beg Harry and Gloria for help. Worst of all was the atrocious idea of what terrible things one human was capable of doing to another.

Grasping his wife's hand, Harry Sleep began to cry.

CHAPTER-6

Behavioral Analysis Unit Supervisor Josh Corner watched as his last, and best, candidate exited his office, her limp more noticeable than when she'd entered. He supposed that sitting for long periods might cause her injury to freeze or stiffen up. At the age of thirty-two and in good shape, it had to be an injury. At least that was his best guess. He was pushing thirty-seven, and his bones were creaking just a bit more than a few years ago, but he could still move without a limp. Manny would be proud of his powers of deduction.

Josh opened Belle Simmons's file again. She had been born and raised on the rough side of Columbus, Ohio, attended the University of Michigan on a full academic scholarship, graduated with honors, then received her master's in abnormal psychology and a doctorate in forensic biology at Michigan State University. She'd worked in the Metropolitan Police Department in Washington, DC, for five years and had begun to build two reputations: one as a brilliant investigator, the other as quirky. Both worked for him.

First she had worked in the crime scene investigative unit, then as a detective specializing in biological and psychological profiling involving special crimes. Her insight, according to her two supervisors, was instrumental in solving far above the normal percentage of cases.

Her answer to his last question was still bounding around in his mind as he closed her file.

"Miss Simmons," he'd said.

"Call me Belle, Agent Corner," she'd answered, grinning.

"Okay, Belle it is. What makes you the best fit for this job?"

Belle had stared at him, tilted her head, and then entertained a slow smile. Her actions somewhat reminded him of Manny when he was sorting things out. Another plus.

"Something I learned growing up as a young black girl in the less affluent side of Columbus was to assess a situation as quickly as possible. More than once, my well-being, and perhaps my life, depended on learning and applying that skill. Let me use that learned ability here. The BAU doesn't need another profiler like Manny Williams. There aren't many out there like him anyway."

She'd leaned over his desk, her dark eyes sparkling. It was impossible not to see Whitney Houston in that expression.

"What the BAU *does* need is someone to complement him and the rest of the staff. I've read the bios and researched Sophie Lee, Alex Downs, Dean Mikus, Manny—as if anyone in the business needed a refresher course regarding what he's about—and you. You all have your strengths and weaknesses, as do I, but the thing is, if you allow it, I can help make your group a better team. A stronger entity. I've been places, literally and figuratively, that you all haven't. Besides those facts, I'm a great shot, adore old Motown music, love staying up until all hours of the night, and am a practicing gourmet cook."

As she spoke, Josh heard the words, but he also heard something deeper—a genuine desire to participate, contribute, and learn. Honesty and humility with a dash of confidence was an impressive combination.

"Great answer," had been his response.

"I know." Belle had grinned, confident.

It had been all he could do to not smile or laugh out loud. The woman was better than good at reading people.

"I'll be in touch."

"I can't wait."

Then she'd left.

Sipping his second cup of coffee, he leaned back in his leather chair. "She just might be what the doctor ordered," he said under his breath.

Adding a new BAU member to replace Chloe Williams had been a tough sell, but the new assistant director, Beth Watson, saw the value in adding to the team. Josh was thankful she'd come around. Budgets were still tight, but she had made it happen.

He told Manny about his plans to add another profiler, and he'd shared it with the group—they all thought it was a great idea. More input meant faster crime-solving. No ego about infringing on someone's space or upsetting the chemistry of the current team. Just *yeah, it will be good for everyone.* Belle was right. Men like Manny were few and far between. Not just the profiler that bordered on Sherlock Holmes-esque from time to time, but who he was on the inside. He continued to teach Josh about life, and Josh was pretty sure Manny knew it.

Leaving his coffee on the desk, Josh put on his dark-blue suit jacket and headed toward the personnel department on the fifth floor. He thought about the perfect time to call Belle. Maybe today, maybe tomorrow. He hit the elevator button, shaking his head. Giving Belle one more day to think he was still trying to make the right decision was akin to attempting to fool Manny. She *knew* she was the one. So did Josh.

Having a full, six-member crew for the BAU would be a welcome draw of resources. It was like being back in the saddle again.

Chalk one up for his team, and him.

One hour later, Josh pushed through his office door. Under his arm was a full background check and report confirming his decision regarding Annabelle Sasha Simmons. Nothing in her personal or professional life could be much better in terms of keeping her life clean and uncluttered. Hell, her credit report was better than almost any he'd reviewed. She did purchase a ton of books for her Amazon Kindle, but excessive reading wasn't a flaw. If so, he would have fired Manny and Dean long ago.

The wisp of nostalgia made an unexpected prod as he sat at his desk and glanced at the blinking message button on his landline. He used to read fifty books a year. He couldn't remember the last time he'd sat down with a good thriller or something supernatural and got lost in it. Josh promised himself that he'd indulge soon. Maybe even tonight, after the boys and his very pregnant wife were down for the count.

A glass of wine, the dog at his feet, and a good book might make the rest of the world go away for a while.

"This could be really good, Corner," he said out loud.

A brief ripple of excitement coursed through his body as possibility evolved into sure-fire intent. He'd use his tablet, download the proper app, and get to it right after he tucked in the boys.

Taking a pen out of his pocket, he hit the play button on his phone. Cell phones were wonderful, but after a couple of breaches in the security system, the Bureau had decided to reduce the availability of cell phone numbers to only a few organizations outside of the FBI. The vast majority of law enforcement agencies around the country and the rest of the world were on a need-to-know basis. They were still using the old-fashioned way to contact the FBI: an answering machine.

"Special Agent Corner. My name is Investigator Eduardo Munoz. I work for the Mexican Ministerial Federal Police."

Josh's ears perked up as the investigator's near-perfect English greeting demanded his attention.

The FBI usually only received calls from Mexico's Federal Police when their problem had to do with serious drug cartel issues spilling over into the U.S.

"This has nothing to do with the usual cartel inquiries. Please bear with me as I explain. I received a call from the Cozumel director of police. They have . . . an issue, and I'm hoping your BAU can offer some insight. Please return my call at the number listed on your machine. Thank you."

Glancing at the phone's blue digital display, Josh wrote down the number, stopped the next message, and made the call.

After one ring, Investigator Munoz picked up. "Thank you for returning my call, Special Agent Corner."

"No problem. I don't get calls every day from other countries asking for help, especially Mexico. What can I do for you?"

"I like it that you get directly to the point, señor. My longtime friend is director of police in Cozumel. Do you know of Cozumel?"

"I know that it's a great vacation spot, and it beats the hell out of most of the U.S. during the winter months. But I've not been there."

"You're right on the weather, and the beaches are wonderful. I spent six years in Chicago getting my education and training. I've experienced the difference. I prefer the warmth of Mexico."

"I understand that," said Josh.

Munoz continued. "Cozumel is a sleepy island that deals mostly with tourists and cruise ships. Our crimes are mostly pickpockets, a few local muggings. Too much tequila and some traffic issues are part of it. And while the cartels are moving north, the Yucatan has not had to deal with them much."

Munoz grew silent, and Josh heard him exhale. "The reason I'm calling is that we now have three unusual murders in the span of three days. We also have three other local citizens missing. We've done our work and are sure this spree killing has nothing to do with drug trafficking or territories, at least to this point."

"Are you sure?" asked Josh.

"Yes. We have grown very accustomed to those crime scenes. These killings are not in that manner. In fact, I'd say they are, in many ways, more disturbing."

Switching the phone to his left hand, Josh pulled a pen out of his shirt and began to write. He didn't care for where this conversation was going, but curiosity forced him to ask the next question.

"I understand how tied up the Federal Police are with cartel and drug issues, but why us? Certainly you have profilers and investigators that can step in and give a hand."

"I'm it, Agent Corner. I'm all our government saw fit to dispatch to Cozumel. You're right. Mexico—as does your country, unfortunately—has its share of angry young men who are prone to spree-killing and mass-murder tendencies. Not counting any developing serial killers we don't yet know about."

Munoz released a breath. "As of this moment, we have six such crimes. Four in Mexico City alone. Mexico has one hundred twenty million people, Agent Corner, and we simply don't have enough investigators to handle them all. Twenty-one million in Mexico City's area alone. You can guess where our resources are sent."

"I can. What is it you would like us to do?" asked Josh, poised to write.

"I would like help with profiling this killer. I have my own ideas. But someone like your staff member, Agent Williams, would be of great value."

"And you just happen to know that he's on Cozumel at this very moment, yes?" said Josh.

"It is true. We check all foreign visitors when we begin our investigations. It is a routine procedure that you know very well. Imagine my surprise when I saw his name on our list of visitors."

"He's on his honeymoon, Mister Munoz. I can't ask him to do this, especially given his workaholic inclinations. He won't be able to stop with just a profile."

"I understand. All we require is his input. Then we'll leave him to his vacation. You have my word."

Josh let the last sentence hang in the air. Munoz's word didn't concern him. Josh had promised Chloe that the world could get by without the Guardian of the Universe for a few days. In fact, he'd given the whole BAU a chance to get away, and now this?

Munoz interrupted his thoughts. "Agent. I feel you wrestling with this decision, and I respect that. But please consider that two or three hours of Agent Williams's time may save lives. We will make sure his stay is unmolested and without concern after this. I believe it a fair trade. After all, is that not the reason we're in the profession of police work?"

Releasing a sigh of his own, Josh found it difficult to disagree with his Mexican counterpart. He knew he'd have to give Manny the choice. If his friend found out that someone needed help stopping a killer, no matter the circumstance, and Josh hadn't told him . . . well, talk about a shit list. Besides, Manny had taught him well. Living was a gift. Their fight was against those who steal that gift. Even if it got in the way of the personal life they enjoyed so little.

Josh understood that.

"I'll send him a text with your number. It'll be his call entirely."

"That is all I can ask, and thank you, Agent Corner."

Hanging up the phone, Josh shook his head. He might as well call and have his gravestone prepared. Chloe was going to put him in the ground. Or make him wish he were dead.

He'd do what he said, but he'd wait until the morning. The least he could do was give Manny and Chloe a night before he sent him Munoz's info. The morning would simply have to be soon enough.

Glancing down at his still blinking phone, he realized that he hadn't checked the other message.

Josh pushed the message button, and then stopped it, struck with an idea he seldom entertained. He was going to go home early.

One insane situation for the day sufficed. He had to finish getting Belle Simmons on board, and that would remain his priority. But he could make that call to her while leaving the building. God knew he had about a billion vacation days to take. Today was as good as any.

The thought of spending the rest of the day with his wife and boys and getting started early on a good book had taken over. He was now on a mission.

One more glance at the blinking light on his phone told him he was right.

Impetuous wasn't really in his makeup, but it would be today.

"Tomorrow is another day," he whispered and stood and left his office, taking the note with Munoz's information with him.

CHAPTER-7

After spending twenty minutes in the resort's large van, the driver's ability to successfully negotiate San Miguel's traffic brought into question more than once, Manny found himself in the unique lobby of the Casa Palms Beach Resort.

The design was quiet yet alive with Caribbean and Mexican culture. The full-wall mural on the south side of the lobby depicted the orange sun setting over the teal Caribbean waters, shadowed by a sailboat heading directly into the larger-than-life orb. The mural was not only well done but gave a sense of sailing off into the peaceful embrace of the horizon.

He ran his hand through his hair and did his best to take the symbolism to heart. He felt himself relax a bit more.

Chloe clasped his hand.

"Penny for your thoughts?"

"Sure. I'm pretty cheap."

"And easy," said Chloe, smiling.

"That too," he said, mirroring her grin.

"I'm just trying to get into all of this. I sometimes forget just how perpetually wound up this life we lead can become. I'm reminding myself to relax and kick out the junk at least for a few days."

"I'll see what I can do to help. I think the first thing we should do, after the other four get back from scouting out the pool, is get a strong pina colada, put on our bathing suits, and get a wee bit sunburned," said Chloe.

"The first thing?" he asked, winking.

"Oh, yeah . . . well the second thing then," she giggled.

"That sounds great. And you've had that whole pool thing planned, right?"

"I have. We just need to get this luggage to the room, and I need to make a call to Mum."

Manny looked at his wife. "You mean when *we* make the call, right?"

"Yeah, whatever. I just have to make sure he ate and—"

Chloe, and the rest of the guests, were interrupted by the rising sounds of a distraught woman at the far end of the marble counter. *Distraught* didn't cover it actually.

More like *terrified*.

The fiftyish lady in the red-and-blue-flowered dress shifted her weight and removed her wide-brimmed hat, releasing her long, brown hair. She reached out to grasp the arm of the thin clerk.

"You don't understand. He would *never* be gone this long without letting me know where he is, never."

Her accent indicated she was English. Her articulation indicated she was probably well educated.

"Missus Rathburn. I'm terribly sorry that you can't locate your husband. But we have searched the property, and he is not where we can locate him," answered the clerk, trying to maintain a professional air.

She wasn't making it easy, and her tears were adding more pressure.

"Pedro. You said your security people didn't see him leave. That means he's here somewhere. Right? I demand that you look again. He may have fallen or God knows what."

Pedro grew more nervous. "Please come to the office. We can discuss what to do there, Missus Rathburn."

Her voice rose higher. "I don't want to come back to your bloody office. I want you to call the authorities and keep looking for my Aaron. We've been coming here for over twenty years. You owe me that much, Pedro."

Manny sighed. So much for taking the relaxing to the next level.

Leaving the lobby and going up to their fourth-floor room was the smart thing to do. This wasn't his problem. Her husband was probably sitting on some secluded section of the beach, right?

That sounded fine, yet his instinct told him that wasn't true.

Releasing a breath, he looked at the ceiling fan. For the love of God, he was on vacation.

But Manny's whole being ran on helping people who couldn't solve issues on their own. Studying her actions, his empathy had kicked up a notch. He knew he'd want some help if he were in that same situation and who better than he and his crew to offer that aid?

He glanced at Chloe. She released his hand and sighed. "Ya just can't help it, can ya?" she whispered.

There was no anger in her voice. Only understanding. She got it. She got *him*.

He kissed her full on the lips then walked over to the counter.

"Excuse me. Maybe I can help."

The woman turned toward Manny, and his heart broke. His life's work had consisted of reading people in all states of flux and circumstances. Some were calm, some were extremely emotional, but in every case, as he'd relayed to Sophie more than once, a person's eyes will unveil more in a few seconds than their tongue could in hours.

This woman loved her husband. He was almost as important to her as air to life. He guessed they'd been together for a time and probably had no children. The possibility of losing him was only rivaled by the horrifying concept of being without her best friend, alone, for the rest of her life. Either all that was true or she was the best actress on the island. He didn't think she'd taken any acting lessons.

She had no idea where he was. If something seriously had happened to him, she wouldn't be a suspect. Their bond seemed far too strong for that.

"We can handle this, *senor*," answered Pedro with a tight smile. "I'm—"

"No! You can't handle this, Pedro. He should be on this bloody resort somewhere." Mrs. Rathburn turned back to Manny. "Who are you, and how in heaven can you help?"

He stuck out his hand. "I'm Manny Williams, and I'm a special agent for the FBI. I have some experience in locating missing folks and the like."

"FBI?" she asked, her eyes filling with tears again.

"Yes. I'm here on a short vacation. Listen. I'm sure your husband is fine."

"You don't know that. This is not like him. I'm . . . I'm scared."

He took her hand and she let him. "Come sit with me over at those chairs, and tell me what's going on, okay?" he urged softly.

Without another word, and with a grateful nod from Pedro, Manny led her over to two chairs, and they sat down across from each other. As they did, Manny noticed a slight man with sunglasses and a bright yellow and green shirt watching both of them intently.

The man, who looked as if he could be a local, saw that Manny had noticed him, quickly turned away, and headed down the hallway toward the pool. The same hallway Sophie, Dean, Alex, and Barb would be walking to get back to the lobby.

Filing what he'd seen away for later consideration, he turned his full attention to Mrs. Rathburn.

"Do you want some water or tea?" he asked.

She shook her head, her demeanor still distraught, but she seemed better. "No, thank you."

"Okay. Again, my name is Manny. I didn't catch yours."

"Oh. I apologize. I'm in such a state. My name in Penelope, but call me Penny, please."

"Penny it is. Penny, I want you to take a deep breath and tell me why you're concerned, and when you first believed something was wrong."

The lobby began to return to normal activity while Chloe and the others, who'd made it to the lobby, stood close enough to hear his conversation, but not too close. Nothing like having trained FBI agents in your inner circle.

He caught a glimpse of Sophie's face and noticed her wink. Times like this, he thought she knew him better than anyone else on the planet. Hell, she probably did.

"Aaron always goes for an early morning jog. Except this morning he said he was taking a day off and wanted to go down and walk the beach. He told me he'd be back to take me to brunch. That was five hours ago, Mister Williams. He's NEVER done that before. Do you understand?"

Manny did. Once again, he was captured by the complete emotional attachment she had for her husband. Soul mates was an overused phrase in his mind, yet she seemed to have found hers.

"So that was around ten. When did you get the hotel's staff involved?"

Reaching up to whisk a stray tear away, Penny leaned toward Manny. "I . . . I called Pedro's office about noon. He should have been back far before then. No one's seen him since."

"Did you ask the staff to review any security cameras they might have on the beach or property lines?"

She nodded. "I didn't think of that. But Pedro mentioned that the security people had reviewed the video and didn't see him anywhere in the area he said he was going."

"How about a car? Did you and Aaron rent a car?"

"Why, yes, we did. He likes to have his own transportation. He sometimes embarks on little treasure hunting trips to the shops on the island. He likes unusual souvenirs. I hardly ever go with him, however. I'd rather read a good book at the beach or the pool."

"What kind of souvenirs?"

Penny stared at Manny, her impatience spiking higher, as she looped her hair behind her ear. "Please don't take this the odd way, Mister Williams, but what does that have to do with anything?"

"Probably nothing. I only want to get an idea of what your husband is like. It helps me get a mental picture of where his priorities and actions could take him."

The dubious look stayed a few more moments. She then raised her eyebrows and clasped her hands together. "You're the expert, I suppose. Aaron collects figures of jaguars and black panthers. We have two cats and a dog in our home, and he's much more of a cat person than me. He has a sort of fixation with jaguars. He says collecting the figurines reminds him of his babies."

"I see. I get that. I'm a big dog man myself."

Manny reached out and touched her arm; she seemed to unwind more. He'd learned to never underestimate the touch of another human when folks are distraught. It could force people to realize that they weren't alone, even though their perceptions could lead them down that road.

"I'm sorry, Penny, but I have to ask. Did you and Aaron have an argument or some tiff?"

"No. We did not. We seldom disagree on things, let alone argue about them. No, Mister Williams, that is not how Aaron and I operate our relationship. We believe life simply too short to engage in that kind of thing."

"Great. And that's an admirable trait. Has he been under any stress lately? Job? Family?"

She exhaled. "Yes. We recently lost a close family member. It was quite devastating. I believe the worst is over, and he's seemed to be back to normal the last month or so."

"That can be tough. My condolences."

"Thank you, Agent."

"Okay. I have one more question. Did you see if the car was still parked where he left it?"

"I didn't. But one of the security team said it was still on the property."

"Good enough. Now, I need you to do something for me, okay?"

She tilted her head and actually gave him a quick smile. "Thank you for helping, Mister Williams. I finally have the mind that something will be done to locate my Aaron. So of course. What is it?"

"I'd like you to go down to the beach and look around. Take your time and go over every inch of where Aaron said he was going, okay?" Manny asked softly.

She raised her hands in protest. "I've been there twice. I don't see the point."

More of that insistent impatience rising to the top. He could see she was struggling to control it and doing a pretty good job, considering her state of mind.

"You were upset and worried about Aaron. You were looking but not really seeing. Does that make sense?"

Penny stared at her hands for a few seconds. "When you say it that way, it does make sense."

Her bright, dark eyes sought his. "If I might ask, Mister Williams, what will you be doing whilst I go back to the beach?"

He gave her his best reassuring smile. "I'm going to talk to Pedro and the head of security and give them a couple of ideas of where to search."

Penny's eyes grew larger. "Search? So you believe he's missing?"

Quickly shaking his head, Manny continued to smile. "Absolutely not. My guess is that your husband is sitting in a quiet little place, drinking tea, and relaxing in this incredible sunshine. People are sometimes prone, in environments like Cozumel, to reflect on life and want to be alone. We just have to find out where that is."

"Do you really believe that? You are right. He can be a deep thinker."

"I do."

Manny motioned for Pedro, who'd been leaning on one of the lobby's pillars.

"Pedro will send one of his folks out with you, and you can search together. Two sets of eyes are better."

He stood, and she followed suit. Then she stepped over to him and threw her arms around his neck.

"Thank you, Mister Williams. I feel bloody better about finding him."

"You're welcome. I look forward to meeting your husband."

"As do I . . . introducing him to you," she answered softly.

With that, she turned away from Manny and joined a female security guard, and they headed toward the pool door and the property's beach.

Pedro, accompanied by another man, a larger local with a shaved head and piercing, brown eyes accenting his grey uniform, stepped to him.

"Thank you for helping to calm her down, Mister Williams. I'm sure her husband will show up shortly. This is Ramon Torres, our head of security." Manny shook hands with both of them as he sensed Sophie and the others gather behind him.

"Glad to help. Listen. I think that Aaron Rathburn never made it to the beach."

Torres nodded. "I think that is right."

His accent was heavy, but he spoke clear English.

"Having said that, I'd like to see your parking lot's security video from this morning, if you don't mind."

"Why?" asked Pedro.

"Just a hunch."

Just then, the bellhop appeared from around the corner near the elevators, the wheels of his cart squeaking as he approached.

Manny turned to Chloe. "We need to help this woman. I'll be up in fifteen minutes. I promise."

"Of course you will." She kissed him again. "If it's sixteen, it'll be a cold night in paradise, don't you know."

Leaning closer, he whispered in her ear. "I love you, and this will be the best five nights of your life."

"It better be."

He turned toward Torres and felt Sophie approach on his left.

"I'm going with you. Dean will get us settled in. I'm going to make sure you get this done and then lecture your ass on the fine art of vacationing. Got it, Williams?"

"I do. And thanks."

"You two have at it. I'm heading to the beach," said Alex.

"We'll be there shortly," said Manny.

Five minutes later, they were sitting at the security monitors in the back office. The odor of stale smoke and fresh coffee reminded Manny of how things were when he first broke into law enforcement. The smoke was gone, but coffee seemed to be the life force of every cop on the planet.

Torres sat down and hit a button and the first monitor came to life. The videos were in color, even though the feed was grainy.

"So, did you actually go through all of the footage or just check to see if the vehicle was still in the lot?" asked Manny.

The security chief looked down at his hands and back to Manny.

"We did not search the video. We didn't think it necessary. I sent one of my people to verify that the car was still there."

Fighting the urge to grab him by the shirt, Manny turned to Sophie and gave her a quick glance: *what the hell is wrong with these people?* Obviously, the hotel's security staff wasn't taking this very seriously. He thought that could be a mistake.

"Mister Torres, I'd like to see the footage from ten this morning until an hour ago. Can you get that quickly?"

Torres's face reflected his almost indignant attitude. He heaved a deep sigh.

"Yes, I can. Our technology allows it. But I still think it unnecessary."

"Noted. Please humor us, okay?"

Torres sat down at one of the monitor stations and hammered the keyboard for a few seconds. The monitor came to life, showing three cars near a line of palm trees on the west side of the parking lot.

"Mister Rathburn rented the white Lexus on the end of that row," said Torres.

He pointed to the lower left corner of the screen. "At forty minutes after eight this morning, the car was sitting in that spot near the tree line. Our guests like to park there to keep their vehicles out of the sun."

He hit another button, and the images raced ahead. He stopped fast-forwarding as the time stamp changed to twelve thirty.

The white Lexus suddenly reappeared as the video eased to a complete stop.

"As you can see, *senor*, the automobile is still there."

Manny leaned forward and then quickly glanced at Sophie.

"Do you see that?"

"See what? The car? Of course I see the damn—"

With her index finger, she reached out and touched the screen.

"Shit, Manny," she said.

"What is wrong?" asked Torres, his voice rising higher.

Exhaling, Manny ran his fingers through his hair. "See those trees? The car is now in a different position since this morning . . . you can tell by looking at the trees. The Lexus was moved."

CHAPTER-8

He touched her picture and smiled. His tears had stopped haunting him, at least for the time being. His composure could be a sign—maybe he was getting used to the idea that she was no longer his, even though he still found it hard to believe. Giving up one's anchor isn't easy.

When she had been in his life, she offered tremendous security to him. She accepted him for what he was and where he was during that time in his life. Her eyes were gentle and her caress, tender. Her words were like a breath of life. Never angry, always understanding. She'd truly loved him, hadn't she?

Love was a word thrown around far too frequently without the deep reservoir of meaning it truly held. Love wasn't about the physical, although the expression of intimacy between them had been significant. She had taught him love was about giving oneself totally to another. To consider one's needs and wellbeing far above your own was an art long forgotten by most. Not by her. She'd mastered that part of their relationship and had taught him in the wake of her actions.

But no more. She'd been away from him for six months, and his life wasn't the same.

It wouldn't be again, he suspected.

He'd called her cell phone often, but all he heard was her voicemail message. She did not return one call. He supposed he knew that she wouldn't, but hope and faith had played many for fools over the years. He was simply another in that lineage.

At least he got to hear her voice when he called.

Gently, he placed the picture face down in the seat of his vehicle and climbed out.

The SUV was still parked in his large garage, away from any potential eyes. He moved to the back, pushed the button under the handle, and watched the large tailgate rise.

Staring in the back, he tilted his head and frowned as realization pounded at the door of his sanity. This would be the last one. The last step toward reconciliation. Whatever came next, he'd welcome with open arms.

His task would be finished, his offering complete. Then maybe, just maybe, the peace he sought would arrive with the fanfare he desperately coveted.

Hope and faith.

Reaching to close the door, he hesitated, and then stretched out his hand, stroking the man's head.

"Do not worry, my friend. Tonight, when the moon is full, you will give your all to right the wrongs that plague this world. Your noble sacrifice will be an experience that you will take into the next life, as the Great Priestess has said."

The man's eyes were half open, perspiration teasing his forehead and upper lip. He mumbled something through the red bandana covering his mouth.

Reaching into his pocket, he pulled out the syringe and pulled off the needle cover.

"Sleep now. Tonight will be amazing."

After the injection, he closed the door and headed toward the garage door leading to the house.

Indeed, tonight he would finish what he started. Let the gods see his earnest.

He smiled as he walked into the afternoon sunshine.

"May evil fear what comes for them," he whispered.

CHAPTER-9

Torres swore in Spanish and then rewound the video to 9:50 a.m.

Manny and Sophie moved closer to the screen, Manny standing directly over Torres's shoulder. Before he gave his own frustration another thought, he spun Torres's chair in his direction.

He understood he was on vacation, and he understood that in the security world and in law enforcement in general, you usually got what you paid for, but to ignore a woman in that much duress was just poor work. It pissed him off far more than it should have.

"Let me get this right, you didn't go back and review every inch of the video before you talked with her and Pedro? I actually sort of get that for the first hour or so he was missing, if you believed this was nothing too serious. And I can see how you wouldn't have noticed the car being in a different spot. But what the hell were you thinking when he didn't show after the first two hours? Never mind, don't answer that. Anything you say will just sound weak-ass and idiotic."

"Manny, take it easy," said Sophie, touching his arm. Her smile grew, however.

The security chief sat in his chair, not moving, his eyes narrowing. Manny was sure he was contemplating the possibility of getting another job on the island after he decked a guest.

After a few moments, Torres smiled a humorless smile, his voice cold, his dark gaze colder. "We are not the FBI, Agent Williams. We are a small island off the main grid, as you Americans say. We do what we do with what we have. We didn't believe this situation serious. The FBI is called when the crime is already committed and someone tells you that they have a problem, yes?"

Manny took a deep breath, checking the emotion that had attacked him without warning. His intense reaction would be something to reflect on later.

He spoke softer. "Yes. You're right and I'm on vacation, but I could see by her body language and the tone in her voice that there was something wrong. You and the resort's staff should have been able to detect that. Good God, you're in the people business."

"That is perhaps true. We did what we felt necessary. Discussing this judgment of our inaction further will delay what we need to do. Now, would you like to see the recording or talk more?" asked Torres, still as cold as ice.

It was Manny's turn to smile without humor.

"By all means, *Senor* Torres."

Torres turned back to the screen and began to move through the video at triple the normal speed. Two minutes into the review, a man wearing a white, wide-brimmed hat flashed onto the screen.

Torres stopped and reversed the video to where the man first appeared. Then the security chief began moving one frame at a time until there was a clear shot of the man bending over the driver's door of the Lexus.

The man had a dark tan, was fairly well built, and from what Manny could tell was over six feet in height. He wore plaid shorts with a teal island shirt, and as Manny and Sophie bent closer in unison, Manny noticed a key in the man's hand. The time stamp indicated 10:17 a.m.

"Is that Aaron Rathburn?" asked Sophie.

Torres nodded. "It is him."

"He's obviously getting ready to go somewhere. Let's find out when he comes back," said Manny.

Torres moved the video forward, and they watched the Lexus pull out of the lot and disappear to the left of the resort, heading toward San Miguel. Fast-forwarding again, the car reappeared. Torres manipulated the video to when the car first appeared and slowed it to normal speed.

The Lexus swung into the area in front of the trees, two spots over from where it had left. After the vehicle rolled to a stop, the door opened almost immediately. The man who got out was wearing the same hat, shirt, and shorts as Aaron Rathburn. He glanced slowly in several directions, keeping his face away from the camera, and then walked toward the right, moving at a leisurely pace, almost strolling.

Manny frowned. Keeping his face away from the camera looked intentional, but it could have been just a coincidence. Also, Rathburn was walking *away* from the resort, not in the same direction he'd come from at 10:17. Why? There was something wrong.

"Please rewind to just when he stepped out of the car and pause the video," Manny said.

Torres swore again. He must have noticed what Manny had.

"I think you'd better contact the local authorities."

"I believe you are correct, Agent Williams."

Torres ran his finger over the video as if he needed to be convinced one last time that the man who had exited the car was shorter than and smaller than the missing Brit.

There was no denying that Aaron Rathburn hadn't returned the car.

CHAPTER-10

It had been ages since he'd laid eyes on her. Untold, uncountable years, it seemed to him. He simply couldn't remember exactly how much time had eroded away. Time, the great con artist, and no one is immune to its favor or its curse.

He shifted his weight, taking another sip of coffee. Who was he kidding? He knew exactly how long it had been.

Twenty-nine years, four days, and about eleven hours. He missed her virtually every second they'd been separated. His dreams kept her image in his mind, and his hope kept her in his heart. Yet, those weren't the same as being near her. The true scent of her hair, the gentle touch of her hand, the beautiful curve of her face were no match for his imagination.

No man had ever missed a woman's presence more. Not a one.

He sighed.

Wondering if *she* missed *him* was no longer on his radar. If that was the case, she would have made an attempt to see him. Or at least written. That's what lovers did.

Perhaps she simply wasn't able to bear the thought of him in the state to which he'd been reduced. That often happened to relationships like theirs. He'd seen it over and over again in his home away from Galway, Ireland.

Closing his eyes, he refused to go down a road that wasn't his to take. People could experience so much despair—merely the thought of seeing their soul mate in compromised situations would bring on a deep depression. Perhaps even suicidal tendencies.

He ran his right hand over the jagged scars on his wrist.

In the end, however, when his mind had cleared, he was relatively sure her reasons for not seeing him had nothing to do with missing him. Her decision appeared to be far more disconcerting. The only logical conclusion he could marshal was that she'd found someone else. Wasn't that what had separated them in the first place?

Suddenly, the thought of that possibility rocked him like it hadn't in years. The peace he thought he had made with the idea of infidelity was a shadow in his precipitous, crimson anger.

To hell with a woman scorned; what of him?

Clasping his hands together, he scowled like a rejected school boy who had asked his secret heartthrob for a date, only to receive a *what the hell* look and a cruel laugh of rejection.

Slamming the coffee to the floor, he reached for the knife resting on the passenger seat and began to exit the car. The door swung open five inches, and then it stopped. He stopped.

He closed his eyes, fighting tortuous memories far more vivid than they should be. The experts said his anger should be gone. They proclaimed time as the crowned healer of healers, and he'd had enough time.

My ass. I don't feel healed.

Slowly closing the door, he inhaled, freed the breath, inhaled and released two more times, then let go of his emotion. Control was returning, for now. Besides, he needed to focus on the positive, the good aspects of their long-distance reunion.

He did, and again found her face in his mind's eye.

In spite of what had happened . . . no matter the reason for their separation, he had to release the past and see the future for what it could become. Their separation had been a casualty of life's experiences. It wasn't her fault that the two of them weren't able to fully develop what they'd begun almost three decades prior. Abnormal circumstance was the true culprit regarding their separation. Nothing more.

He wiped his sweaty palm on his black jeans, tugged on his earlobe with his free hand, and brushed his long, silver hair from his forehead. Reaching for the dash, he lifted the small, powerful camera, fingering it nervously. Yet he wasn't nervous. Excited was the more appropriate word.

Separation had indeed made the heart grow fonder.

She'd aged some, but who hadn't? Yet it was still *her*. And she was as beautiful to him now as she had been then. More captivating. More . . . desirable.

The object of his intense affection stepped off the stoop, opened the rear door of the SUV, and loaded the baby into the car seat. She halted, said something to the blond-haired, teenage girl standing on the passenger side of the SUV. They both laughed, then entered the Chevy Traverse.

The vehicle backed out of the driveway and headed west. Waiting a moment, he slipped the car into gear and started after them.

He could hardly wait to see the look on Haley Rose Franson's face when, at long last, they met again.

CHAPTER-11

"Just keep your ass moving, boy. You're not getting involved in this. Chloe will kill you dead. Dead, get it? And I don't have that many friends, *comprende*?"

Sophie kept both her hands in the small of his back, ushering him down the hall like a six-foot first-grader heading to the principal's office.

"Okay. Okay. I get it. I had no intentions of getting involved any deeper. But we had to help Penny. We had no choice," he said, looking over her shoulder.

They continued walking toward the elevators. "Don't give me that shit, Williams. *Hello-ooo. This is me-eee.* I know what you were thinking."

"Do you now?"

She rolled her eyes. "What did I just say?"

He laughed. "Looking into our crystal ball again, are we?"

"Yes, I did. As if I needed to. Damn, a blind man could read your face."

"That bad?"

"Yep."

His friend shrugged. "You're right though. We had to help her, and we did. Security and the locals will take it from here . . . as screwed up as they might be."

Hitting the elevator's UP button, he glanced at Sophie.

She was right on both accounts, as usual when it came to reading him. Over the years, she'd gotten to know him better than all but three people on the planet. She understood what motivated him and how his mind led him—and her along with him—down the paths they'd taken as a team and as close friends.

Those experiences had led to her next correct assumption.

The scale of difficultly at *not* taking over the full investigation regarding Aaron Rathburn was a full-blown ten on the workaholic gauge. The locals, led by Torres, were going to screw this up. A man could die in the wake of their ineptitude.

Sophie waved her hand in front of his face. "Hey, right here. Stop it. Damn, Manny, just stop. You can't keep doing this crap. Chloe, and the rest of us, *need* you to enjoy us away from the job. Away from that dark shit that drags you in."

The elevator opened, and they stepped in.

"I know. I can do this. But—"

Sophie reached up and put a small hand on each side of his face. "No buts, other than Chloe's, and maybe seeing Barb's and mine, are going to be on your radar for the next five days. Understand?"

There was no mistaking the quasi-anxiety in her voice.

He put his right hand on hers. "What if they screw this up, and Rathburn dies because of it?" he said softly. "How do we live with that?"

"We live with that because you can't be everyplace at once. None of us can, except your God, as rumor has it . . . and the last time I looked, there was only one God of the Universe. He's not taking replacement resumes, right? Come on, Manny. People do things to people every day. We can't stop that. You helped them find a serious lead for Rathburn. The rest is on them. Let it go. Besides, there is more than one way to save a life. Yes?"

She stepped back as the elevator door slid open. They locked eyes. For a moment, he believed she was talking about saving his family's life by being there for them, but then he realized it was him she was speaking of, his life.

Point, set, and match.

He finally nodded. "Right, on all accounts. I get it, at least in the brain. Not so sure my gut agrees with you."

Pulling him from the elevator, they headed down the marbled floor toward their rooms.

"That's okay. Despite popular opinion, you ain't so damned perfect. Just get with the program, okay?"

"Deal."

"I have one more question," she said, stopping at her and Dean's door. "This is important, so pay attention."

"Fire away."

"Should I go topless with my thong at the pool? I mean these puppies should be seen, right?" said Sophie, grabbing her breasts.

It was Manny's turn to roll his eyes. "Seriously? That was your question?"

"Damn right. Nothing more important than keeping the fire alive in a relationship. Dean likes the look, so I thought I could share it, ya know?"

Kissing her on the cheek, he headed for his room and his waiting wife. "Some things probably shouldn't be shared, Sophie," he said.

"True, but these need exposure." Then she laughed.

Her door opened and closed. Sophie was out of sight, but the smile he wore said she wasn't out of his mind. Wisdom and wit in the same conversation was a trick reserved for only a few. Sophie may own that one.

Manny turned the corner and stopped, his smile evaporating in a New York second.

The door to their room was completely open. Chloe was nowhere to be seen, but the gaping doorway didn't tell the complete story. Quite the opposite picture in fact.

A man stood in the center of the entrance, glowering at him.

CHAPTER-12

Belle Simmons kissed her cell phone, listened for the Marvin Gaye tune that served as her ringtone to reach her ears again, then picked up the phone from her desk. After wiping the face of the phone clean with a tissue, her finger hovered over the green button that said she'd take the call.

She cleared her throat and sent the butterflies packing, most of them anyway. This felt like the first call from a boy.

Anyone worth his or her salt—working in the criminal-profiling world, that is— had dreamed of this phone call at least once in their lives. Some, like her, had more than dreamed. Obsessed was more like it.

It wasn't just the FBI moniker stamped on the caller ID. Not even the jets and instant respect associated with a unit like the BAU. That was all pretty intense, yes. But it was mostly about working with the best, and no one was better at this insufferable profiling game than Manny Williams. It didn't hurt that he was easy on the eyes either.

Who says God doesn't answer prayers?

Wiping her clammy hand on her jeans one last time, she pushed the green oval on her phone.

"This is Belle."

"Agent Corner here, Belle. Are you ready for this?"

That was a fine question. It held more meaning than *let's get your ass to work.* She shivered with anticipation.

The answer was the same as it would have been ten years ago or ten years in the future.

"I am, Agent Corner. I am."

The brief pause caused her to frown. Hesitating in situations similar to this was usually an unconscious gauge of a deeper emotional reaction than the quick, insincere *glad-you're-aboard.*

"Sorry, Belle, got sidetracked for a moment. I'm glad to have you joining us. But I have to ask again: are you *sure* you're ready for this?"

Am I ready for this?

She stared into space.

Her heart and mind were more than ready. Her logic was somewhat iffy. She could play it safe and stay where she was. She'd still be the big fish in the little pond and that had benefits. But playing safe had never been something she'd embraced. She rubbed her leg as an affirmation to that thought.

She wasn't totally sure where this *yes* would lead, but did it matter? Really? She'd grown past her current position. Well, that wasn't quite right. She'd grown up, eager to ride the next train.

"I've never been more ready, Agent Corner. When do I start?"

"It's Josh. Are you giving notice?"

"My bosses have been on notice for five years, Agent. I can come in tomorrow."

"That will work. Eight a.m. sharp."

Her heart fluttered as the butterflies left her stomach. "I'll be there, Josh. I can't thank you enough. You've made me the happiest person on the planet."

This time the hesitation was intentional. She could tell by the way he inhaled.

"You know the salary and benefits, but there are three other points, Belle."

"Enlighten me, Josh."

"First, you got this gig because you're talented and can help us do what we do even better. The next thing is to pack a bag good for three nights, minimum. You'll need to throw it into the car or the jet in an hour's notice."

"Okay. Thank you, and the bag is already packed. What's the third thing?"

"I want you to hold off on the thank-you for six months."

It was her turn to hesitate.

"Why is that?"

He exhaled. Her new boss spoke slowly.

"No one ever thanked the guards for tossing Daniel into the lion's den and covering up the pit."

CHAPTER-13

Manny's eyes flashed to the wall by the open door, double-checking the room-number plaque. He was in the right place.

He stepped closer, his eyes never leaving the man, who apparently was a local, dressed in khaki shorts and a bright green and teal Banana Republic shirt. That wasn't all; he sported a shoulder holster cradling a pearl-handled Beretta 92s.

Law enforcement or drug cartel? Would the cartels be that blatant and obvious? He knew that none of the Mexican cartels' scopes of influence had truly gone this far north, but who could say for sure?

Law enforcement was the logical assumption.

He frowned.

But why? Did this have something to do with the missing Aaron Rathburn? Good God, he'd just left the security office. His experience told him most foreign law enforcement didn't, or couldn't, react this quickly. That glove didn't fit either.

Never taking his eyes from the taller man, Manny walked faster.

"Chloe?"

Nothing.

Four steps from the self-appointed sentinel, Manny returned the man's glare. Anger pulsed in Manny's temples. Maybe a little morsel of fear as well. He still couldn't see his wife.

"Chloe? Talk to me."

One stride from the man, and Manny had already braced for the imminent, unavoidable physical confrontation.

Chloe popped through the door.

"Manny. Relax. I'm fine."

Her expression told him she was telling the truth. But there was something else underlying that expression.

My wife is doing a slow burn.

Despite the man's size, Manny grabbed his shirt with both hands and slammed him into the wall, holding the stranger in a tight grip so that he couldn't reach his weapon.

"Who the hell are you?"

"Wait, Manny—" said Chloe.

"Wait indeed, Agent Williams. I'm Inspector Eduardo Munoz with the Mexican Federal Police."

The man's calm, dark eyes told Manny he was who he said he was. Manny held tight. Just because someone was a cop didn't mean he had good intentions. Especially in another country.

"Really? Where's your ID?"

"In my shirt pocket. If you'll let me go, I'll show you. I'm not one of the bad guys, Agent."

"Yeah? That's what they all say."

Chloe put her hand on his shoulder. "Manny, I've seen the ID. Let the poor man loose. He's been polite, even though I don't like why he's here."

The touch of Chloe's hand was electric, as always. The sound of her voice reassuring. He felt his anger subside as he reluctantly released Munoz, patting him on the chest.

Stepping away from the Mexican cop, he was choked with the realization that this was the second time in an hour the lid had popped from his temper. Getting angry was nothing new for him, or for anyone for that matter, but to have it happen this close together suggested some underlying frustration.

No shit, Williams. You mean like having another vacation screwed with?

Maybe his pissy attitude had to do with his not-so-fond memories of being used as a knife holder during his prior stay in a Caribbean Resort.

Thinking something may have been wrong with Chloe didn't steady his mind much either. Throw in a security staff that wasn't qualified to work at any mall in America, let alone protect the resort's guests, and one may have a motivation or two to be angry.

"I apologize, Inspector. I'm probably a bit too cautious, but we've had a reason or two over the years to keep up our guard."

"I understand, Agent Williams."

"Do you really? We're here to get away for a few days, and so far, the script hasn't gone as it should," said Manny.

"Yeah well . . . that's not all the inspector's fault, is it?" said Chloe, a morsel of that Irish fire flashing in her eyes.

"True. But we couldn't let that woman go on like she was without stepping in to see what we could do, right?"

"You mean *you* couldn't let it go."

He shrugged.

Sighing, she took his hand. "It's one of those love-hate traits that makes you Manny Williams, and a reason I love you."

"I thought it was my good looks and my black Lab."

"See, you still have much to learn about me, man. I do love that dog though."

Manny squeezed her hand. "I do. But I'm sure that the Mexican authorities don't really care about all of that."

Turning to Inspector Munoz, Manny searched his face and felt his stomach tighten. This man had a full meal on a small plate. He thought he was here to discuss the missing Brit, and maybe Munoz was, but that was hardly the complete story.

The inspector rubbed his stubbled face with both hands and gave Manny and Chloe a tired smile. "Your perceptive and lovely wife said you would discover my intentions before we sat down. That is unless you've already received a call or text from Agent Corner . . . if you had, then you'd be informed of the reason for my visit."

Manny shook his head. "I've not heard from Josh in two days. He promised to give me, and the rest of the unit, time off with no interruptions."

Munoz nodded. "He said as much when I called."

Turning to Chloe, Manny saw that she knew exactly why Munoz was at their door.

"Well, since I've received no contact from Josh yet, I'm assuming he was going to give me a day to relax and then send your information. But you obviously don't believe you can wait that long."

"I do not believe waiting is an option, Agent."

The expression on Munoz's face grazed desperation, but he was keeping it together. It was obvious he was a patient man, and his heart for his job was genuine. Yet, as Manny knew intimately, this line of work can rip that heart away and stomp on it like an insect.

"And let me guess, it's simply a stroke of luck that we happen to be on your island, right?"

Staring at his hands, Munoz spoke quietly. "Fate has its own agenda, Agent Williams. I don't smile at the fortunate circumstances because there are so many other unfortunate situations that don't end with the finest of results. You and your wife and friends vacationing on Cozumel, at this moment, may balance those unfair scales somewhat."

Manny ran his hand through his hair. The man obviously needed help. Profiling help.

He was overrun with the urge to say "no" and take his wife by the hand, shut the door, and lock the world out. It could be just the two of them. Sex. Pina coladas. The beach. The pool and whatever else they wanted to do, or not do. But it would never be just the two of them. At least for any extended time.

Jen. Ian. Sophie. Max. Sampson. Alex. Josh. Dean. Haley Rose. Even Louise. These people had shaped, and continued to mold, his and Chloe's lives. They were their support system and would always be with them. Good or bad. Never mind the perverts and hardcore psychos and unrestrained animals that he and Chloe had encountered in their line of work.

Then there were people like Munoz. The people who weren't afraid to do what it took to make this world a bit better. He'd gathered enough courage to ask for help—and not wait to ask for it. Something Manny could always learn more about, asking for help. Weren't they on the same team?

What choice did he truly have?

Bowing and stretching his hand to the door, Manny smiled. "Step inside, Inspector. Let's talk about what's on your mind."

The Mexican cop returned the smile. "Are you sure you want to know?"

Then Munoz walked into the hotel room.

Manny glanced at Chloe. She shook her head and followed Munoz.

Closing the door behind him, Manny realized it had only taken about three hours to get this vacation off to a rocky beginning. He prayed he was wrong and that the rocky start would only be a temporary glitch.

Could they actually get that lucky?

CHAPTER-14

Alex looked at Dean, grinning. His friend was sitting completely upright in a pool chair, feet on the concrete, concentrating on his laptop resting in the empty chair to his right, the one he was saving for Sophie, but those actions weren't what drew his attention to Dean, again.

The forensic tech extraordinaire, without question, owned the most unique look at the resort's sparkling, ten-thousand-square-foot pool. The man was as white as the proverbial snow storm, accenting his purple-and-red-paisley swim trunks. There was a wide, white streak of sunblock running down his nose, and some of it had trickled into his dark beard, making it look like he'd left part of his BLT to eat later. Throw in the white ball cap and white socks under his brown leather sandals, and you had . . . well, you had Dean Mikus at his very best. And worst.

"He's one of yours, right?"

Alex glanced at his wife Barb, who was lying on her stomach, already turning the warm Mexican rays into a darker tan.

His smile grew wider.

"Yep. White skin, classy garb, and toss in a sense of healthy sun protection, and you've got him covered."

"Just him?"

He looked at her again. She was as beautiful as ever. Her orange bikini accented the perpetual tan she seemed to carry year round on her almost perfectly shaped body.

"What do you mean?"

"Nothing, honey. Nothing," she said softly.

"Hey. I burn easy, and I need this hat to protect the dome."

"Yep."

"And who said socks weren't okay with sandals?"

"No one important, honey. But you are at a pool."

"True. And my feet are getting hot. Okay. Maybe I'll take them off."

"That's fine. Maybe the sweatpants too. Like I said, it's a pool."

"Whatever. That leaves a lot of skin exposure to UV rays. I'm not sure that's totally safe, Barb."

She sat up on her elbows. "Let me tell you what's safe and good for you. If you don't take that shirt and pants off and put on a swimsuit, I'm going to be your worst nightmare. Got it?"

He sighed. She looked harmless, but. . . .

"Okay. Okay. Damn. We're on vacation, and you're getting tense. Just relax. And, by the way, what's in it for me if I strip down to pool-boy clothes?"

"You *do* know what happens to the pool boy when the cougar of the house gets a good look at him half naked, right?"

"You mean like in the movies?"

"Yep."

"Be right back."

Five minutes later, Alex was back in the chair beside Barb, green bathing trunks loose around his thighs, his skin glistening with 50-SPF sunblock. His bucket hat pulled a little lower.

She turned her head and looked his way.

He smiled.

She smiled.

"That's better, pool boy. Momma's got a surprise for you later."

He was feeling warmer, and it wasn't just the sun.

"Surprise, huh? I can't wait."

"Wait for what?"

Looking up, Alex saw Sophie standing beside him, floppy hat on her head, a pink beach bag draped over her shoulder, and a tight, one-piece swimsuit covering her body.

"None of your business. It's a personal family activity thing."

Sophie took off her sunglasses and rolled her eyes. "Good God, Dough Boy, I know what the hell that means, and I don't want that image in my head. What's wrong with you? You should have lied to me. You could have said it was about dinner or some damned thing. Now I need a brain scrub."

"Oh, your warped Asian brain needed a scrub long before now. You know that, right? Hell, maybe even a lobotomy. And don't call me Dough Boy."

"Really? A lobotomy?"

"You actual know what that means?" asked Alex.

She turned around and patted her rear. "Right here, Dough Boy. Or should I say Snow Boy. Damn, you make Mikus over there look like a poster boy for Coppertone."

"Whatever, wench. At least this is the real me."

"What? Are you talking about my girls? That's it. I'm kicking your ass."

"How about margaritas first?" suggested Barb.

By then, Dean had wandered over. "That sounds great. Everyone want one?"

Sophie waggled her finger at Alex. "You're damn lucky your wife has a great mind. You were about to be a statistic."

"Yeah? I'll try not to lose any sleep."

"You do that. But like Manny says, you got to be on your toes. When you least expect it . . . *bam* . . . I'll be all over you. No one talks about the girls except Dean."

"Now *I* need a brain scrub," said Alex.

Dean finished ordering from the poolside waiter and then sat down at the foot of Alex's deck chair and motioned for Sophie to come closer.

"Okay, drinks are coming. Speaking of statistics and girls, how'd it go with the lady in the lobby?"

Barb turned over and sat up. She was watching Sophie.

Alex suddenly felt uneasy but tried not to show it. His wife was no dummy.

"Well, we got a few minutes in without work raising its ugly head," said Barb.

Sophie looked up toward the afternoon sun, slung her bag to the pool's deck, and sat beside Dean. "It went okay. You know Williams. He found a couple things the security people missed, and it's pretty obvious her husband is missing and hasn't just run off somewhere."

"How so?" asked Alex.

Sophie told them what had transpired with Aaron Rathburn and the stranger who returned his car.

"Shit. Did Manny get that look in those baby blues?" asked Alex.

"What do you think?" snorted Sophie. "He's like a damn perpetual clock. He just can't shut down. I climbed on his case for a few minutes, and I think it helped. But you know about tigers changing their stripes. Doesn't happen."

Alex did know about that. His good friend—the BAU's and maybe the rest of the world's Guardian of the Universe—simply wasn't wired like most folks. He guessed that was a good thing. If Manny thought like normal people in this job, he'd probably be in a sanatorium.

"So is he going to get involved?" asked Dean.

"I don't think so. I reminded him that Chloe and he needed a break . . . and to take one, for crying out loud. The authorities can handle this. We're on vacation," said Sophie.

"Let me guess. He said he'd try, right?" said Alex.

Letting out a breath, Sophie nodded. "He did, for what that's worth."

"Ah. Well. I'm not sure how to say this," said Dean, blocking the sun with his hand. "But should we see if the locals can use our help?"

Standing, Sophie reached down and clutched his beard. "Are you nuts, son? No! The locals *can* handle this. They're cops. They have inspectors and shit. Manny and I helped them get some leads and a timeline. That's enough, got it?"

"I agree," said Alex, glancing at Barb. "We're here to recharge. Josh let us come on this vacation together and said the world can wait. So, you know what? The world can wait."

Alex watched as Dean slowly put his hand on Sophie's. "I hear you both. I'm just saying, if we were that woman, wouldn't we want some help?"

"We got her some help, right, Sophie?" asked Alex.

"We did. They're way ahead of the game because of the BAU," she said softly.

The waiter reappeared and dished to each of them a salty, lime delight.

Alex took two long draws while watching his feet, the awkward silence deafening.

Finally, he broke it. "Listen. You and Manny did your civic duty. Let's not get jammed up in anymore of this. God knows we'll have a few things to get caught up on when we get home, okay?"

"Fair enough," said Dean.

"So let's change the subject," said Alex.

"Deal. But let's not talk about who dressed either one of you men. You both look like something straight out of *this ain't how you do it* magazine," said Sophie.

"Hey. We're practical. But changing the subject works. When are Manny and Chloe coming down? We can get an early dinner and then go to the casino or something," said Dean.

"He didn't say. But it shouldn't be too long, unless, of course, Chloe has already killed him and stuffed the body down the laundry chute," said Sophie.

Just then, Alex felt the phone vibrate in his front pocket, telling him he had received a text.

"Speaking of the devil . . . that must be him telling us he and Chloe are on the way down."

He pulled the phone from his pocket and felt the grimace take over his face.

The text was most assuredly not what he expected. Not even close.

He read it again, just to make sure he was seeing it correctly. He was.

I NEED YOUR HELP. NOW.

CHAPTER-15

Standing on the modest wooden porch of his bungalow, he noticed the afternoon sun was sinking closer to the blue horizon. As it descended, his excitement rose. This would be one of his final acts of obedience and contrition.

Contrition.

It was such an unusual word for his situation, yet nonetheless accurate. After all, did he not hold at least some partial culpability for his circumstances, and hers? If not directly, then by the act of not acting?

If he'd not turned his head and ignored all the obvious signs, he may have staved off the eventual outcome of their separation. So, he was at fault on some level.

Many would disagree. They would say the outcome of his journey was inevitable. His opinion on the subject, however, was the only one that mattered. Thus he walked proudly on this road he had reluctantly, at first, chosen.

He set his glass of wine on the wicker table and bowed his head. He had finished many tasks in his adult life, but this, the two sacrifices to come, would be an achievement worthy of any he'd accomplished. What came next could be even more monumental, but one must take life one step at a time. His training, and she, had taught him that.

He picked up the glass, watching the sun reflect through the wine at just the right angle, causing a tiny prism of light to dance against the white wall. Turning the glass slightly caused the colors to completely disappear. He marveled at the notion that he was able to change the appearance and perception of the sun by a mere twist of his hand. Yet, that was the very essence of his next task, to change acuities with a twist of his hands, was it not?

Smiling, he finished the wine.

A mere twist of his hand.

CHAPTER-16

"What the hell is wrong with ya, man? We're on holiday here. Is there some part of you that doesn't get that, for crying out loud?"

Manny sat on the edge of the king-sized bed, his guilt right beside him, watching his wife pace, her face red, her hair flipping around her head each time she turned away from him.

Pissed and beautiful.

Pissed wasn't the proper term. In fact, he was sure the English language had no word that captured the essence of a woman scorned in a very special, romantic resort in the Caribbean. Perhaps rage or fury or wrath combined into one elicit term would cover it, then again . . .

An Irish woman at that.

On vacation.

She spun away again, and he almost smiled.

Not good, Williams. She'd better not see that smile if he still wanted to enjoy more of his life.

"We leave Ian for a few days . . . and that was tough enough, don't ya know. But I say to myself, I say, 'Chloe. It'll be worth it." I'll get to wear bathing suits that will make the other men at that pool think you're the luckiest man on the damned planet. We'll get some fine time alone, together. We'll talk. We'll laugh, we'll drink, we'll dance, and we'll get naked and have wild, unchecked sex so often that it just might kill a normal man."

His heart picked up the pace.

Kill a normal man?

She reached over and grabbed his face with both hands. There was no fire like the jade flames leaping from his wife's eyes. For a solitary, brief moment, he thought he really might be a dead man here.

"But *ohhhhh no*, you can't get with the damn program, can ya? Don't look away from me when I'm talking to you man, got it?"

"Yes, ma'am, I get it."

"And who said you could talk? I am NOT done. I'm. Just. Not. Finished. With—"

She stared at him as tears formed in her eyes. After a few moments, her face began to soften. A little at first then completely.

He held her hands with his.

"Better?" he asked softly.

"Yeah, maybe."

She moved closer and kissed him with those startling lips, and he felt his world spin. Her touch was special, but those kisses were the kind that never left his mind.

Those lips were the drug most men sought to ease any pain.

"I love you more than anything, you know that?" he asked.

She searched his face. "I do, Manny. I do."

"And do you remember in Galway, the night I sang to you?"

More tears.

"No woman could ever forget that. Good God, you rescued me."

He nodded. "I still think you've got the who-rescued-who part turned around. But do you remember what I said about having issues and sometimes you'd hate me?"

"I do. I also remember you said that you'd try," she said softly.

"This is it, Chloe. This is the best try I have. I can't imagine a life without you, ever, but I can't escape the idea of helping to make the world a little safer, a little more secure. The fact that there are people in a great deal of pain, and I can help to ease that pain, is consuming. I . . . I'm sorry."

She kissed him again and then sat on his lap.

"I know. And it is part of what drew me to you . . . well, that and your fine bum."

"Thanks. That's good to know."

"Listen. I'll always be jealous of your time and of this damn profession. But I get it, mostly. The Guardian of the Universe has to do what he does, but it doesn't mean I always have to like it. I'm Irish, so I get angry at things I can't control."

"I promise it won't take long. You heard Munoz. They want us to help with a profile and that's it."

She rolled her eyes.

"I wasn't born yesterday, Williams. That's it, really? And you promise? We've been here five hours, and you're involved with two investigations. That's two more cases than bathing suits you've seen me in. And now you're about to involve the whole BAU."

He sighed and pulled her closer. "I can't wait to see you in those suits. I'm trying, Chloe. I promise to do my best to be the man you want for a few days."

"Oh, you fool, you are the man I want. I just want more of you."

They held each other until the knock on the door said it was time to get back to the real world.

Chloe stood then bent over to pick up the hot-pink bikini that had fallen from the bed, her backside virtually in his face.

He swallowed hard.

She stayed bent over a bit longer than necessary, then stood, smiling.

"There's plenty more where that came from, whenever you think you can handle not working."

"Kill a normal man, truly?"

She put her hand on his and raised it to her breast. He felt her strong heart racing with excitement.

"You know what they say about making-up sex, right? You'd be daft not to see exactly what that means," she whispered.

Standing, he kissed her again, then headed for the door.

After a few steps, he stopped and looked her way. "For the record, I'm dedicated, not daft."

"Dedicated, huh? We'll see."

I must be fricking crazy for agreeing to do this.

He opened the door and watched the rest of the BAU team stream into the room. Barb Downs held Alex's hand, walking side by side with him wearing a look Manny understood. She was as good at keeping her emotions at bay as anyone, but she was clearly disappointed in his request to assemble. And she hadn't heard the worst.

But they *all* knew, didn't they?

"This better be some kind of *I can't find the rest of my luggage* problem, Williams," said Sophie.

He shook his head. "Nope. That's not it."

"All right, you're having a tough time and need a couple of those little blue pills?" she asked.

"No, not that either, and why is it always about sex?"

"That's what I keep saying," said Alex.

"And I keep saying that sex and money, mostly sex, makes the world go around. Look it up," said Sophie.

Alex shook his head and then smiled. "You know, for once, I'm wishing she was right."

"Yeah, maybe I do too."

"So let's get to it; why are we here? Is it about the missing man, Rathburn?" asked Dean.

Manny started to say "no," then checked his response.

The two sets of circumstances didn't look related in any way, but the fact that Rathburn was missing, and Munoz had similar kidnappings before he had bodies, made Dean's statement relevant. Manny had no proof, only a feeling, but for him that was often enough. He decided to choose his words carefully.

"No. Rathburn wasn't why we received a visit from a Mexican federal investigator. Inspector Eduardo Munoz has a problem and needs a bit of help."

"Shit. So he knew we just happened to be vacationing in Cozumel, if you call five hours and fifteen minutes a damn vacation, and figured he'd take advantage of the BAU's presence?" Sophie's pretty face scowled like some angry, old-fashioned school teacher.

"That's about it. He called Josh first, and Josh apparently was going to give us a day, then let us decide if we wanted to spend a few hours helping this man. But the inspector didn't want to wait."

"How kind of our boss," said Sophie.

"Hey. I appreciate that Josh was trying to let us get settled," said Manny.

"So this Inspector Munoz must be desperate if he couldn't even wait twelve or fifteen hours," said Dean.

Manny nodded. "That's what we thought too."

"Is he? Is he that desperate?" asked Dean.

"And you just can't help yourself," said Sophie.

"Sophie. You know the answer to that," said Manny.

Glancing at Chloe, Manny turned back to the others. "The Mexican cops have their hands full with all of this cartel crap and have few allocated resources for other crimes, even ones as serious as spree killings," he said softly.

The room grew quiet as his words wormed into the psyches of each person in the room. He knew his friends. He knew Chloe. He thought he knew himself, but when it came to choices like this, making one was more than knowledge; the decision was almost a moral compulsion for them to help anyone who actually needed it.

"Yeah, Dean. I think he is that desperate," said Manny.

"Okay, let's hear it, Manny. What can we do?" asked Sophie, her displeasure with being called to his room apparently fading. Her cop instincts were kicking in.

"Munoz wants a few hours of our time. He has four murders and more people missing in the last four days, counting Aaron Rathburn. He'll give us full access to all he has, forensic evidence as well, and is asking that we build a profile of the unsub or unsubs. After that, he's going to leave us alone. He promised."

"So just a profile, and we can come back to the pool and I can strut my stuff," said Sophie.

"Oh, you need a pool for that?" asked Alex, rolling his eyes.

"Hey, we might even get your skin to look mildly beige, Dough Boy."

"We will all be able to strut our stuff and add some serious color," said Chloe.

Manny sighed. "I can't ask you all to do what I'm going to do, but with all of you pitching in, we'll give him a better idea of who this killer might be and where to search."

It was Alex's turn to sigh. "Yeah, like we can let you do that alone. You might miss something Dean and I can see in the evidence files. As much as I hate to say it, Sophie might be useful too. Maybe."

"Damn right. Oh wait. Are you slamming me?"

"No. Just saying."

"Alex is right," said Dean.

"Chloe is willing to come along for a few hours too," said Manny.

He stepped toward Barb. "You are invited too. You're not a cop, but I've seen enough of your insight. You can add something to the discussion."

Barb's face lit up then simmered down to a less excited state. "I'd rather be at the pool or shopping, but I came here to be with Alex, so I'm in. I just don't need to look at any crime-scene pictures."

"That's a deal. So I guess we're all in."

"Like you thought we wouldn't be," said Chloe with a half-smile.

"Hey. It's still your decision. But I'm glad you're willing to take a few hours to help," said Manny.

"When do we do this?" asked Sophie.

He looked at his watch. "Twenty minutes. Munoz will have a van down front."

"Damn. You really do have us pegged."

Smiling, Manny took Sophie's hand. "Profiler, remember?"

She shook him off, but the sparkle was still in her eyes. "No touching me. I'm trying to be pissed. Just so we have this right . . . we do a profile and we're done, right?"

"That's right. I told him we're out of there after that. And if we do our job, he'll be able to do his."

Manny's phone shook, telling him he had a text. He read it and shrugged.

"I guess they're a bit early. Our chariot awaits. Let's change and meet in the lobby in ten minutes."

"*Done after that.* Is that what you said?" said Alex, moving toward the door.

"I did."

"Whatever," said Sophie, following Alex.

The friends filed out of the room, and Manny took Chloe's hand.

He hoped he could keep his word this time.

CHAPTER-17

Sampson's huge, black face rose high on the other side of the wide bay window on the front of the house, his deep bark serving as a greeting Jen Williams had heard a thousand times before. Maybe a million. There was a particular comfort on hearing the big dog make a fuss over the Williams family members whenever they returned. She loved knowing that the Big Dog was watching out for them.

She sprung out of the SUV and hurried around to get to little Ian's car seat before her granny, Haley Rose, beat her to it. She pulled open the door, and Ian broke into one of those grins that melted hearts and took names. She returned that bit of sunshine with a grin of her own and then kissed him out of pure compulsion.

"Hey. You got him out at the mall. It's my turn," said Haley Rose, struggling with her seat belt.

"So sad, Granny. You have to be quicker with the seat belt thing. Besides, you never let me hold him when we're home."

With that, Jen released the straps and whisked Ian out of his seat, hugging him tightly.

Never did she think that a brother some eighteen years her younger could bring out such a sense of love and protection. She guessed her dad was right about the whole maternal instinct condition and how much she was like her mom in that regard.

She thought she liked that comment from him the best. She missed her mom terribly, even after almost three years, but Haley Rose and Chloe were doing a bang-up job of taking that edge off.

Her thoughts veered to her dad. His love had a wee bit to do with that too. Then along comes Ian and the void was even less.

Louise Williams was never far from her heart, but Jen had learned that life goes on. Her mom wanted her to move on. Her dream had said so.

Ian giggled. She felt his eyes probing her face, then she laughed out loud.

"You're just the cutest thing on the planet, aren't you?"

"Well, you got that part right for sure," said Haley Rose.

She'd exited the front and retrieved the shopping bags from the rear of the SUV, and was now standing very close to both of them.

"Was Chloe this cute?" Jen asked.

"Ahh. Now that'd be a question to consider, but never ask a woman if someone else's baby was cuter than her own, even a grandbaby as handsome as this one." Haley Rose winked. "But I'll say what Ian's mum would say . . . hell yes."

Jen shook her head and headed for the mailbox with Ian in her arms. "I'll see what the mailman brought."

"Good thought. I'm going in. These shoes are gettin' a bit heavy. Be careful."

"Yes granny. Like, what can happen twenty feet from here to there?"

"Nothing, just making sure."

Then Haley was inside telling Sampson to move his big, black arse and to stay down. Jen heard her swear a second later. Sampson had things under control . . . his way.

Pulling open the box, Jen took out a couple of advertisements and a small package she'd been waiting for.

A blue compact car driving slower than normal passed the front of her home. She peered into the driver's window and began to wave with her free hand, then stopped. At first, she thought the car belonged to her friend, Stacie Wells. There was more than one car like hers in the neighborhood. But Stacie wasn't piloting the car.

Someone else entirely sat behind the wheel.

The older man with the long, silver hair grinned and waved a large hand ever so slowly as he rolled by.

She frowned.

His yellow, toothy grin was much closer to creepy than friendly.

The life lessons she was taught early, especially with a cop for a father, came to the forefront, and she backed closer to the house, didn't return the wave, and for a reason she didn't quite understand, sought the back of the car to memorize the plate number.

That didn't happen.

As Jen Williams spun around and hurried for the front door, she wasn't sure what was more disconcerting—the fact that the man's grin was spooky or that the car's license plate number was covered with black paper.

CHAPTER-18

"Dammit, Williams. I know I've mentioned this before, but no one shows a woman a good time like you. I've been waiting my whole life for the opportunity to sit in a Mexican jail with no air conditioning and inhaling the stink of stale, funky God-knows-what," complained Sophie.

"What? This isn't on your bucket list?" asked Dean. "And you can relax. I think a couple of those odors are just coffee and cigarettes . . . and a couple bodily fluids that'll need a spectrometer to sort out, but I'd say urine and feces isn't out of the question. Probably a few more options."

Sophie stood from her chair, wiped her hand across the back of her plaid shorts, and looked behind her at the chair she was just seated in. "Great. Just freaking great. What kind of bodily fluids did you say? I'm okay with a few of them, but really?"

"You're treading in real deep water, Dean," said Manny, smiling.

"Yeah, but it's warm, and I've learned to swim," he said.

Sophie's eyes narrowed as she looked to Manny then Dean. "Are you yanking my chain, Beard Boy? If you are, you ain't touching the magic stuff for the rest of the week."

"I'm shocked you'd think I'd do that," he deadpanned.

"Shocked, huh? We'll be talking later . . . and that's *all* we'll be doing."

"Hey. I'm only messing with you a little bit—there is smoke and coffee, and maybe some other stuff."

Dean looked at Alex, who was sitting across from him. Manny hadn't seen a look for help like that from Dean since Vegas.

"He's right," said Alex, pointing to the stucco wall over Manny's shoulder. "That stain right there, the big green one? I think that was a bottle of alcohol that grew some mold and they couldn't get it clean or . . ."

"Or what?" demanded Sophie.

"Or someone peed on the wall because they were upset with the cop that brought him in," said Manny.

"See? I'm telling the truth. Mostly," said Dean, pulling at his beard.

Moving away from the chair between Dean and Manny, Sophie sat on the other side of the table with Chloe and Barb.

"I don't trust any of you anymore. I can smell stuff on my own, but your opinions are like politicians, full of shit. I'm safe over here."

The warped, wooden door to the simple interrogation room opened, and Inspector Eduardo Munoz entered carrying a stack of green files. He was followed by a younger male officer in blue, pushing a rickety, four-wheeled cart with three more stacks of identical folders, except they were colored red, blue, and yellow. That wasn't the extent of the contents of the cart.

On the lower level were stacks of photos on one corner, and on the other, six copies of a book titled *The Mayan World.* On the top of each volume were small cards, apparently used to mark specific passages in each book.

A couple of hours?

Manny's best guess suggested they might be in this small room, away from the sun, beach, pool, and margaritas, for longer than that. His "uncomfortable meter" inched higher. He'd promised his friends just a short time away from the resort and their vacation. This wasn't quite what he'd envisioned.

Munoz placed the files on the desk. He stood straight and began rubbing his back. He then scanned the six people in the room.

The man had the gift of reading people quickly. Manny could tell he'd already, at least to some extent, figured out the strengths and weaknesses of each of them. The fact that he lingered on Barb a moment longer told Manny he knew she wasn't BAU. Munoz also had done his homework because none of them had name tags. He wouldn't need them.

The inspector exhaled, folding his hands in front of him. "My friends, I can't thank you all enough. I know how much time away from what we see and do for a living can mean. For you to give up some of your free time is very much appreciated. *Gracias*."

"We're here to help," said Manny.

"You could have hired a maid though," said Sophie.

"Yes. I'm sorry this room isn't what you perhaps are accustomed to, but it is the best we have."

"Yeah, well, I suppose we've seen worse, except for the sticky stuff on the chairs," she answered, shifting in her seat.

Manny leaned forward. "By the look of the material you brought, we might be giving up a little more time than we anticipated."

Munoz shrugged. "It is your decision. I brought all that we had, plus some reference publications describing the Mayan culture and its very strong influence on our island."

Frowning, Manny's mind began to run. "Why bring the books? Is there an influence of Mayan history involved with this spree killer's MO?"

Instead of answering Manny's question, Munoz stepped to the cart, pulled out the books, and stacked them on the table. He then picked up the files and passed them out to everyone except Barb, even though he had one more cradled in his arm. He hesitated and then placed the file on the corner of the table, causing the table to wobble against the hard floor.

"I'll let you decide, Missus Downs, if you believe reviewing the photos and descriptions of the murder scenes are something you choose to explore."

He then turned in Manny's direction. "I'll not answer your question. You do what you do, as they say, and tell me what you think is transpiring."

"That makes perfect sense to me," said Manny, his mind growing more uneasy.

The Mayans were notorious for ritualistic human sacrifices, particularly against their enemies. Yet they were considered a bright, intelligent people as well.

If this killer *was* emulating some form of Mayan influence, that could mean these murders held a personal significance. Not a good thing.

He shook off his racing thoughts.

The facts.

They simply needed to focus on the facts to build this profile. Yet, in cases like these, there could exist, and often did exist, a blurred perception between facts and the killer's intent. That was the trick, wasn't it? To sort out that line between reality and the killer's world.

"Okay, we'll get to work," said Manny.

"I'll take my leave. I'll be in the outer office when you need me."

Barb stood, placing her hand on Alex's shoulder. "I'm going with him. I . . . I'm okay discussing some of this with you, Alex. But I'm not ready to see the stuff in these files. Not yet, at least."

"Hey, we get that, honey. We're not ready for it most of the time either," said Alex, putting his hand on hers.

"I'll take a taxi back to the resort and hold a few chairs for you all at the pool," she said flashing a humorless smile.

"That's what I'm talking about," said Sophie. "Sun and pool works for me."

"No need for a taxi," said Munoz. "I'll have one of our officers escort you back to the Casa Palms."

Munoz waited for Barb to step toward the door before he followed her. As she reached it, she turned back to Manny. "Not too long. I want to enjoy my husband before the week is over, okay?"

There was a pleading in her voice. Another tiny piece of his heart broke.

The stark realization that not everyone was convinced they had to be the Guardian of the Universe was driven home. The guilt wouldn't go away unless he got his people out of here quickly. Even then, the guilt wouldn't dissipate entirely. It never did. But it would be better.

"I promise, Barb. I promise."

"I know you do," she answered.

Then she disappeared through the door.

Munoz took two more steps and stopped.

"There is one more thing. There is another missing-person report other than Aaron Rathburn.

A woman who worked in a downtown office building did not report to work this morning."

"Why is that unusual?" asked Dean.

"She worked for one of the missing men, Samuel Rozen."

CHAPTER-19

Making another note on the front of the file, Manny set the pen on the metal table with a small clank. He then crossed his hands on the top of the orange folder and stared at them.

His were strong hands, he thought. Not those of a younger man, but one who had passed that stage and was onto the next. He was in better shape now than at almost any point in his life but had worked hard to get there.

Maybe going through what he and Chloe had experienced in Puerto Rico elevated his awareness of just exactly how mortal humans were—and taking care of himself was now a bigger priority. Life was too short, precious.

He recalled how he'd thought that way when he finally awoke from surgery and discovered the tip of metal from the broken knife blade had been successfully removed and his life intact. He had another opportunity to live. Not just be alive, but to *live*. He was grateful for that opportunity and would always be—that God thought him worthy to make a difference. He supposed getting another chance was one of the reasons he sat here with the others, in this life that meant so much to him. That and his workaholic tendencies.

At any rate, he spent more time in the gym and far less eating what he shouldn't. Well, except for those chocolate chip cookies that Chloe seemed to pull from some oven in Heaven. He thought he could smell them even in this dungeon posing as a conference room.

Was there anything better than warm cookies and a huge glass of milk?

Looking back at his hands, he wondered if even the training he'd put them and the rest of his body through had produced enough strength to open the file. Despite any notions to the contrary, seeing people in the way he'd see them in these files never got any easier. But if not him and this crew, then who?

Looking around the table, he saw the identical struggle on each face of the members of the BAU.

We must be crazy.

"You all know the drill. Let's take as long as necessary to effectively review the reports and files, and then let's get to it. Obviously, there are other situations Munoz is working, like the office worker's kidnapping, but that isn't why we're here. That information could shed some light on what this unsub is about, however," he said. "And oh, by the way, thank you all again."

"You're welcome. Just make sure Josh checks on the medical plan and that my therapy sessions are covered," said Dean.

Manny nodded. "That could be true for each of us."

He glanced at Alex and saw that he was looking at the door through which Barb had left with Munoz. His friend had to be wondering if he should be the one taking her back to the resort. He knew he'd be thinking that way.

"Are you okay, Alex?" he asked.

"Yeah," he sighed. "Let's just get this over with."

"I couldn't agree more," said Chloe.

With that, Manny opened the cover of the combined case files. The rest of the BAU, and Chloe, followed suit as they began the trek into a world they'd traveled numerous times before. Yet, that landscape changed constantly because the author of this kind of heinous behavior had concepts based totally on their discernment of reality. That was the trick, nonetheless, finding out what made these unsubs tick.

Staring at the first set of photos, Manny ran his hand through his hair. His thoughts immediately reflected what his instincts had already grasped.

What were these folks thinking after they were hit with the stark realization that they were about to die? Of regrets not expressed and apologies not made? Was God real? Have I served my purpose here? Will I see my loved ones? Why me?

Manny fought for his ever-increasing emotional purchase. These photos revealed people, human beings who aspired to live a decent life.

The images allowed them to look back with satisfaction when old age made its inevitable appearance.

Reflecting a moment on his own reality again, he knew those musings, and much more, had riffled through each of the victim's heads.

A distorted reality? Is that what this desolation was about? He bit his lip and began the journey from the emotional to the more analytical profiler mode that proved a conundrum in every sense of the word. He wondered, for the millionth time, if his ability to turn off the sympathy and concentrate on the facts and actions made him less human.

His almost-involuntary glance at Chloe, and all she represented in his life, said "no." His love for her and Jen and Ian defied any thoughts of him lacking in humanity. Quite the opposite. Love, or perhaps the lack of it, defined us all. He was simply well equipped for what he did. Although he wondered why God would equip anyone with tools like he and the BAU possessed to solve crimes like these. Those abilities could send one on a fast track to a rubber room.

Manny slowly turned the pages of the file containing the first victim's pictures and corresponding reports. He let out a breath as his eyes darted toward the gaping wound at the rib cage just below where the heart once existed.

Then to the blank eyes that saw nothing.

Then to the ancient bowl that contained remnants of that heart that once provided life.

He saw it all in a blink that felt like eons.

He continued to turn the pages until the case file was semi-implanted into his brain. He repeated the process with the next three files, which were remarkably similar in detail. They were related in another way that was impossible to escape; each of the victims screamed for justice to be delivered. He prayed the men and women in this room could help.

At the end of the thick folder were a few details of the latest kidnap victim, but he decided to follow his own advice and stick with the details of the murders, for now.

Munoz had obviously gone through the process of having the reports and notes translated into English, although some of the paperwork was still difficult to read. Another example showing Munoz was doing his best to stay on top of this investigation.

The others were progressing through the information. There were a few disgusted grunts. At one point, he heard Sophie swear, then again, but his crew stayed on task. They would all see something the others had not focused on, and that mix would be essential to finding this killer, as always. The only thing missing from this BAU gathering was Josh Corner and his insight.

Going back to the beginning of the file, Manny slowed his pace the second time through, which was his own personal custom. Yet the impressions and analysis from what he'd seen were already forming a portrait from the void of nebulous facts and details that filled this case. Obviously, the killings were related and ritualistic.

Each victim, three males and one female, had been killed the exact same way. Each photo was unique, but remarkably similar, right down to the length of the incisions.

He'd done a little research on the Mayans and their habits while getting ready for this trip, but these weren't the type of details he'd been researching. He knew, as was the case in most ancient and some modern cultures, there were different acts and sacrifices for different prayer requests to particular gods. These killings seemed to fit that pattern.

The island of Cozumel had been a gathering place for fertilization rituals, for females, among others, in which most Mayan women in the region gladly participated. They came to deliver proper respect and offerings to a goddess whose name he couldn't recall at the moment, to insure the prosperity of a large family.

I must be getting old.

He reached for one of the books Munoz had left and began searching the colored three-by-five cards, which had particular passages bookmarked. After pulling a few cards, he found what he was looking for. The goddess's name was Ixchel. It translated to "she of the rainbows."

As he read the text, he learned that she was depicted as a peaceful deity that represented fertility, midwifery, and medicine, but was subject to the will of greater gods and powers, particularly Itzamná, the Mayan creator god and god of fire.

He sat up straighter. This god wasn't the only one that held spiritual power over Ixchel. The god Kukulcán, a colorfully feathered serpent divinity, who seemed to be a co-creator with Itzamná, was also powerful. The description of this god was ubiquitous and sketchy; nevertheless, he was credited with numerous traits. The one attribute that got Manny's attention was the possibility that he resided over sacrifices as a god of war.

Scowling at the perceived image of the god, he closed the book and flipped back a few pages in the case file to a two-page spread, which contained several pictures of the surrounding area, maybe six feet from the second victim's head resting on the sacrificial altar.

The second picture on the right side of the page showed two feathers, one blue and one green. Each was approximately the same length. That was telling enough, but the Mayan symbol just to the right of those feathers forced him to lean even closer to the photo.

He then turned back to the book and pulled the page showing the image of Kukulcán he had just reviewed. He moved it closer to the photo that Munoz's people had taken at the crime scene. He ran his finger over both images several times but wasn't totally convinced he was right.

"Alex. Slide your magnifying glass over to me please."

Alex shrugged, started to reach into his pocket, looked at the prostheses that served as his left hand, then switched to his right. He extracted the glass and slid it across the table.

"What did you see, almost?" Alex asked.

"I'll tell you in a minute."

Manny ran the glass over the photo, staring until if felt like his eyes would burst from their sockets.

It took a few moments, but his heart skipped a beat when certainty showed its face.

Centuries of rain and weathering had taken its toll on the carving, but there was no mistaking the shadowy image in the photo.

What was the god of war doing in a temple of fertility and peace?

CHAPTER-20

For the third time in ten minutes, while Ian wiggled on her lap, Haley Rose watched as Jen stood from the sofa, walked over to the bay window, pulled the beige curtains to the side, and searched the street of the quiet neighborhood. Each time, her step-granddaughter clutched her cell phone, turning it over and over in her hand like a stack of chips at a Texas Hold Em table.

Haley Rose had seen Jen do that trick a few times in the past, when she was anxious about something at school or talking about her deceased mother.

Neither of those situations had arisen today.

"What are ya doing, lass? You'll be making your old Maimeo more daft than I already am if you keep that up."

Jen began to close the curtains, looked one last time, and drew them shut. She stood by the window, staring at her sandals. "Sorry, Granny," she answered as she plopped down on the sofa. "Just a little of my dad in me, I guess."

"Whatever does that mean?"

Haley Rose watched Jen's face as she seemed to be debating how to choose her words. Then Jen shrugged.

"Well, if paranoia is a family trait thing, then I've inherited the mother lode."

"Do tell."

Jen sat beside her. "Okay. When I went to get the mail, this car drove by real slow, and like, I thought it was my friend, Stacie Wells. She has a car just like that. Anyway, I started to wave, and I actually thought the car might stop because it was going so slow. Except it wasn't her.

"So it wasn't Stacie. Is that a problem?" asked Haley Rose.

Again, Jen was taking time to pick the proper words. Yep. Just like that dad of hers.

"I'm not sure. He was older, like in his fifties."

"Careful girl. Careful."

Jen tilted her head and smiled. Yet, she stayed focused. "Not like your fifties. He was a lot . . . I don't know . . . like, harder? He wasn't bad looking, I guess, and he had long, gray hair, but his grin and his stare . . . I guess they were just kind of creepy, ya know? Plus there was something covering his license plate so I couldn't see the number."

Haley Rose nodded, trying to hide the thoughts spawned by an imagination that had instantly and uncontrollably rambled to one of those places parents, and in this case, grandparents, feared the most.

A man watching your granddaughter so closely that she could make out his facial expressions was disconcerting, to say the least. Add to that the fact Jen had been carrying Ian when it happened, and one could call it a recipe for panic.

"It could have been anything, Jen. He may have been lost, or maybe he thought he recognized you, right? I don't know about the plate situation. Maybe some kid was pranking him so the cops would pull him over. That's not a new trick."

Haley Rose's voice sounded confident, she hoped.

"I suppose. You're probably right," answered Jen, releasing a breath.

She began flipping her phone in her hand again as Sampson came into the room and sat by Jen's feet, leaning against her leg. No doubt he sensed her anxiety.

"But?"

"It's just . . . well, I don't know about that, granny. My dad says go with your gut when you're not sure what to make out of something. I don't know what that man was doing, but I don't think he was a good guy looking for directions or anything."

Moving Ian to her other knee, Haley Rose got a better look at Jen's expression. Manny had a gift for the "feel" about people. It wasn't a far reach to think that his daughter had inherited Manny's insight to people's emotions and their intentions.

She saw a trace of Chloe in Jen's expression as well. Chloe, while at home in Galway, would often make some of the same observations about people. And she'd been right the majority of the time.

Her angst rose.

Changing dirty diapers, feeding Ian, watching him laugh, rocking him to sleep, eating pizza and cookies, feeding the Big Dog, and shopping with Jen had been her complete agenda for the week. She'd been prepared for those situations, but a possible stalker or some pervert who had a hunger for young girls or babies was not on her list of things to do. Not even remotely.

She took a deep breath.

"Jen. I believe you, but I think this was a random situation, so let's not get our pretty new lace panties in a bunch, right?"

Her granddaughter looked at her for a moment then broke into a real grin. "Good Lord, you're right. I'm sorry for maybe, like, overreacting."

"Given what's happened to you and Manny the last few years of your life, I'd be way worse than you. So let's bake a batch of those oatmeal-raisin cookies that I can almost taste, and try on those new clothes we spent your dad's money on."

Jen jumped up, smiling. "Oh. That sounds great. I'll get the mix out of the pantry."

"Mix? Oh, girl. We don't do mixes where I come from, don't ya know. You are about to get the baking lesson of your—"

The ring of Jen's cell phone interrupted Haley Rose.

Jen looked down at the display, and her smile grew wider.

"Speak of the devil. It's Stacie. Wait 'til I tell her about that car and stuff. I'll be right there, Granny."

Haley Rose felt her tension disappear as she took Ian to the kitchen, put him in his high chair, and walked to the pantry. She dug out the flour and a box of oatmeal, grabbed a bag of raisins, and then returned to the table.

This baking lesson was going to be far better than worrying about some psycho driving by the house.

Reaching for the cupboard door next to the table, she rattled two pots around before she found the cookie sheet, checked to make sure it was clean, then turned back to the table.

"These cookies—" She stopped in midsentence when she saw the expression on Jen's face. Her granddaughter stood in the archway leading from the family room, her face pale, and her eyes moist. The phone was clutched so tightly in her right hand that her knuckles had morphed white.

"What's wrong?" asked Haley Rose.

"That was . . . was Stacie's mom. Stacie got mugged this morning after track practice. She's okay. But she's in the hospital right now."

"Good God. I'm so sorry." She rushed over and hugged her.

"That's not all."

"What?" said Haley Rose, putting Jen at arm's length.

Wiping at tears, Jen looked her square in the eyes.

"The mugger stole her car."

CHAPTER-21

"Wait for the rest of us to finish, will ya?" said Sophie, giving Manny one of her infamous evil-eye looks.

"I'm waiting. I'm only doing what you all should do. I found something that doesn't fit, at least with what I understand about the Mayans. You know how this works. Pieces and then a completed puzzle, we hope."

"Well, do it quieter. I'm concentrating here," said Sophie.

His loquacious friend then looked around the table, closed her file with a thump, and put her pen on the table.

"I've seen enough though. How about the rest of you?"

Chloe followed suit by shutting her file, then pushed another of the books that Munoz had provided toward the center of the table. "I'm ready. I might be rusty, but I've got an idea or three."

"Yeah, you mean the kind that will get us back to the pool, colorful drinks, and the ocean? That kind of idea?" asked Sophie.

"There's that," she answered, smiling.

Alex glanced at Dean and raised his eyebrows. "How about it, Dean? You ready?"

Dean didn't answer right away. He stroked his beard, adjusted his teal-paisley driving hat, glanced at his notes, and then pursed his lips.

He flipped back to an already dog-eared page in one of his files, shook his head ever so slowly, then shifted in his seat.

"Damn, boy. You look like a fifty-year-old who needs a potty break," said Sophie.

Her husband looked up and offered a small grin. "Well, that makes sense. I have to pee, but that's not the driving force behind my apprehension."

"Want me to hold your hand and take you to the potty so we can get on with this? I'll make it worth your while later," said Sophie.

"Hey, best offer all day, but I think I can manage."

Manny knew there were subtle signs in these files that could cause a forensic expert like Dean to be reluctant to discuss the cases. Alex's action had displayed some of that behavior as well, but Dean was hung up on something more plausible than the general distastefulness of the cases.

"What is the driving force then?" asked Manny.

Dean turned to glance at Alex, then he focused on Manny. "I'm not quite sure; there are circumstances and physical evidence that doesn't seem to fit, based on what I understand about hot weather and physical evidence."

"I saw a couple of things too," said Alex. "But our job is not to critique the Mexican police. We're here to profile, right?"

"We are. So let's give them our best and get out of here. Right after we take a break," said Manny.

After a five-minute break, the five huddled around the table with full glasses of iced tea and a batch of sweet bisquets, still warm from the bakery. The heavenly aroma reminded Manny of how late in the day it was becoming—he was ready for an early dinner.

He piled two more on his plate and pulled his notes to his right side.

"Ready?"

"Hell yes," said Sophie. "You go first and we'll fill in the blanks or whatever."

"Sounds good."

Exhaling, Manny began, although it felt extremely odd to profile a killer that he had no real opportunity to investigate, let alone bring to justice.

"This killer is meticulous. He's a male, between twenty-five and forty. Not tremendously big, but because of the way he pulled the hearts from the victims' chests, he has strength in his hands. I'd say he works with them or has training that requires that kind of hand strength to compete."

"Like what?" asked Alex.

"Maybe martial arts or something similar. There is another possibility, I guess. He could have spent some time in a wheelchair or on crutches. Those are specific conditions that could cause immense strength in hands and arms."

"That may fit with one thing I've seen in a couple of the photos," said Dean.

"You mean the way a couple of the footprints show a subtle pressure on the outside of his feet?" asked Manny.

"Yeah, that utterly clear imprint near the foot of the first victim's murder scene indicates that he could walk with an ever so slight limp," answered Dean.

"Or that he had some orthopedic problem with a knee or ankle," said Alex.

"So far we have a man of average- to below-average size, who has had or still has a problem with walking. Anything else with the physical?" asked Manny.

"Yeah, maybe. The report on page five shows a couple of hair sample pictures. Although the DNA test had no hit, there is a difference between the victim's hair and a few found at the scene," said Dean.

Everyone turned to the page Dean had mentioned, and Manny saw what he was speaking about immediately. Running his hand over the photos, he shook his head.

Damn. I missed that one.

"I don't— *Ohhh,* you mean the two on the left are more curly or wavy?" said Chloe.

"Yes. That's not all. The color is not as dark, as black as the victim's. That might mean the killer has a different genetic origin than the victim, who was born in Mexico. It's not unheard of to have some genetic diversity in any closed population, but it could be something."

Alex leaned over, resting his prosthesis on his file. "So are you recommending a DNA test to determine the proper haplogroup?"

"Yep."

"What the hell is that?" asked Sophie.

"I'll tell you," Dean interjected. "Parents pass on certain genes to their kids. Within that genic make-up is a group of genes that can determine what ethnic group you may have originated from. You know, what area of the world your earliest ancestors came from."

"So there is a chance that I'm *not* Asian? You mean I could be like Scandinavian?" said Sophie, batting her eyes.

Manny laughed out loud, joined by the others.

"I'm not sure I'm ready for a short Scandinavian woman with dark hair and a smartass tongue who tosses throwing stars," said Manny.

"But you're okay with an Asian woman who does, right?" said Sophie.

"Only *one* Asian woman who does those things. I don't think the law enforcement community could handle two," said Manny with wink.

"Yeah, and don't forget it," said Sophie.

"At any rate, that might give us more insight to the physical appearance of the killer."

"So you think we can add Caucasian to the mix?" asked Chloe.

"Yeah, I do," said Dean. "It's something more for them to look at."

"Anything else with the physical side of this killer?" asked Manny.

He waited. The silence suggested it was time to move on.

"This man is bright. He understands timing. The reports say the police are still checking for any video evidence of the kidnappings, but he seems to avoid public and private surveillance cameras and congested areas. That makes him an opportunist or a well-organized unsub. Even though the police haven't found a link with the victims yet, there could be one."

"Tell me why you think that, over just random kidnappings," said Chloe.

Manny felt the enthusiasm build as the killer's puzzling motivation became clearer.

"His methods are very precise. Each incision, each placement of the bowls where he burned the hearts, every knot he used to tie the hands and feet were virtually identical. It is as if he practiced and practiced so that when the time came, emotion wouldn't play a role in his decision to kill these folks. Even his kidnapping method was identical, with the exception of Samuel Rozen's."

"You mean with the way he subdued them or how he isolated them?" asked Sophie, her eyes intense.

Manny nodded. "Yes, both of those. He didn't use chloroform, according to the toxicology report; instead he used bromoform, which is a little more harsh but easier to find outside the U.S."

"Hell, if he were bright enough, he could have created his own concoction," Alex added. "To do that, he would have had to know the victim's weight so he knew how many parts per million to mix in the solution."

"Not to mention access to the chemicals and a place to create it," said Dean.

"The potential to do that, mix the bromoform, makes this killer one smart cookie," said Alex, leaning back with a scowl. "And that makes me nervous."

"Remember, we're talking possibilities here. Having said that, I'm sixty-forty this sicko is bright enough to blend the bromoform correctly. That adds another layer to this one, but also could narrow down the search parameters," said Manny.

"An academic?" asked Chloe.

"Possibly. There are a lot of bright people out there and the Internet is the giver of all knowledge. Let's keep going though. I want to continue to focus on his precision," said Manny.

"Yeah, good idea. I hear the pool calling my name," said Sophie.

"Me too. The markings and the irritation on the nose and mouth of each victim shows me he probably used the same cloth to cover each victim's face," said Manny.

"That would indicate he was comfortable and feels safe keeping everything to the same pattern," said Chloe. "So I'm aboard with all of that. He's a total creature of routine."

"As they say, you can write it down. As if we needed more proof, he kept the rituals the same. And though it's almost impossible to tell the exact moment of death, each one of these folks died within a few moments of the incision," said Manny.

"The blood curation analysis around the wounds says you're spot-on with that," said Alex.

"None of that indicates a relationship to the victims. It just shows he killed them the same way," said Chloe.

"You're right," said Manny. "He could simply be looking to act out."

After taking another swallow from his tea, Manny reached out and pulled one of the reference books Munoz had provided.

"I looked up some of the ritualistic processes he uses, and this man seems to be completely in tune with those methods associated with Mayan sacrifice. Right down to the ceremonial burning of the heart. He knows exactly what he's doing. As much as he tried, he's still not perfectly consistent with all of the victim's circumstances."

"Like what?" asked Sophie.

"Fair question, so let's look closer. There are some minor inconsistences, like body position and the fact he was more physical with the men. For another example, the locations of each murder are remote parts of the island but not so far off the beaten path that they weren't inaccessible. It looks like he was trying to hide them. The exception seemed to involve the first murder in San Gervasio. That's a pretty public arena."

"Could it be he was not hiding the bodies so much as hiding what he was doing?" asked Chloe.

"That's a great point," said Manny. "None of the bodies took more than five hours to locate, if the time of deaths are correct. And each was found in the morning hours, which on the surface might indicate he was offering the sacrifices to a particular god."

"How does the time matter?" asked Dean.

"Well, if he were offering his worship to the fertility goddess Ixchel, there wouldn't be a particular time and most certainly not human sacrifice. If these were sunrise offerings, he would have been making his sacrifices to the Mayan sun god, Kinich Ahau."

"But you don't think that was it," said Alex.

Manny shook his head. He was always surprised at how discussing details of cases cleared the muddy waters swirling in his head. There was odd magic at work to be sure.

"No, I don't. He might want us to think that way so we stick with the premise he was sacrificing to be blessed each morning. But I saw something else at the first murder scene that didn't really make sense to me."

"Which was?" said Sophie.

"There was a small, block stone that showed an image of one of the major Mayan gods, who doubled as the god of war. That should never be in the location it was in, given the type of altar this one was intended to be. I believe our killer put the carving in that spot in the wall. I think he actually took out a stone and replaced it with that one. The scrapings around the stone look fresh, and the stone looks a trifle newer," said Manny.

"Is that what got your attention when you asked for Alex's magnifying glass?" asked Dean.

"It was."

"Why would he do that?" asked Sophie.

"You tell me."

Sophie's wheels were always turning, but this time they were racing. Her eyes darted around the table, and then she settled on Manny.

"Okay. A god-of-war offering might indicate the killer was at war with someone and might want to be blessed in that war. That concept's not far from some of the practices in Asian cultures," she said.

"What else?" asked Manny.

"The fact that he spent time putting the stone where it was means he probably knew it would be seen . . . or else he's really new at this and simply screwed up."

"Since that one was his first murder and the other victims were found in less conspicuous locations, I vote for mistake," said Chloe.

"I'm not sure yet, but it could be," said Manny.

"If that first one was a screw-up, and he's maintained his pattern since then, it means he's far more comfortable in the private surrounding than in a public setting," said Sophie.

"That could be a reflection of his personality, so it adds to the puzzle," said Manny. "But let's go back to the war concept. Why do wars happen?"

"Because politicians feel safe in those damned chairs and thousand-dollar suits and can send grunts to do their dirty work," said Sophie.

"That's partly true, but politics aside, wars are fought because someone perceived a wrongdoing from another party, right?" said Manny.

"True. So this is a war?" asked Chloe.

"I don't know. It's worth consideration though. He could simply be another deranged killer that has his own reasons. The key will be if the Mexican police can find a link to the victims. Plus there are two more inconsistences that get my attention."

"Do tell," said Alex.

"The photos with the feathers in them . . . the feathers are different colors and lengths. That could be significant in terms of where they came from and what they were used for," answered Manny.

"Munoz's people should be able to do the legwork and find out who makes the feathers. That should be easy," said Alex.

"They will, I'm sure. The other situation that seems odd to me is: why do two of the victims have Mayan jewelry around their necks and the others do not? Why not garnish them all the same way? Anyone who goes to this length, in their warped thinking, would likely do something like that to each victim."

"A different message for these two?" asked Sophie.

"Maybe. I'll make sure Munoz's people analyze the necklaces and their intent, if he's not already on it."

Manny finished off the tea and closed the file, but his mind was restless, like they'd missed something. He wondered again about the way the killer had deviated from his pattern with the jewelry. It didn't fit. Sophie interrupted his thinking.

"Wait, I know that look. You think those inconsistencies are intentional, don't you?" asked Sophie.

She was right on again. "It could be. Of course, that begs the question why. Someone this meticulous doesn't make mistakes like that. He must have a reason. Maybe even to persuade us to chase our tails some. I'll throw it into the report to Munoz, but I think we're ready to get him a profile."

"So let's get this right. We have a man with ridiculous knowledge of the Mayan tradition, who may not be that big, sort of young, may have had a limp or some shit, makes mistakes on purpose, and randomly kills people because he's at war with them? Right?"

Manny laughed. "You're pretty much right on, but I'll add a few more details based on what you've all deduced."

He glanced around the table and started to thank everyone, but before he did, he was struck with something Sophie said. He swore under his breath.

"What?" asked Dean.

"Damn it. I missed something," said Manny, scanning the group. "These *aren't* random murders at all. He knew each one of these people."

CHAPTER-22

For the third time, Haley Rose reached for her phone to call Chloe. She was no cop, but she was smart enough to know that the theft of Stacie's car and the subsequent drive-by of this house was no fluke. Fishy was fishy and, in her experience, usually led to more than an innocent coincidence. Things like that could be totally different than they appeared to be. She'd learned that lesson the hard way in Galway, more than once.

Taking a long look at Jen holding Ian and kissing his neck, which caused him to belly laugh, she wondered again if her wisdom was sound. Maybe the drive-by *was* nothing after all—just some happenstance forcing her own mistrust to take control of her still bruised emotional state.

After debating again whether to bother Chloe and eventually Manny, she put the cell phone in her pocket.

Losing Gavin in Las Vegas those months ago hadn't helped her outlook on life, and she had to throw that in the mix. They hadn't actually been an item, but the man had been comfortable to be with. In her book, that was a building block for a serious relationship, something she didn't have much luck with. Not even a secret kiss of the Blarney Stone had delivered on its promise.

After all she'd been through, maybe she was still a smidgen distraught.

Maybe not.

The look in Jen's eyes had been remarkably Manny-like. No fear, simply pain at what had happened to her friend. But there was something other than that. There was anger. It was simmering—no question—but well controlled.

Jen's complex emotional response had been the driving force for Haley Rose to pick up the phone in the first place. Yet, how could she bother them and most assuredly ruin their vacation with a few maybes and possibilities? They got so little time away together.

But what if. . . .

She ran her lip against her teeth. She couldn't make this decision alone. She didn't have to.

"Jen. I've been stewing over this for too long and need your help. What do you want me to do, darlin'?"

Jen stopped rocking Ian and turned toward Haley Rose. Her eyes were steady and her face relaxed.

"Well, we called the LPD and told them what we saw. They said they'd send patrols every once in a while and put out an APB on the car. But we both know that's because of Dad and Chloe, mostly. So maybe they think it's no big deal."

"That's probably the truth, girl."

Shifting Ian to her other hip, Jen kissed him again. He laughed again. "We can't go see Stacie at the hospital until tomorrow, and it's getting close to Ian's bedtime anyway. Even if you call Dad or Chloe, when could they get here? Twelve or fifteen hours at least? Unless they get the BAU jet to go get them and bring them back, that's still eight or nine hours, right?"

"Aye, you've been thinking it through, I see."

"Just putting a little common sense to it, that's all. The chance of this guy being, like, a problem for us is slim."

Jen bent down and stroked Sampson's head. "I thinking messing with this version of the Big Dog wouldn't be healthy for anyone either."

"Another good point," agreed Haley Rose. This girl could go to work for law enforcement already.

Striding across the floor, Jen handed Ian to Haley Rose and then disappeared down the hall toward Manny and Chloe's bedroom. She returned a minute later with something in each hand. Haley Rose felt her pulse climb and clutched Ian closer.

Laying the items on the table, Jen stepped back and smiled. "We have these, just in case."

"It's been a spell for me, Jennifer Williams. I'm not sure I can handle one."

Jen picked up the Berretta 92s and managed it like she was born with one in her hand. "Dad made sure I was an expert shot after we . . . we lost mom. I've got more training hours than most cops. I know how to use them. But you used to shoot, right?"

"I did. It made me feel safer with Chloe, her cousin Meav, and me in the inn."

"It's still the same, Granny. Point, click off the safety, and protect yourself."

Haley Rose glanced at the table and then back to Jen. It was impossible to stifle the smile that spread like morning sunlight across her face. The girl wasn't going to have any trouble with unwanted advances from young men in college. Usually teenage girls have a measure of trepidation when it came to discussing issues like shooting someone to protect themselves.

Not with this one. Yet, preparing to shoot someone was a far cry from pulling the trigger, she suspected.

Still, she felt a surge of pride accompanied with a twinge of sadness. Growing up faster than one needed to grow up was always a crap shoot. Yet, Jen seemed to accept the realm of being the child of a gifted cop. Maybe she was even destined to follow him into the world of protecting universes and fighting evil forces bent on having their way.

Shifting the now sleeping Ian over her shoulder, Haley Rose reached for one of the weapons and was surprised how comfortable it felt in her hand.

"Okay, young one, your logic is good. Between Sampson, you, and me, we'll make it a day to regret if anyone tries to make life tough for us."

"I'm sure he won't, but it never hurts to be ready, like Dad says."

"Your dad's right. So let's put this wee one to bed, finish baking those cookies, and order a pizza. I'm hungry, and my sweet tooth is yelling for a fix," said Haley Rose.

Jen's face was fairly beaming. "Don't forget that butter pecan ice cream," she said, laughing.

"Oh my, yes. We'll be fat but happy and sassy, don't ya know."

With that, Haley Rose took Ian into his room, and Jen called the number to order pizza.

"It'll be a good night," Haley Rose whispered to young Ian, gently settling him in his crib.

****

He stood behind the large lilac bush, wringing his hands. The fragrance was one he knew well and, he had to admit, one of his favorites, even though it had been years since he'd actually enjoyed the presence of a live Lilac. It was just one more reason to believe God had intended him and Haley Rose to be together.

It had taken some effort to get this close to her, especially since the teenager had no doubt called the police after he took her friend's car. He hadn't really meant to rough the girl up, but she wasn't cooperating and that damn pepper spray only served to piss him off.

Kids needed a good smacking around from time to time anyway. That's what his papa had said. He was no worse for wear, was he?

Moving a step to his left, he got a better view of the kitchen window and Haley Rose standing there with that teenage brat and the baby over her shoulder. He thought his heart might burst. Each time he saw her, his love for her seemed to grow in ways he hardly understood.

Absence truly did make the heart fonder.

Watching until she disappeared and the young one closed the curtains, he moved from the backyard to the street two houses down and climbed into the four-wheel-drive truck he'd relieved from another idiot who had far too much handed to him.

Turning on the radio, he found a station that was speaking of lost loves and songs dedicated to them.

How appropriate. But his love, their love, wouldn't be lost much longer, now would it?

"No, sweet Haley Rose. Not much longer at all," he whispered.

CHAPTER-23

"Great. Just when I thought we were getting our collective asses out of here," said Sophie, sitting back into her chair.

"We'll be gone soon," said Manny.

He reached over and squeezed Chloe's hand. "We've still got time to hit the pool or beach, and I can still see you in one of those awesome swimsuits."

"Lucky you," she said with a wry smile.

Manny's anticipation climbed another level. He wondered if she would always have that effect on him. He hoped so.

"I think I can safely speak for all of the heathen men in this room that I'd like to see all of our women in a bathing suit at the beach," said Dean.

Panning the room, Manny couldn't help feeling like he'd struck gold when it came to his BAU members who doubled as his close friends. Dedication was an understated word when applied to this group.

"Agreed. So let's wrap this up. To do that we need to look at the unsub's motivation."

"I thought we did," said Sophie.

"Partially. We need to look at the rest of his thought agenda. Wars aren't waged against random foes, like Sophie's statement indicated. Wars typically are waged against a particular target, a population or a segment of people, for instance."

"So his selection of victims isn't based as much on opportunity as selection? That's certainly not unheard of. We've experienced those types of killers before," said Chloe.

"Most spree killers are motivated by bloodlust. Serial killers usually have a type of victim in mind, but their logic can be so twisted that it's impossible to discover the reasons for their actions entirely," said Manny.

"I see what you're saying. This guy is cutting two paths that don't usually fit together," said Sophie.

"Right. Spree killing is not serial killing in most instances. But through the god-of-war carving and the succinct pattern he uses, even though this has happened very quickly, I think he's targeted his victims and there's a common denominator."

"There doesn't seem to be any mutual demographic that I can see. Other than living on Cozumel," said Alex. "Two of the victims weren't even born in Mexico."

"That's true, but there's something that connects them," said Manny.

He hesitated, wanting to take this angle much further, but the red flag—time—kept grabbing his attention.

He glanced at his watch. Three hours thirty-five minutes. It was time to wrap this up.

We're here for a profile, and that's it, Williams.

Pulling the phone out of his island shirt, he dialed Munoz.

The phone barely had a chance to ring before he heard Munoz's voice.

"Inspector. We're ready," he said. Then he put the phone in his pocket.

"That's it? We don't dig deeper? You know, like where this guy might find these people and all of that other stuff?" asked Sophie.

"We've done our part. We're not the investigators; we're giving Munoz another tool to work with. Finding the link with these people is not our job. And honestly, as much as this case intrigues me, I'm on vacation and want to feel what that's like."

"Good God. The world just may have stopped spinning," said Alex, grinning.

Manny got the message and returned the grin. "Isn't that a song or something? Listen. I can do this. You all just have to help me through the door when we're done, okay?"

The door opened, and Munoz, followed by two other men and one woman, approached the table.

"You and your people have seen into the crystal ball, Agent Williams?" asked Munoz.

"Perhaps some. This killer is unique with how he operates, but we think we can help you narrow the path to find him."

Munoz spoke Spanish to his associates, and they immediately took out notepads and pens.

"Please share with us."

"He's between twenty-five and forty. Not a large man, but has strong hands and arms. That makes us believe he may have had or still has some orthopedic problems, based on the footprint pictures. He's extremely meticulous and knows the Mayan culture like few do. He could be an expert or an amateur expert. I'd check places like the college science departments. You have museums; maybe he works in one. Of course, he could be here on vacation or could have come in from the mainland each day, but I believe, because of the way he knows the island, he lives here."

"I suspected some of this. His knowledge is extraordinary," said Munoz, nodding.

Reaching to the file of the first victim, Manny pointed at the image there.

"It appears that he changed out one of the carvings at the altar of the first victim, and it shows the god of war instead of the plain stone that should be there. That could make this apparent spree action more like a war. Not a typical spree killer, but one who has a target group."

"Who knows the reasons for this kind of psychological snap? But something set him off, and he has his own logic for picking his victims. We believe that means there's a link between the victims, and you'll have to discover that link in order to get to him, I suspect."

"You have no idea what that link could be?" asked Munoz.

Manny shook his head. "I think you'll have to dig into the background of each of the victims for that. You have the tools. I can even call Josh Corner and have him get the research team in Quantico involved. Not sure it will help, but it might."

"Thank you. That would be helpful. Anything else?"

Scanning the group, Manny exhaled, running his hand through his hair.

"I think he's Caucasian. Not native. He is obviously deeply entrenched in the idea of the Mayan culture. Almost obsessed. I believe if someone were exposed to the island's purposes and past, they wouldn't be as devoted to the ways and precision of the sacrifices. Fertility prayers and offerings are a mile away from the ravages of war. I also believe him to be a bit of an introvert based on the possible leg issues. Most folks with physical ailments are not happy to be seen in public. That means, in my estimation, he doesn't exactly fit the typical outgoing personality that many of these killers learn to adopt."

Munoz tilted his head. "Very insightful, Agent Williams."

"There is one more thing. I know you'll have your folks run down the feather types, etc. But I'd do something else."

"Yes?"

"The knife he used to make the incisions. The blade was obviously sharp, but unless I miss my guess, he would have used an ancient Mayan dagger with as much significance to the sacrificial order as possible. It would make him feel more like the priest he is emulating or perhaps thinks he is," said Manny. "See if you can locate some of those blades."

Munoz nodded to his female assistant, and she rushed out the door.

"We will begin working with who and what we have available. You all have been of tremendous assistance. Thank you for your efforts, agents."

He reached out his hand to Manny, who hesitated and then gripped it.

The room seemed to sigh with unrequited relief. None of the BAU members or Chloe spoke. It was as if breaking the silence would bring them back to a different reality—that they weren't truly finished with this case. Manny knew what they were all thinking. The handshake sealed the deal, right?

That's it. We're out of here.

"Good luck," said Manny.

"Our fortunes have greatly increased," said Munoz with another one of those tired smiles

Manny recognized as a reflection of his own world every so often.

No rest for the weary.

Shaking everyone else's hand in turn, Munoz thanked them individually. Sophie didn't give him the chance for a handshake. She hugged him and then held him at arm's length.

"We're out of here and thanks for not pushing us further. Williams here doesn't know when to stop."

"A curse and a blessing, to be sure," said Munoz. "Let me get you back to the resort. I'm sure Missus Downs is anxious to have you all join her."

Getting behind Manny, Sophie pushed him toward the door. "You first. I don't trust you bringing up the rear. We could be here another two days."

Manny laughed.

She was right.

They reached the warm air of Cozumel and the street where a fairly new, blue and white police transport van awaited them.

Manny helped Chloe up the step and then settled in beside her, holding hands and making small talk.

Just as Alex reached the door, his phone went off to the ringtone of an old Chicago love song. Barb was calling.

His friend pulled the phone from his pocket quickly, almost in panic mode. Manny didn't blame him. What they'd just gone through in the meeting room would put anyone on edge.

A moment later Alex's stress evolved into a grin. "Yeah, I think we can do that. See you soon."

He hung up and plopped down beside Sophie.

"What was that?" she asked, sitting close to Dean.

"She wanted to know if a six-thirty dinner was good and could we handle a couple of bottles of expensive champagne."

"Oh. I love how that woman thinks," answered Sophie.

The drive back to the resort was without incident. They were even able to see some of the old, quaint shops littering downtown San Miguel. Including one called The Jaguar's Lair. It was an old book and antique shop advertising links to the Mayan past. Manny made a note to visit the shop. Bringing home an actual piece of history for Jen appealed to him far more than trinkets made in another nation. There was something else. He wondered if Aaron Rathburn had been in this shop. It was worth the effort to see. He'd give the information to the hotel's security staff. Maybe Torres could get it right and check to find out.

They reached the resort and waved as the van left the property.

"Let's get to that dinner," said Dean. "I'm starved."

Glancing at the door, then both sides of the driveway, Manny saw nothing suspicious. Nothing, or no one, that needed his attention or the BAU's expertise. The feeling was as foreign to him as a good night's sleep.

He shook his head. That was really it. The profile was all Munoz truly wanted. Nothing more. No more bodies that screamed to him for justice. No more photos that caused his guts to clinch and forced him into another emotionless, cold world. No more psycho heads to worm inside and discover logic that defied logic.

The choice and circumstance to be free was exhilarating.

"Manny? Are you ready, man?"

He sighed. "I think I am. Let's do this."

Chloe kissed him on the cheek, and they followed the others inside.

Tonight was theirs, and nothing could change that.

CHAPTER-24

The midnight moon, although not quite full, reflected a silver glow from the sheen of the lush plants. The tiny clearing had all of the light necessary to complete the task. It was finally here. The culmination of all of those long hours of planning. Of working out details. Of righting what was wrong.

His heart was prancing a hundred miles per hour, yet he saw his purpose and his goal as clearly as ever.

Stretching his hand to his side, he felt the steel of the long knife and the shorter one beside it. The blades were cold, but the night was warm and full of promise. Promise that he prayed would end the hell that had begun those months ago.

"Of course it will," he whispered. "The gods never lie."

He laughed softly. "Gods indeed."

He approached the middle of the clearing and stared at his feet. Slowly, he removed his feathered headdress. Then the matching ankle bracelets. Then the wrist and armbands. Lastly, the leather loin cloth and ceremonial chest plate.

With each subsequent removal of his dress, he felt his freedom return. It was as if the chosen deities had designed this costume—and the successive ritual—to bind and restrict rather than to free.

Tonight, he would be free, at last.

Slowly, he dropped to his knees, reaching for the knife from his discarded cloth.

There would be no prayer this night. No thought of which god he should please and which one would be offended. To hell with gods that would claim his allegiance and then allow him to beg for something they could never deliver. No, not this evening. Not in this circle of light he'd so carefully planned and created. This was *his* world for an evening, and he would take from it what he desired. *All* that he desired.

Without warning, her face rose from the opulent underbrush just mere feet away. Her look was the same. Her eyes were soft and kind, her mouth displaying the electric smile that had comforted him and defused life's most problematic situations. Together, they had been one; separated, they were lost. Hadn't that been her favorite quote to him?

He watched as her image moved closer, then melted into the misty light. Once again he was left to wonder why she'd departed from him, again. But he dwelled on that for only a moment.

Reality had made headway in his mind as well as his heart. She'd left him, and he at least understood that desires and actuality were as far apart as east and west.

Steeling his thoughts, he moved his mind to the current task at hand. Literally.

The two scarlet blankets had been placed with precise care, as had the bound occupants now lying upon them.

The woman's eyes showed no fear, no emotion at all. It was as if she expected her walk on earth to end this way. Maybe she was right. Didn't we all have some inkling of when and how this walk would end? He thought so.

The man was still struggling to free himself, although the drug had taken much of his fight. His expression was still haunted by disbelief and recognition, even in his state.

There was silent begging in the man's eyes. As if their past would save him.

It would not. He was dead wrong.

He smiled at his two companions. "No more worries. No more. You will both be free."

Freedom dances to many tunes.

Tears began to roll down his face at the thought of his words.

"Tonight. I will be free," he whispered.

He raised the knife, hesitated, and then ripped it through the air, over and over again.

CHAPTER-25

He gazed at her arm as it rested across his chest, his hair creating a thin mat caressing her forearm and hand. His index finger performed a slow dance over her wrist and down to her fingers. His stomach did its best to tame the butterflies that had suddenly appeared.

The touch of a woman . . .

Manny had been awake for fifteen minutes, the bright morning sun proving to be the alarm clock he'd never really needed in his life. He supposed his internal clock was a witness to his perpetual state of mind, where the wheels were always turning.

During those fifteen minutes, he explored a world he seldom had the opportunity to pursue. He raised his eyebrows at that thought—not exactly right. Maybe he'd had opportunity but simply hadn't seized it. His mental state was a hurried blur at most times, infinitely moving from one problem to the next. But not now. Not this morning. This moment wouldn't be another casualty of his endless appointments.

He listened to Chloe breathe, watching the rise and fall of her breasts, and found a quieting rhythm in both. He explored the warmth of her body as her legs rested against him at the thigh and hip, all of the while counting the freckles on his Irish wife's nose. He gently brushed her long, red hair away from her face to get a better look at the woman who had saved him from the life he'd feared after Louise had died.

A life alone shouldn't be on anyone's horizon.

Chloe shifted in her sleep, smiling at a dream world he couldn't see, but it reminded him of the previous night. As if he really needed a reminder.

The evening had been everything he hoped it would be. The fabulous dinner of lobster and steak served with a special Caribbean spice. Spectacular. Although he wasn't much of a wine connoisseur, he doubted he'd partaken in a wine smoother than the pinot noir the waiter had recommended.

Great wine, great service, and the soft ambiance that only a private balcony overlooking the ocean could offer had forged a permanent pleasant memory. Never mind the opportunity to indulge in such a meal with his closest friends, which only added to the unforgettable evening.

Yet all of that had not compared to the way Chloe had stolen the night by quite simply being Chloe.

Not because of the strapless jade gown that fit like it had been tailored for her alone, and how it matched those incredible eyes. Or the face that had caused everyone at the table to steal secret looks, including him.

Not because of her full, infectious giggle bursting with the Irish cadence that caused everyone at the table to smile wider or laugh louder, especially when she told one of her stories of growing up in Galway. He remembered being mesmerized with just the way her mouth had moved when she spoke.

Not because of how she held his hand under the table or the way she ran her hand along his thigh when they shared a moment that was theirs alone. Not even the fact that they'd fit like a hand and glove when they slow-danced to the talented band whose specialty, it seemed, had been to entice couples to fall deeper in love with one another.

It hadn't even been the sight of her slowly removing the tight-fitting gown strictly for his benefit, teasing him in every possible way.

All of those things had accented the night's experience, but none of it compared to the idea that she was *his* wife. That she'd taken him to be hers, despite the obvious baggage Manny Williams had brought to the table. Extensive baggage.

He glanced at the claddagh wedding ring on his left hand.

Extensive was right. She'd inherited a teenaged daughter missing her deceased mother, a black Lab the size of a hippo, a group of friends that probably wouldn't be classified as normal in any circumstance, and a husband who thought the world needed him every waking moment—and then almost losing him before they could celebrate a full day of marriage.

Not to mention a new job after having to leave the BAU and the new son that came less than a year later.

Looking at the ring again, Manny sighed. Chloe definitely got the short end of the stick, but here she was . . . and she was here to stay.

"If you're thinking of having your way with me again, you'll have to wait."

Turning her way, he fell into the smile that had captured his imagination from the beginning.

"What? I have to wait for you to perform your womanly duties?"

"Yeah. I think it'd be best if I made you exercise some patience. I don't want ya to get too much of a good thing. It might kill ya."

He nodded as he reached over and kissed her. "You're such a good wife. How long will I have to wait?"

"Well, I need to go powder my nose and put on that short, red teddy you like, so how's three minutes work for ya?"

"I think I can wait it out. It'll be hard though."

She reached under the sheet and squeezed him. "Just checking to see just how hard it'll be."

He caught his breath. "How am I doing?"

She answered with a kiss as soft as an ocean breeze. He felt it right down to his toes.

She slid out of bed and stood, smiling at him. "I think I'll cut the time in half. You do seem a bit needy."

Two minutes later, Chloe moved to his side of the bed, wearing the lacy red teddy and a look in her eyes that told him he was, once again, the luckiest man on earth.

An hour later, Manny stood on the balcony facing the Caribbean Ocean, watching the sun rise to its almost unfathomable splendor. He'd been fortunate to travel much of the planet over the years, and had seen a few natural wonders, but there wasn't anything quite like a sunrise that warmed both inside and out. Especially after last night and this morning.

"Careful, Williams, you just might get used to this," he breathed.

He sipped his coffee and turned his ear toward the room. Chloe was singing an old Irish ballad in the shower, and it sounded wonderful. She sang the archaic tune with sprinkles of the ancient Gaelic language that seemed to belong to another world.

He supposed it did.

Manny was struck with the realization that the Irish did a wonderful service to their youth by reminding them often of their roots. He was almost jealous that he had nothing like that to pass on to Jen. Although she'd already begun to show signs of being her father's daughter, there was no language or ancient history to send her way. Ian would have a chance to learn from his mom and grandmum.

Ian.

Manny felt his emotion rise at the thought of him. He hadn't gone many nights without seeing his son. Ian was in good hands, and everything was quiet on the home front, according to Jen and Haley Rose, but that didn't stop a quick pang of missing-my-boy from making an appearance.

Sighing, he siphoned more coffee from his cup.

There was simply no way to cover all of the bases for men like himself. Maybe buying an island and living in isolation was the answer. He laughed.

"Yeah, that would work for you," he said out loud.

Chloe began the next verse, and her sweet tones caused him to shake his head. Add singing and use of Gaelic to the other obvious gifts his wife possessed.

Turning back to the ocean, Manny watched a freighter steam along, maybe two miles out. Just to its left was a much bigger vessel, getting larger by the second.

A cruise ship was approaching the island, bringing another boatload of bright-eyed tourists eager to see what Cozumel had to offer. The excited passengers were in for a treat.

Nothing was perfect, but the cruising industry had shrunk the world with affordable prices, allowing folks from all walks of life to see places they may never have had an opportunity to . . .

His thoughts were interrupted by something out of the corner of his eye.

Just to the right of the small, white sandbar that stretched some eighty feet out into the ocean was a yellow rubber raft rising and falling with the waves.

His pulse rose as he studied the raft, which appeared to be anchored. And each time the waves caused the raft to rise, he could see what appeared to be someone lying inside.

He strained his eyes. There was something, but what? Two hundred or so feet was simply too far for him to pick out the details.

At that moment, an older woman walking the beach with her black poodle must have noticed the raft too, because she picked up the dog and began to walk the long side of the sand bar.

He waited. She was about to get an eyeful that would send her to the therapy couch.

Stepping inside, he moved to Chloe's backpack and extracted the small binoculars she had intended to use to look at the wildlife when they visited the ruins at San Gervasio.

The scream told him he hadn't acted quickly enough.

Dropping the empty case onto the bed, he hurried to the balcony, bringing the binoculars to his eyes in one motion.

The woman was sprinting back to the beach as a few early morning beachgoers began to gather toward her.

He waited impatiently for the wave to rise.

As the ocean suspended the raft in its perfect rhythm, he felt the breath leave his lungs. He continued to stare, because what he'd seen was almost too much for him to get his mind around.

Maybe his eyes were playing tricks on him.

After the next gentle wave, he caught the view again.

His eyes weren't playing tricks.

Another torrent of screams confirmed that fact.

"Damn it," he whispered, wondering again why his world was filled with such things, even on vacation.

It was as if Satan and God had a bet on how much he could handle and whether he'd go crazy from this sort of thing before he checked out.

He continued to stare through the binoculars as the next wave rolled a foot higher, giving Manny the most direct, horrifying view of the two bloodied bodies taped to the raft.

CHAPTER-26

Watching how Munoz moved, how he took control without appearing as if he had, Sophie found it plausible that this man, this inspector, was indeed as gifted as Manny suspected. The more insane the circumstances, the more Munoz slowed things down; and it didn't get much crazier than this. His mannerisms were extremely Manny-like, maybe better.

The inspector pointed to the raft, directing three of the blues to bring it all the way up to the beach. Sophie held her breath as she got a closer examination of the dead man and woman fastened to the bottom of the rubber boat.

What kind of sick bitch dreams up this stuff?

After all that she'd seen during her time as a cop, that question was still valid in her mind. She was starting to believe that maybe these unsubs weren't really people at all. The Underworld *had* to be missing a few demons.

Each of the two victims had an incision under their ribs. Just like the others. Obviously the same killer had been at work, with a different twist.

Despite the fact that seagulls had been picking at the victims, their bodies were relatively intact. The man was missing an eye, and the woman's lower lip was virtually gone. Once Sophie got past the other missing chunks of flesh over the pair's arms, faces, and legs, they resembled actual humans.

Outrageous as it seemed, she felt a calm come over her while she began to compartmentalize the situation in the way Manny had taught her. It wasn't easy, ever, but she'd developed a better understanding of what it meant to remove the emotion and start looking at the facts and details.

For a stint, at first, Sophie had thought her long-time friend had shown her how to develop this ability to solve murders more quickly. To make sure no detail was lost because of the physical appearance of the crime scene.

Maybe that had been true to some extent, but she realized Manny had been trying to protect her, to save whatever sanity she had left. She loved him for it, but . . .

Holding Dean's hand, she stole another look at Manny. The torment in his eyes was almost unfair. That single look, one she'd perhaps never truly noticed before, revealed to her an epiphany that was almost overwhelming.

For Manny, it wasn't simply that someone had committed a crime and had to be put away before they could do it again. It was more. This man, this profiler extraordinaire, truly cared for these victims. He'd never met them, never spoken with them, but he was heartbroken over the fact that he'd never have the chance. He hated that this killer had taken something from the world that wasn't his to take.

She bit her lip in frustration at her own lack of understanding.

Damn. No wonder the man never got a good night's sleep.

She sought his face again, and the look of anguish was gone. Just like that. It was replaced with sky-blue pools of determination. Add in a purposeful hand through his blond hair and Manny Williams was in full BAU gear.

A sudden sadness captured her heart.

His vacation was over.

There was only so much unopened alcohol one could expose an alcoholic to before the addiction was all that mattered. Manny was no alcoholic, but instead was driven by something entirely different. Was empathy an addiction? She supposed anything could be.

Manny had told her something once after they'd overeaten in celebration of ending a case, when she'd joked about getting fat right there on the spot. He said there wasn't anything truly evil in itself. The way that particular object or obsession was used dictated its potential. Food was good. Too much food, not so good. A measure of sympathy was great. A boatload of that empathy could cause a madness she doubted she could truly understand.

The workaholic Guardian of the Universe, who was her closest friend, was no exception when it came to his vocation and purpose and how it related to addiction. She sighed softly.

Turning her back on the boat, the ocean, and even Dean, she walked directly to Manny gripping his arm with both hands.

"Can I have a word with your hot ass?"

His eyes fixed on hers, and if she'd had a scrotum, it would have grown rigid in a microsecond.

The chill assured that.

"Not now, Sophie."

"Yeah now. You owe me."

"Huh? For what?"

"'Cause I've been your friend for twelve years and that ain't easy. So get your ass over to my office," she said, nodding away from the group of cops and the BAU.

"Yes, you have. And I love you for that. But we're staying right here."

Manny's voice carried that quality he invoked when it was truly time to listen. She wasn't sure it was intentional, but the effect was impossible to ignore.

Holding his hand, Chloe stood silent, expressionless, reflecting nothing, but Sophie was sure she felt everything Manny was suffering.

"I need to speak to you all," said Manny.

Sophie watched Alex, Barb, Dean, and Munoz step through a few feet of sand, drawing closer and eventually forming a tight circle. Sophie thought the action resembled a noose tightening around someone's neck.

Resemble, hell . . . it *was* a noose. The question was whose.

"I spoke to the inspector after he arrived, and I'm afraid I have a little more work to do here," he glanced at Chloe.

The fiery redhead's countenance remained expressionless. Sophie was impressed. She was thinking of kicking Manny's ass for Chloe.

"Since yesterday, Munoz's people, and with the help of the FBI's databases, have identified several possible unsubs who live on the island. He's asked me to interview them, and I've agreed."

The waves lapped slowly to shore, the only exception to the silence in the circle. Sophie wasn't sure what everyone else was thinking, but the voice in her heart was screaming.

Enough was enough.

She began to speak, resisted, and then settled down the way Manny had taught her. He deserved to be heard, *then* she could run the throwing star up his rectum.

"Why in hell can't you just leave it alone? You've done your part."

Sophie snapped her head around. She didn't expect the source of the comment to be who it was.

Manny looked at Barb with the unwavering expression of softness and determination that was his trademark. To Barb's credit, her expression didn't waver either.

"Good question Barb, and I'll answer it."

He walked over to the raft and the two bodies, pointing at the scene with a long finger.

"This wasn't random. The killer did this with a purpose. The MO was the same, but why put them in a boat and anchor them just off this beach? This time of the morning? Why not in the jungle where all of the others were found?"

"Hey. You're always saying we can't put logic to illogical situations," said Sophie, feeling the edge fall from her frustration. The man was going to tell them why, and she knew she wasn't going to like it.

"True, I do. But we also know killers like this man have their own lucidity, their own set of rules or twisted logic that, in the end, identifies what they're truly about. This spree killer has evolved into something else entirely, in my opinion. He's gone completely against what is comfortable and expected for the kind of killer we profiled yesterday."

"How?" asked Dean.

Manny shifted his feet in the sand and nodded. "He seemed content to work in the comfort of the dark and leave the bodies in more remote places. Even the first victim found on the altar at San Gervasio was placed on the ruins in the very back of the property. Now he takes the time to risk someone seeing him actually put the bodies on public display like this."

"Did anyone? You know, see anything?" asked Alex.

"My people are still canvasing the area, but nothing so far," said Munoz. "He may have come from the north, which is still fairly remote. We are checking out every possibility. He is, however, very clever."

"You didn't answer my question," said Barb.

The sigh Manny released, intentional or not, gave Sophie another peek into the torture inside Manny.

At that moment, her heart broke for him. He truly *was* haunted by his obedience to the demons only he could see.

Chloe moved closer to him. She had seen it too.

"Remember I said this display of the bodies was intentional? That his logic was his own?" asked Manny.

"Yes," said Barb. "We all heard that."

"I believe his intention was for us, the BAU or maybe just one of us, to see the bodies first."

CHAPTER-27

Josh Corner sat at the antique mahogany table his wife had just finished restoring, eating his onion bagel, sipping his chai tea, and scrolling through the pictures on his phone of his two sons and his pregnant wife as they enjoyed the previous afternoon in the park at the end of their street. There was even a couple of silly selfies, one with each of his boys that caused him to laugh for the umpteenth time.

Charlie and Jake were now seven and six, growing like weeds and changing daily.

He took another long draw from his cup.

Once, several years ago, he had a t-shirt made from a picture of them. Both boys laughing like kids do at that age. Odd as it seemed, that shirt had brought some order to his chaotic existence.

"Time for another one," he whispered, scrolling to the next shot. Josh supposed he'd better do it soon. It wouldn't be cool in a year or so; his boys would most certainly remind him of that.

Touching the screen, he went to the next album and continued to treasure the pictures that stopped time and forbade the future to make an appearance. Each shot gave him another thankful reason that he'd listened to his "Manny" voice and taken the day off. The world had turned another revolution without him and all was well. Imagine that.

The vibration and synchronized sound that alerted him of a new text disturbed his thoughts.

Without looking at the source, he turned the phone on its face and finished his bagel. It was most certainly another day where his services would be required, but not just yet. A good bagel was hard to find, and he would enjoy this one until the savory end.

Five minutes later, he flipped the phone over and saw that Manny had texted him. He read the two-liner, frowned, read it again, and sensed his feel-good morning begin the process of totally disappearing.

Josh. I need some info and help with a couple of things.

Call me when you get this.

What the hell does he need my help for? I haven't even sent him Munoz's info yet.

"Shit. Munoz," he said softly.

The man couldn't wait one damn day? Hadn't he asked the inspector to leave Manny and his BAU alone for one day, at least? Hadn't Munoz said yes?

Josh slowly shook his head. Hell, maybe Munoz hadn't agreed. The more he recalled their conversation, he was sure the inspector never said any such thing.

Reaching over to the other side of the table, he turned Tim Ellis's latest Parish and Richards novel on his iPad over in his hands. He'd enjoyed much of it last night before he fell asleep in his chair. He'd fulfilled part of the promise to himself. He wondered when he'd have an opportunity to finish the story.

Placing the iPad face down, he studied Manny's message a second time.

He knew the unrelenting sense of near desperation that sometimes accompanies cases like the one haunting Munoz. In fact, there were times, especially pre-Manny, that he would have taken almost any other resource than what the Bureau offered.

If he'd done the math correctly and this killer was a true spree killer, then there were probably six bodies instead of four by now, or there would be shortly.

A tinge of guilt tapped him on the shoulder. He'd delayed talking to Manny so the man could keep crazy at bay, but Munoz had acted to save lives. Maybe Munoz was right in his decision.

Shaking off the thought, he hit Manny's number on the speed dial and waited. Maybe this had nothing to do with the crimes in Cozumel. Maybe his friends needed another couple of days to rest up.

"Yeah, and maybe the earth is flat," he whispered.

The phone rang twice, then Manny answered.

"What kept you?"

"I was getting some more beauty sleep."

"You're going to need it," said Manny.

Josh could almost see the grin on his face.

"Yep, especially at seven ten in the morning," said Josh. He exhaled. "What's up, Manny?"

"You probably know. Thanks for trying to give us a day without the sick part of the world getting in the way, but it didn't work out so well."

"Munoz?"

"Yes. He's pretty persistent."

"What happened?"

"We did a profile for him yesterday and thought we were finished. We had a wonderful dinner last night and expected today to be a beach-pool-margarita day."

"And?" asked Josh, cringing.

"The two bodies in the raft outside our resort sort of changed our plans."

"Manny, you can—"

"You know better than that. I, we, can't just let this go. I think the message of where, how, and when the bodies were dumped is intended for us, the BAU, or at least for the cops . . . maybe. The way he did it suggests that. Or he's just a daring dumbass that might go to the next level of his devolvement. Either way, I need some background checks on a list we've compiled. And something else."

"I'm already reaching for the travel bag. I'll bring the sunblock."

"Thank you, Josh. One more thing. We didn't bring any weapons."

"Shit, Manny. Are you going to need them?"

"Maybe," said Manny quietly.

Josh felt like he'd been punched in the stomach. Once again, this escape was turning into a workaholic's dream. And becoming dangerous as well. *Just damn great. No more vacations for any of them . . . ever. At least not with Manny.*

On top of that, Chloe, not to mention Sophie, would probably shoot him and Manny and Munoz with one of the Glocks or Berettas he was bringing. He didn't blame them.

"I'll handle it."

"Thanks. See you in a few hours."

Manny hung up and left Josh staring at the phone.

"No rest for the weary," he muttered, dropping the phone on the table.

Sliding the chair back, he started toward the bedroom where his wife slept, then stopped, turned back to the phone, and dialed another number.

"Are you ready to go?"

"Now? Yes sir, Agent Corner."

"Meet me at the airport in one hour. We're going to Cozumel."

"Yes sir, I'll be there. Cozumel to boot? Oh, hell yes."

Josh hung up, knowing she'd be there before him.

"Welcome to your first ride with the BAU, Belle Simmons," he said softly.

CHAPTER-27

"No, Miss Franson, we didn't find the car or the man who attacked Stacie yet. But we will."

The handsome young officer was holding his hat in his hand as Haley Rose held Ian on her hip in the hospital's waiting room. The sound of his voice was almost reassuring. Almost. But she'd been around a block or two herself and knew most of the cases like this one, where the attacker actually got away at the scene, were never solved.

"Thanks officer. I hope ya do. He sounds like a real winner, he does."

"Yes ma'am, he does. Stacie was able to give us more information about him, and she saw enough to do a sketch for our police artist. The fact that Jen got a look at him will also assist the artist."

"Do they ever really help, the sketch drawings?" she asked, shifting Ian to her other side.

The officer smiled. If she didn't know better, she'd say he was a tad flirty. She'd had worse things happen to her in the States.

"Surprisingly, it does. Someone will say that looks like my Uncle Fred or Cousin June. It's enough to at least look into a possible suspect, and sometimes it pans out."

"Then it'd be worth the effort, I suppose. Can she . . . is she . . . Stacie, I mean, ready to dig into that?"

"She's a resilient girl, so I'd say yes. She's described him and with Jen's input, they should come up with a good composite. Stacie mentioned this morning that he had a smell about him, sort of like fish, so maybe he works in a butcher shop or does something in the fish business. She also said he had an accent. She wasn't sure what kind of accent, but we can help her with that too."

Haley Rose nodded, and then held the young cop's eyes in her own. "Did he— ?"

"No. He didn't rape her. He only touched her because she didn't want to give up the car, she thinks. That's when he threw a couple of punches." The cop held her gaze. "It could have been worse, Miss Franson, much worse."

She shuddered. Lord have mercy, that might have been Jen just as well as Stacie Wells. This situation reminded her that no matter what a parent or grandparent did, you couldn't be there every moment. Visions of Chloe being shot those years ago in New York and Meav escaping Argyle with her life danced into view, as if to confirm her thoughts.

As if she needed any reminders.

"That's not the last of the questions we have, Officer . . . ahh . . . Shaw."

Haley Rose and Officer Shaw turned to see Jen standing behind them, arms folded, eyes red, but the tears long gone. Replaced by a determined look far too old for a young woman to carry.

Shaw looked at Haley Rose and then back to Jen, his eyes darting to the floor, his hat turning circles in his hands. He then looked back to Jen, a rehearsed smile attempting to cover his discomfort at what may come next.

"What other questions, Jen?"

"Well, the first one is: why do you think this guy drove by our house?"

"That *is* a good question, and I think it was simply random. Stacie only lives three blocks from you, and this guy was in the neighborhood."

Haley Rose felt her own indignation rise. Her Irish temper tugged at her mouth.

"Excuse me, but how dumb do ya think we are?" asked Haley Rose. "The man takes her car at the mall and drives back to the neighborhood to where she lives with no thought of being recognized, and that's a random thing?"

"Yeah, and he just happens to slow down in front of our house?" chimed in Jen.

"Listen. It's not unusual for these guys to do something like this. Criminals don't always go back to the scene of the crime, but this guy might have been curious about where Stacie lived," said Shaw.

"Why would he do that? I mean if he'd wanted to take his act a step farther, why not just toss her into the car and do what he wanted to do when he had the chance?" asked Jen, taking the thoughts directly out of Haley Rose's mind.

Rubbing his jaw, Shaw looked at Jen with an air of impatience.

"I can't answer that for sure. Who knows exactly what these people think? Sometimes they tell us, and when we catch this guy, maybe he will."

Jen crossed her arms and stood taller. For the second time in a day, Haley Rose was reminded of Jen's heritage.

"Can't answer that for sure? What happened to common sense? Like, even I can figure that one out."

It was Shaw's turn to cross his arms. His neck had started the gradual scarlet ascent to his face. Jen stepped closer to him.

"Suppose you clue me in, child."

"Suppose I do, cop."

Haley Rose began to move between them but stopped, lifting Ian to her shoulder. She wanted to hear what was coming next from Jen's perspective, for one thing; but for another, the large backbone of this teen had suddenly made her very proud to be Jen's step-granny.

"That man driving by our house did it on purpose. The weirdo *wanted* to see what was going on at our house, for whatever stupid reason. That makes me think that maybe Stacie wasn't the real target here. Did that ever cross your brain?"

Shaw rolled his eyes. "Really? That's what you think? That your friend was a smoke screen and he really wanted to visit you? Why would he do that? And why didn't he stop by and say freaking hello?"

"I'm not sure. Maybe he wasn't ready or something stopped him from doing it. Listen. I saw the look in his creepy eyes. He wasn't just checking me or granny out, you know?"

"Young lady, that's why you go to school at your age and trained professionals solve crimes. Do you hear how you sound?"

"Yeah, I do," she said softly, eyes flashing.

Officer Shaw did a double take, his air of arrogance brought down a few steps simply by Jen's demeanor.

Haley Rose had to admit that those three words had been very compelling.

"I don't—"

"Wait," came the voice from the white, tiled hallway.

"The three of them turned in unison to see Stacie standing there, her long, black hair combed to one side, her mother and father standing like sentinel bookends.

The right side of her face remained swollen and red. The stiches running underneath her orbital bone past her nose to the corner of her lip told more of the details behind her attack. Haley now understood Jen's tears. She was holding back a stream of her own.

"Don't let this conversation upset you, folks," said Shaw. "Sometimes people think they know more about how cops work than we do."

Stacie stepped away from her parents, standing on her own, legs apart, hospital gown swaying at the bottom. Haley sensed a measure of determination and even defiance in that brave, wonderful step. In that moment, it became more difficult to hold back her emotions.

Stacie's parents didn't bother to hold back, letting their tears flow.

Speaking slowly, her voice distorted from her injuries, Stacie confronted the officer. "Yeah, that's true, sort of. But this time, she might be totally right."

CHAPTER-28

"Missus Rathburn is resting quietly for the moment. One of the hospital's staff nurses will stay with her until she's ready to take the next step," said Investigator Munoz.

Manny nodded, feeling the escape of whatever air remained in the happy balloon that was supposed to be this trip.

The woman in the life raft was not positively identified yet, but Munoz's people were relatively sure it was the woman missing from the first victim's office building. The man in the yellow rubber boat wasn't as difficult to ID.

Aaron Rathburn had finally been located.

The Brit had been missing for almost exactly twenty-four hours and, oddly enough, or perhaps not, was found floating in this raft, right near the resort from which he'd disappeared. The irony wasn't lost on any of them, especially Manny, if it was irony at all.

"I don't suppose Missus Rathburn will be making any future trips to Cozumel," said Manny, standing in the sand beside Chloe.

He didn't blame the woman. Escaping this island, right now, had been an overwhelming urge for him as well. Hell, maybe it was still a good idea.

"I believe you are correct, Agent Williams," said Munoz. "The resort, and Mexico, will help her in every way possible. When we can release the body, we'll ship him home for her as well."

"She won't think so at first, but your support will be a tremendous burden from her shoulders," said Manny.

The ocean breeze freshened. The scent riding the wind would have been an invite to experience more of it, except for the circumstances surrounding this unique beach gathering.

Glancing at his friends for the one-hundredth time, he tried to get a bead on the states of mind of each.

Barb had gone back to her room, but Dean and Alex stood to his left, talking quietly. Sophie sat a few yards away, moving her feet back and forth in the white sand, staring at her purple sandals.

This wasn't what any of them had envisioned when they landed in San Miguel two days ago, but life doesn't always play with an even hand or on an equal playing field. He knew that as much as anyone. He also knew his friends had a choice here—even though he'd made his, they hadn't.

People were dying. Any way he cut it, that circumstance was far more important to consider than a few days of vacation. Guilt had no say when it came to keeping people alive.

Turning to Munoz, he watched as the inspector got his fill of the teal beauty of the Caribbean Sea.

He looked back to Manny. "Tell me more why you think this was intentional. The staging of the bodies virtually outside of your rooms, I'm referring to, and not just a random act."

"The fact that one of the victims was Aaron Rathburn forces me to rethink that a little. The killer could have been just bringing the man home, so to speak."

"But you still think you are correct?" asked Munoz.

"One of the first cases I worked in Ireland, before joining the BAU, had something similar," said Chloe. "The woman was killed, her throat slit, and stuffed into a small, red wagon then left in front of her home for the whole family to see. It was related to a previous drug-war killing, and it was clear there was a message regarding whose territory was whose."

The calm and strength in Chloe's voice was music to Manny's ears. She wasn't going to kill him until they got home, he hoped.

"That could be it. He may be thinking that very thing. This is my island, and I can do what I want. But there could be something else here."

Just then Alex and Dean, side by side, made the five-step journey to where Manny, Chloe, and

Munoz were talking, Sophie dragging a step behind them.

"What do you want us to do?" asked Alex, rubbing his right hand over his prosthesis. "It's not like this vacation is going to actually be one now, so we might as well get to it."

"That, and the fact that this display of the bodies was entirely too close to home . . . kind of forces us to get involved," said Dean.

Sophie sighed. "Damn it, Williams. You're just a magnet for this shit, aren't you? But, as much as I hate to admit it, these men are right."

Manny nodded. "Let's get to it then. Dean and Alex, we need to see if we can get you some semblance of a crime-scene kit."

"I'll take care of that." Munoz spoke in Spanish to one of the local blues who then headed off toward the parking lot, jogging.

"Vámonos," Munoz yelled, and the local blue began running.

"Thank you. We need to process the raft again, and I'd like you two to go over Rathburn's rented Lexus. Obviously his kidnapping and murder are related to the other killings, so let's see what shows up," said Manny.

"When we get the kit, we'll do the car first. The saltwater may have tainted everything in and around the raft, plus Munoz's people have just gone over it, so I'm not sure that's worth the effort," said Alex.

"Take a look anyway, then the car," said Manny.

"You were saying that there could be something else to leaving the bodies here like that?"

"Yes. But before I forget, Josh is on the way, and he's bringing more info on our possible suspects."

"Couldn't he just fax them? Damn, that's a long trip to deliver some paperwork," said Sophie.

"I guess he doesn't get a break either," said Chloe.

"That, and he said he has a surprise too."

"What? Another vacation?" asked Sophie.

Manny shrugged. "We wish. He didn't say, but he'll be here in a couple of hours or so."

The officer Munoz had sent to get the kit for Alex and Dean returned, breathing hard, and placed it at Alex's feet.

Dean picked it up, looked at Alex, and then rolled his eyes. "This ain't mine, but it'll have to do."

"It'll work," said Alex.

"Before you go, I want you to know why I think both bodies ended up here," said Manny.

"Speak," said Sophie.

"There's a reason this killer broke his protocol—or more accurately, why it *looks* like he broke away from his meticulous methods. For example, with the woman . . . he didn't leave her in the jungle or even put her somewhere near her home or work building."

The frown on Munoz's face made him look twenty years older.

"What are you saying?"

"I'm suggesting he may have wanted these two found together. It's possible he sees them as a pair, for whatever reason."

"You mean like an affair?" asked Dean, scratching the side of his face.

"I don't know for sure, but maybe we need to rethink Mister Rathburn's motivation for leaving the resort so early yesterday. We need to do our best to find out. If these two victims were an item, then it would partially explain the killer's display."

"We'll see what the car has to say," said Alex.

Munoz's phone rang. He walked away and then came back after fifteen seconds.

"We have the first three interviews set, beginning this afternoon. That should give Agent Corner time to land and get settled."

"Okay. I guess we have a few hours. So you'll— ?" Manny saw the look on Sophie's face and stopped.

"What's going on, Sophie?"

"You know, there could be another reason for the two bodies. Remember that case in New Orleans where the guy stepped up his agenda and started killing more people before he bit the dust? He'd escalated his pissiness and wanted to take out more county workers."

Running his hand through his hair, Manny thought about what she said.

"That's a good angle, but he said he was going to kill them all before he quit."

"Right," she answered, tilting her head. "That's my point. What if he killed these two off, together, because he's done?"

CHAPTER-29

"What does that mean, honey?" asked Stacie's father, moving closer to his daughter.

"Yes, please tell us why you'd say that," said Officer Shaw, his lips twisted doubtfully. "I can't wait to hear this."

The young cop had taken an almost defensive stance, with legs spread, jaw set, dark eyes intense. Haley Rose found the handsome young man far less appealing than a few moments earlier.

"Good God Almighty, Officer Shaw. Is this how ya make people comfortable so they'll confide in the authorities, man?" she asked, eyebrows raised.

The blue didn't even glance her way, but Stacie did. Jen's friend offered a quick frown while studying Haley Rose's face, more precisely her mouth, and then turned back to Officer Shaw when he spoke.

Odd, yet given her trauma, nothing would appear totally normal to young Stacie.

"I'm not here to make people feel comfortable. I'm here to catch whoever did this. So, I'll ask again; why would you say that?" Shaw said.

"What crap! Never mind talking to him, Stacie. I'll call the LPD and have them send someone else that's not a total ass," said Jen, walking to where her friend and parents stood.

Shaw's face finished turning red, yet his voice stayed calm. "Have it your way, but it will take time and, in case your stepmother hasn't told you, we're short-staffed. That means maybe tomorrow or the next day maybe," answered Shaw.

"Fine," said Jen evenly. "We don't need the attitude."

Shaw shrugged and headed for the door, then stopped, heaved his wide shoulders, turned around, and gave his head one shake as if to clear his mind. He came back to where Jen and Stacie stood.

Haley Rose shifted Ian to her other shoulder and waited.

"Listen. I'm sorry. We're working long hours these days, and this is the second case like this in two days. We had another last night. We don't think it's related to yours, Stacie, at least not yet. The victim was an older man sitting at a stoplight a couple of miles away from your home."

"Could it be? Related, I mean?" asked Stacie, touching her lip.

"We'll see. For now, it's important you tell me what this perp said, okay?" said Shaw.

Nodding slowly, she glanced at Jen, gathering strength. Haley Rose felt her pride swell. Trust, even among friends, remained a precious gift to share.

Taking a deep breath, Stacie quickly clutched her battered ribs and steadied herself.

"I always park on the back side of the mall. Away from a lot of other cars so mine doesn't get all dinged up, you know? He came walking up, smiling.

"He was pretty good looking for an old guy. He had a good smile, but his teeth were sort of yellow. His hair was long and white, like I told you. Anyway, he knocked on the window and asked for directions to the nearest bookstore. I told him Schuler's was around the corner and pointed. He grabbed the door and opened it so fast I didn't have time to, you know, like, react. He said to get out of the car. He needed it. I sort of got mad and told him no way. That's when he hit me, the first time.

"After that, I saw stars and stuff. The next thing I knew I was on the ground and he kicked me getting into the car. He kicked me again when I didn't get out of the way . . ."

Tears moistened her eyes. Haley Rose thought her a brave young woman.

Shaw motioned for her to keep going. "I know you've told me most of this, but two or three times telling it helps."

"Okay. Anyway, when he bent down, he hit me again. Then he said that I wasn't the only date he had for the day. That I was, like, holding him up."

"Date?" asked Shaw.

"Yeah. I didn't know what that meant. I was feeling a little woozy. But then Jen told me that he drove by her house. We just put it together, you know?"

"Makes sense," said Shaw, writing on his leather-bound pad. "Anything else before the department's sketch artist gets here?"

"Not really. I think that's it."

Stacie glanced at the floor then over to Haley Rose. That same odd expression on her face from a few moments earlier.

"What country are you from again, Missus Franson?" she asked quietly.

"Ireland. Why are ya asking girl?"

"He . . . he talked the same as you."

CHAPTER-30

Watching the south end of the airport's arriving flights, Manny saw the white Gulf Stream V circle for its final approach. The thick windows of San Miguel's airport were clear and clean. The Caribbean sun was bright, shedding its warmth for others to enjoy.

Not him, however. For that matter, not Sophie either.

They sat together in hard plastic chairs that did little for his attitude. He guessed not for her's either.

It was official; the BAU was on duty.

"Did you just look at me?' she asked, staring at her phone.

She was playing another game of Words with Friends. Her opponent was probably someone halfway around the world. Technology was becoming more of a world-reducer each day.

"Yes, I did."

"Why?"

"I'm wondering what you're thinking."

"About the case or Josh's surprise or how I'm going to explain to Chloe that you no longer have any family jewels?"

"Let's work our way down your list. The case first."

"I can't wait to get to three." Sophie turned off her phone and swiveled in Manny's direction.

"Okay. I know we did this whole profiler meeting yesterday, but do you really think bringing in a half-dozen clowns to interview that *might* fit the profile is going to lead us to the killer? When was the last time that worked?"

"Actually, that's how several serial killers have been brought down. Gary Ridgeway, the Green River Killer, was finally arrested after the police couldn't find a reason to take him off the 'B' suspect list. He'd been questioned, and he even stopped by the police department when he had one of his soon-to-be victims in the truck with him. Eventually he was added to the 'A' list after another incident with a hooker. Their background information allowed them to focus on him a bit more.

"The same sort of thing happened with John Gacy. Parents of one of the victims had called the police over one hundred times to point a finger in his direction. He'd had a few issues prior, so investigators dug deeper, which led the Chicago police to his door and the bodies under his house."

Sophie shrugged. "All right. It could work. But what if it doesn't? You and I both know that more than half of all serial killers are never discovered, let alone arrested."

"True, but we have a captive audience here. Plus, if you're right and he's done killing, his personality traits will be different than a true serial killer. Remember, I think this is a spree killer. He'll be less outgoing, maybe more soft spoken, and his past might be uneventful. Not like the sick bastards that can't stop what they're doing."

"You keep going back to the fact that he's a spree killer, and I get that, but in the end, something set him off, just like all of the others, right?"

"I think so. But Berkowitz, the Son of Sam killer, was schizophrenic and paranoid, and that added to his delusions. He even thought the neighbors and their dogs were demons."

"So you're going to eliminate suspects, not select one, right?"

Manny nodded, feeling the rush of the chase suddenly pulse through his veins. Putting these people away was like nothing on the planet for him. But at what cost?

Talk about a love/hate relationship with one's vocation.

"That's the plan. If we strike out, at least that's six men we can eliminate."

"Sounds like a plan, but everyone has a plan until they get bitch-slapped," said Sophie.

Manny laughed. "Good point. Let's not get slapped."

Standing, Sophie stretched and then punched Manny playfully on the arm. "Right. That never happens to us."

"Another good observation."

He stood beside her as the Bureau's jet rolled to a stop fifty yards away.

"Let's go see what Josh brought us," said Manny as he moved toward the tarmac door.

"Hell yeah. It might be a pony. Better yet, a crystal ball that gets this case over with so I can go back to the beach with all my organs in place and not being measured for a casket."

There was no smile from Manny on that one. They'd lost people on this path. He didn't relish that situation again. He pushed at the uneasy feeling. It drifted to the back of his mind but didn't leave completely. Then again, did it ever?

Once through the doors, the strong odor of jet fuel combined with the noise of powerful engines reminded Manny of just how well-built airport terminals were.

He glanced into the air and watched as two more small planes circled to land. It was still a true mystery to him how iron vessels weighing untold tons could get off the ground and fly six-hundred miles an hour to then land softly at any given destination.

Before they reached the plane, the door swung open, the steps were lowered, and Josh Corner climbed out, blue travel bag over his shoulder. He stopped and waved at Sophie and Manny, then turned his attention toward the jet as a young woman moved to the first step then navigated the rest, joining Josh on the ground.

Her limp was noticeable. She didn't exactly bounce down the steps, but she had found a way to cope with her condition.

This woman was obviously the surprise, but Manny wasn't sure what that meant.

"Who's that?" asked Sophie as she and Manny approached the plane.

"I don't know. Could be our surprise."

"Shit. No pony."

"I don't see a crystal ball either."

"Hey, she might be it."

Sophie made a beeline to Josh, hugging him and pecking him on the cheek. "Hey, handsome. Good to see you."

"Thanks. You too, Sophie."

Manny reached out his hand and Josh ignored it, giving him a hug that any bear would be proud of.

"Glad to see you too, old man," said Josh.

"Yeah well, it's better than the alternative," he answered, grinning.

Josh stepped back and motioned to the young woman to come closer.

"Sophie Lee and Manny Williams, this is Belle Simmons, the newest member of the BAU," said Josh, his expression beaming like the Mexican sun.

This time Manny beat Sophie to the punch and stepped in front of her. He reached out his hand.

"Nice to meet you, Belle. You're immediately on the prayer list."

Her laugh was genuine and full. He liked her.

"I need all of the help I can get. That works for me. It's such a pleasure to meet you, Agent Williams. I've dreamed of working with you and the BAU for years," she answered, her eyes dancing.

"Just Manny, okay?"

"Deal."

"Get out of the way. I've been waiting for this since Chloe left the BAU," said Sophie, bumping past Manny, shaking Belle's hand. "Hey, Belle. In case you didn't notice, I'm Asian and hot. Since you're black and hot, we're going to be good friends, unless people think you're hotter than me, then . . . well, you figure it out."

Belle laughed again, clasping Sophie's hand with both of hers. "Hotter than you will be tough."

"That's what I'm talking about. She can stay, Josh."

"I'm glad you said that. Otherwise, she'd have to turn around and fly home."

"That's not happening. I'm in Cozumel, baby," said Belle.

Manny wasn't sure the smile would ever vacate her pretty face. Then he was reminded why she was here. The smile *would* abandon her face soon enough. It always did. Still, Belle Simmons seemed even keeled and extremely bright. She was a profiler and not just an investigator, no question.

Tilting her head, Belle watched Manny, and the smile slipped, then returned as fast as it had disappeared. "Am I getting the famous Williams profile?"

"Oh, sorry. But I suppose so. Force of habit."

"I'm looking forward to hearing what you see and what you think you see," said Belle.

"Yeah well, careful what you wish for," said Sophie.

"I'm sorry, didn't hear that," said Belle.

The engine noise had become increasingly louder.

"BE CAREFUL WHAT YOU WISH FOR," repeated Sophie.

"OH. RIGHT," answered Belle, smiling.

The roar grew noticeably louder as Josh pointed to the terminal. "Maybe we should go inside."

Manny nodded and twisted toward the almost unbearable sound coming from the runway.

His heart jumped into his throat.

The twin prop was almost on them.

CHAPTER-31

"Really? That's all we get from this car?" said Dean.

Alex held three bags in his right hand and had four more sitting in the makeshift crime-scene evidence holder they'd constructed from one of the hotel laundry hampers.

"Yeah well, the boat gave us even less . . . and it was mostly tainted too," answered Alex.

"Raft. It's a raft."

"Okay, Beard Boy, raft. You can call it the *Titanic* if you want, but we ain't gonna get anything from it," said Alex, leaning against the Lexus.

The day had grown decidedly warmer in the early-afternoon sun. Dean loved the sun and warmth, but dripping sweat leading to an exchange from his purple paisley driver's cap to a red dew rag hadn't been in the plans for the day. Hell, none of this had. But there was a crease of Manny in every member of the BAU, so here they were.

"I loved that movie," he said, squinting at Alex.

"What? Oh. *Titanic?* Seen it at least six times."

"Get out of Dodge, really? Eleven times for me. But then again I've been single longer."

"True. By the way, how's that married thing working? Don't get me wrong, I love the woman, but we're talking Sophie here," asked Alex. The wry grin was hard to ignore.

Dean started to answer then hesitated. Describing life with his Princess—the type of woman he'd always dreamed of marrying—wasn't that easy.

Her personality was paradoxical to understate, yet her compassionate, insightful light shined far brighter than anyone would guess. She loved with a special verve, and not just the lovemaking, but the emotional part . . . it was somewhere past the red line.

"You know, all I can say is I'm the luckiest man on the planet. I'd do anything for her. She's made my life more than a blip on the evolutionary map."

"Wow. That was romantic, I think. Anyway, glad it's working. She's still a pain in my fat butt from time to time, but she's changed for the better."

"You two are like a brother and sister, so that goes with the territory. But we can talk about this over some cold tea and a huge burger because I'm getting hungry."

Reaching for the laundry cart, Alex tossed in the evidence bags and pushed the cart toward Dean.

"What do you think happened here?" asked Dean.

"Well, we did our best with what we had, and you know how I feel about guesswork, but we may have to do some of that."

"I agree. We might not have a lot of luck IDing DNA from the bodily fluids in the back seat, but we know for sure there was some hanky-panky going on back there," said Dean, wiping more moisture from his nose.

"That was a great song. Tommy James and the Shondells, nineteen sixty-seven," said Alex, grinning.

"Good song. But it was sixty-six, dude," said Dean.

Raising his eyebrows, Alex then nodded slowly. "You're right. Must be the heat."

"It is warm. I got a few hairs from the back and some routine fibers, but I'm not holding out hope," said Dean, running over the evidence bag contents again. "Nothing that makes me want to get excited."

"Same here. That toothpick from the trunk might be something, but with almost no fingerprints, this one will be difficult to unwind. The fact that the killer wiped down the inside and the door handles means he knew what he was doing."

"Hey, we got a couple smudges. That sort of fits this guy's profile though. We knew he was probably bright and well educated. Just once I'd like to get one of those unsubs with an eighty-two."

"True. These guys still make mistakes though, so we might have to guess a little on a couple of things to get to the next step."

Dean thought Manny would be proud of his science guys theorizing about what could have happened in order to determine the next possible steps.

"Let's start with a couple things I'd like to know. First, providing that it's Rathburn's DNA back there; who was in the back seat with him? And second, what did this guy do to overpower Rathburn?"

"I was thinking along those same lines. Let's brainstorm about the back seat. Rathburn had money so she could have been a professional," answered Alex.

"Maybe. But with that kind of money, why wouldn't you go high-end company and at least go to a motel if not her apartment?"

"Point taken, so that could mean that it wasn't a pro, unless he was kinky about sex in the back of a Lexus with a hooker. Assuming that wasn't true, he probably had more than a casual relationship with his partner."

Dean removed his do-rag, ran his hand over his forehead, and replaced the hat. It had become virtually soaked as the sun grew warmer.

"You're gonna smell bad if you keep sweating like that," said Alex.

"Already do. And I got to tell you, you don't smell like the first rose of spring yourself."

Raising one arm and sniffing, Alex reacted with a sour look. "Man, ripe is not the word for it. We've got to finish this up."

"You're right. Not that we're Manny or Sophie here, but if that's the case—that he knew this woman and was having an affair—she was probably younger and hotter than his wife, who, for her age, is no pooch," said Dean.

Alex nodded. "She is a good-looking older woman, and I don't get why men do that to a woman who's been with them from the start. I guess lust is still lust. Anyway, in the event we *are* right, we're searching for a lady who is younger and may have had consistent contact with Rathburn, even when he was home in England."

"Phone record search?" asked Dean.

"Yep. We just need to get the info from his wife."

"That should be an easy sell to her. If she asks why, we can tell her we want to check out who he may have had contact—Wait."

"What?" said Alex, standing erect.

The vision of the two people lying close together in the raft hit Dean as he recalled something Manny had said. "Remember Manny said that the killer may have wanted them to look like a pair, for whatever reason?"

"Yeah . . . oh shit. You think those two were having an affair?"

"It makes sense. She was younger, good looking, and native to Cozumel. If they were, how did the killer know about it?"

Alex sighed. "Good question, but better yet, if he did know about it, what is their connection to him?"

CHAPTER-32

Reacting as if his life and the lives of his friends depended on it, Manny tackled Josh and reached for Belle and Sophie in one motion— except he missed the women. As he hit Josh around the thighs, his glance toward where Belle and Sophie had stood seconds earlier told him why he'd missed. Sophie was already on top of Belle pulling her toward the FBI's Gulf Stream.

"Under the jet," yelled Sophie.

Then she and Belle became a whirling mass of arms and legs, almost completely under the fuselage.

Taking Sophie's advice as quickly as the two men hit the tarmac, Josh and he began to tumble along the hot surface. Manny rolled over something that prompted a sharp pain in his left arm. He tried to ignore it and continued under the jet.

The engine noise from the twin-engine plane heading directly for them grew to an unbearable level. In an instant, Manny realized they weren't going to make it to where Sophie and Belle were clustered. Another quick look told him the tail section would have to do for him and Josh. Yanking at Josh's coat sleeve, he guided him in that direction.

The roar came closer. It appeared that the twin engine was homing directly on him and Josh like some ancient monster looking for its next meal.

"Hurry your white asses!" screamed Sophie.

Another good idea from Agent Lee.

One more twist found him beside Josh, just under the right tail section, hands over his head, praying.

The other plane was practically on top of them. Manny couldn't see for sure, but his instincts said so.

He was correct. The next thing he heard was metal scraping metal as the unavoidable became reality. The FBI's jet shifted hard to the left as hot, fine shards of metal and composite rained on him and Josh. The debris felt like dozens of bee stings inflicted on his hands, neck, and legs. And while those burning slivers were uncomfortable, he braced for what was surely going to be the last sensation he'd ever feel as he was torn apart by the approaching plane's propellers.

How ironic. He was stabbed by a pilot in San Juan, and now here another pilot, only this time using a different tool—a twin-engine plane—might take him out. *What is it with me and pilots?* He waited for the crush.

Except it didn't happen.

To say that the contact between the jet and plane hadn't been what he expected from a full-on collision was an understatement. The screaming of the plane's engines had lessened significantly and continued to recede with each second.

Manny opened his eyes and stared at the creased arc of the FBI jet's tail section directly above them. While that was damage enough, there wasn't any twisted metal with sharp, threatening edges, or the like. It took a moment to realize that the plane had avoided the direct hit with the FBI's jet and was now soaring into the Caribbean sky.

"Are you all right?" came a voice from the steps of the plane near the midsection where Sophie and Belle huddled. The FBI's pilot and copilot had exited the jet and were now on their knees, eyes wide with obvious concern.

"Not counting my need for new underwear, I think we're good," said Belle.

"Yeah, that'd be two of us," agreed Sophie.

The women began to laugh, which caused Manny to join in.

"I think that makes three for new shorts," he said.

"Four. Make it four," added Josh, laughing nervously, but laughing nonetheless.

The copilot looked at the pilot and shook her head. "We almost go up in a ball of fire, and these four are laughing? You're right. These BAU people have slipped a knot."

A minute later, the six of them stood around the back of the jet. Manny reached out and touched the angled, yard-long scrape, which was still warm.

"Did you see what happened?" asked the pilot.

"It was a blur. All we really saw and heard was that twin prop bearing down on us and picking up speed. We hit the dust after that," said Manny.

The pilot nodded. "Grace and I heard the sensors go crazy inside and knew we were in trouble. We had clearance to be this close to the strip, but my guess is that someone had his head up his ass and was supposed to be one tarmac over."

"Well, whatever the reason, we need to file a report and get to the bottom of this," said Josh.

The pilot nodded, replacing his hat. "We'll take care of all of that. I don't think the damage will cause a flight issue for us, but we'll see about getting it repaired, ASAP. The real question is; are you all okay? Really?"

"Hey, I bounced down the runway on a seat in Cleveland a couple of years back. This is a mere out-of-body experience compared to that," said Josh.

"Good point. Don't sweat the report and repair side of this. We've got it," said the pilot.

"Are you sure?" asked Josh.

"Yeah, definitely. We've got this. Oddly enough, this happens from time to time. We'll file the report and advise," said the copilot. "Don't you have some murders to solve or something?"

"We do. Just as soon as my heart rate slows to fewer than three thousand," said Sophie.

As if on cue, Manny's phone started ringing—one of Chloe's favorite tunes. Munoz was on the other end.

"Inspector. How can I help you?"

As Manny listened, he felt his expression grow dark, along with his heart. A few moments later, he hung up, shaking his head.

"Now what?" asked Sophie, not attempting to hide her vexation.

Manny pointed toward the city of San Miguel proper.

"It seems our theory about the killer being finished wasn't quite right."

CHAPTER-33

"You can't call them, Granny. That'd be, like, totally lame."

Haley Rose bowed her head, holding her phone in one hand, a still sleeping Ian in the other arm. They were in one of the private visitor's rooms at the hospital, awaiting the police artist's final rendition of Stacie's attacker, the man who had driven by their house with apparent purpose.

"Just why shouldn't we be callin'?"

Jen paced past her and then came back. "I don't know. It just seems like we're jumping the gun. Maybe Stacie didn't hear him right when he talked to her. Maybe that's not what the sicko meant. And even if that were true, we'd get protection from the cops, right?"

"But what if all those maybes are wrong? What if this man has no top to his elevator? What if he wants revenge on your dad for some ungodly reason? Then what?"

Crossing her arms, Jen frowned then began a tight-lipped smile that eventually flowered.

"Really, Granny? His elevator doesn't have a top? That's your best, ahh . . . analogy?"

Haley Rose shook her head, repositioned Ian, then returned the grin. "You know what your old granny meant. Don't think you can charm me out of this one by bein' clever."

"Charm you? Not me. I'm just saying let's wait and let them enjoy the week, okay?"

She knew what Jen meant, but this could be far more serious than a weirdo who wanted a closer look at a young woman. She couldn't shake the thought that Manny had enemies. All good cops do, but his list was even more formidable.

That was the real issue, wasn't it? She knew full well that if someone wanted to inflict pain or suffering on someone like Manny, the best way was to go after his family. She'd seen it too many times not to think it a possibility. She'd been left in charge of the wee one and Jen, and by God, she'd make sure nothing happened to them, but she wasn't stupid either. No one protects a family like a parent.

"I know, but some things are more important than vacations. Your dad and Chloe would fully agree."

"I know that. Hey, I love Ian too, but Dad and Chloe *need* this time. Don't you see the look on their faces when they're working cases, especially Dad? He *has* to get some of that R and R stuff, or he's going to explode."

Damn. The girl could be an esquire or an attorney already. Haley Rose glanced at Ian, then back to Jen, and sighed.

"Okay. We'll wait to see if that drawing of this warped man helps the LPD find him. But if they don't get him by the end of the day, I have to call."

Returning the sigh, Jen nodded slowly. "I guess that'll have to do."

"And that's against my better judgment."

Jen leaned over and kissed her on the cheek. "Thanks, Granny."

"Don't be suckin' up, but you're welcome. I just hope I'm doing the right thing."

The commotion down the hall captured Haley Rose's attention. She scanned the other end and saw Officer Shaw walking with the police artist. They were looking at Stacie's rendition of the man who held part of her heart in fear. Shaw pointed at the sketch, said something, and watched as the artist nodded in agreement.

She felt her pulse increase as they got closer. She'd finally get her own look at the man who'd been torturing her thoughts for the last twenty-four hours. She wasn't sure if that was a positive or negative just yet.

Standing, she placed Ian in his car seat and turned back to the blues coming their way. The artist had stopped and motioned for Jen to approach. Shaw kept walking toward Haley Rose.

"What is going on?' asked Haley Rose.

"We need a couple more details. It seems that Stacie and Jen didn't quite agree on a few features that can change the perp's image significantly."

"I see. Why is she talking to Jen again?"

"We think Jen got a better look at this man and has a good chance of being more accurate with the details. Stacie is still shaken up," said Shaw.

"That makes some sense."

Shaw moved his hat to the other hand. "There's something else."

"Yes?"

"We're really not sure that Stacie heard what she thinks she heard. We had one of our LPD detectives talk to her again and some of the details of her account changed. When we first interviewed her, she may have been in one of those out-of-body states people go into when they're suddenly stressed."

"Whew. Who wouldn't?"

"At any rate, we want to take a few hours to discuss everything, and that will give the artist time to make the best drawing possible."

Relief from his words wasn't something she had expected. The feeling was welcomed.

"Now that sounds sensible."

By then, the artist had left, and Jen joined them.

Shaw continued, "We think so. The fact that there was a similar assault on a total stranger makes us believe Stacie's attack was most likely random."

"Do you really?" asked Jen.

"I do. People who do what she claims he did just don't really live in towns like Lansing."

"Then again, lad, it may not have been."

Haley Rose felt the chill from the familiar voice before she ever saw his face.

She spun toward the door just as she heard the subtle, sickening sound of a muffled gunshot.

Shaw fell to the floor, the bullet between his eyes sending him to the afterlife.

Then he was next to her. His hand on her arm, his gun in Jen's face, Haley Rose's heart bursting through her chest.

That same, unchanging grin propelled her toward a fear most never experience.

His yellow teeth flashed wider. "Good to see ya, darlin'. It's been far too long."

CHAPTER-34

The man made his way down the stone steps after he exited the office. He stood beside the curtained window, watching until the cop turned the corner.

So they want to talk about the recent murders. Talk to him, specifically. Good.

"You're an expert on the Mayan culture and could offer some insight," the inspector had told him.

The inspector was right on both accounts. He had to admit he was simply brilliant when it came to such things as studying ancient cultures. He supposed it came from the desire to understand human motivation and how it connected with human actions and interactions. It was fascinating what people were capable of doing, given proper motivation.

He laughed quietly.

That fact was one he understood better than most. Stepping away from the window, he headed back to the now empty office and strolled to the very rear. He then unlocked the large steel door and moved into the research room.

Walking to the locked cabinet under the middle table, he bent down, turned the combination lock, and opened the door. He tilted his head to get a better view of two of the most beautiful objects he'd laid eyes on. Timeless. Priceless. Linked by the reason they were created.

He placed one in his belt, the other in his pocket, and pushed the door closed.

The meeting with the police was in less than two hours. That was more than enough time to do what he had to do. Again.

CHAPTER-35

"I'll say this, Josh. You all know how to show a woman a good time," said Belle, climbing into the police cruiser's front seat.

"It's not every day we get new folks in the BAU, so we need to take advantage of our opportunities to scare the living daylights out of you," said Josh.

"Yeah, and it's just like I keep telling you about these damned planes. I'm walking back to Lansing," said Sophie, climbing into the driver's seat.

Recalling his own plane-crash experience a couple of years prior, Josh nodded. "You might be right about that. But until they perfect teleportation, this is what we have."

Then he climbed in the back beside Manny. His friend was smiling, but Josh knew where his mind was streaming. And it wasn't with the near-death experience that had become somewhat common in the BAU's adventures.

"First, let me apologize for this thing screwing up your time off. I tried to keep him off you for a day or so," Josh said.

"That ship has sailed, so we need to move on. People dying and cops in need trumps a little vacation time," answered Manny.

"Maybe. I just hate it that it got this far. But like you said, we're in it now. Where are you with this unsub?"

Manny stared at his hands then looked up at Josh. "Not where we want to be. Most of the time we have an idea about these guys, and we're pretty accurate generally. Just when I think we have this guy figured, he does something else. Why kidnap another person now?"

"Hey, this ain't a precise science. We thought he might be done; he's not," said Sophie.

"Apparently," said Manny, turning back to the window.

Josh wasn't sure what to read into Manny's voice. Yet, he knew that's when the man seemed to do his best work. He took the crazy, unexplainable, and found the connection.

Sophie flipped the police emergency light switch, put the car in gear, and burst out of the parking lot, driving like only she could.

"Whoa," said Belle, laughing.

"I warned you about her," said Josh.

"You did."

"What do you mean, you thought he might be done?" asked Josh, looking back to Manny.

"We thought the killer's traits as serial killer were less important than his obvious spree-killing aptitude. The two bodies in one setting could have, and maybe should have, been his grand finale," said Manny.

"With that in mind, most spree killers don't care who the victim is, but this guy, well I'm not sure, based on what we're seeing, right?" said Belle.

"You're right, Belle, and this heated rush of murder in less than seventy-two hours, ending with two dead, fits the classic profile for a spree killer. But now, there's another woman missing from downtown. She was a clerk at a pawn/antique shop, and the kidnapping has me guessing on just what kind of psycho this is. Serial killer or spree killer or hybrid," answered Manny.

They flew around another corner. Josh clutched the armrest and waited for Sophie to straighten out the vehicle.

"Is her profession out of whack with the rest of the victims though? I saw some parts of the victim files on the way here, but not all of the information was there," asked Belle.

"That's probably a good question. We're still trying to find a common connection, other than we think he knew the victims."

"So he could be a purpose killer instead of a spree killer?" asked Belle.

"Yes. But this abduction doesn't *feel* like a serial killer action. It doesn't fit his profile, either. It's like this kidnapping is some kind of afterthought. Like he's trying to confuse us or gone off the whole devolution trail. I don't think that's the case, either. Afterthoughts, to spree killers, can be dangerous and get them caught, so they don't go there," said Manny. "I'm trying to sort this out."

"But since we don't have a tight connection with the vics, our profile could be skewed when it comes to his motivation," said Sophie.

"That's the problem. It could. When we were in Vegas, Mike was misleading us because he knew what to do as a cop. Yet, his own psychosis wouldn't let him get away from what he was truly about. No matter what he tried to portray to the outside world, his twisted motivation fell into a killing category we can identify. This last act is different because the killer has crossed lines that make no sense to me," said Manny.

Josh listened to his friend talk. There was no emotion, other than for finding the killer. He'd be a liar if he said this side of Manny didn't make him nervous on a couple of levels. But that ability, or will, was what gave the BAU an edge. The Manny Williams edge. Yet, at what eventual cost? This man was going to get his vacation, come hell or high water.

"So is that why you and Munoz set up the interviews?" asked Josh.

"Yes. I know we weren't involved in this investigation from the beginning, and I'm not sure we would have any more idea who is doing this than we do now. No profile is flawless, but we need a place to start."

"You've got Alex and Dean busy too, right?" asked Belle.

"Dough Boy and the Bearded Wonder can come in handy from time to time," said Sophie.

"If this profiling exercise doesn't work out, we could be in trouble. Dean and Alex are hard at it, but it could be tough sledding to gather good evidence here," said Manny.

"You don't sound hopeful with the forensics," said Belle.

Glancing her way, Josh saw that she was picking up on Manny's words and appeared to be heading to the next step. The interaction between these two could be interesting.

"Tainted scenes that have been run over several times by locals, especially in hot climate environments, don't typically yield much. But those two are better than most," answered Manny, taking a quick look at Belle himself. He caught her insight.

This could get *really* interesting.

"I'm not sure about Alex, but I know for a fact Dean has some skills," Sophie said, grinning.

"TMI, Lee. TMI," said Josh.

"Just saying."

"You can tell me more when we get some girl time," said Belle.

"That works for us," said Manny.

Josh looked at Manny. The man had already gone back to staring out his window, his mind now deep in a world Josh only saw superficially.

Then again, who else experienced this profiling dominion like Manny?

A moment later, Sophie slammed on the brakes in front of the beige, rundown policia building where the suspect interviews were to take place. She wheeled into a parking spot and turned off the vehicle.

Leaning over the driver's seat, arm resting on the edge, she sighed. "Okay. We're here. Let's do this right."

As they exited the car, Josh thought about the accident at the airport, the screwed up vacation for his unit, and the fact he had to leave his family for this ride. No pluses there. Seemed like destiny owed all of them a few breaks.

It was time to collect, he hoped.

CHAPTER-36

In the time it had taken for Haley Rose to recognize the attacker, her mind's eye had gone back to when she and Ennis Preston had first met. He'd seemed so harmless those years ago. Quiet, yet funny, handsome as the devil, with his bright, blue eyes and long, brown hair, and a consummate gentleman.

But that had changed in something akin to a lightning strike after she had a casual conversation with one of her guests and laughed out loud at something the guest had said.

Ennis overheard. What transpired over the next few minutes still fell on the wild side of crazy for her.

His face reflecting an evil she'd not seen in any man, Ennis had grabbed her guest by the throat, lifted him from the floor, and dragged him through the front door. She ran after him, screaming to let the man go. He shoved her aside as if she wasn't there. She still had the scar on the back of her head where she'd hit the staircasing.

When she'd recovered from the motes of stars doing the two-step in front of her eyes, it was over. Her guest was dead, strangled, and Ennis sat on the long bench outside of the front doors. She'd never forget how he simply stared at his feet, talking softly under his breath to no one in particular. She wanted to speak to him, but the demon she'd seen raise its ugly head prevented her from moving in his direction. Two minutes later, the police arrived and cuffed Ennis, placing him in the rear of the car.

He'd been convicted, of course, but not before it was determined that he was off his rocker and not responsible, completely, for his actions. After he was locked away, she began to receive two or three letters a week for the next fifteen years or so. She'd returned every one without opening it.

She never saw him again—up till now, that is.

Her mind ran with the thoughts that this man had been Stacie's attacker and Jen's stalker. It didn't take a genius to realize that Ennis had been after her, Haley Rose, and that his actions toward the girls were some sort of message for her, one she didn't really understand.

She guessed she should have been shocked. She wasn't. Surprised, yes, but given her experiences with men over the last two years, an appearance of a crazy ex-lover who should still be in prison seemed to be par for her course.

She turned toward him, and he let her.

Jen was right in her description of him—he was good looking for his age. His white hair was still his, and for the moment, he seemed to be in a normal state of mind. "Ennis, what are ya doing, man?"

He smiled. "Ahh. After all these years, you're as beautiful as ever. We'll talk more, darlin', after we leave this place."

"You know this creep?" said Jen, not taking her eyes from the gun.

Ennis's face contorted into an ugly smile. "Careful, young one. Unless ya want to end up like your cop friend there, get me?"

Jen nodded, but no fear showed in her eyes.

Reaching to Haley Rose's chin with his other hand, he searched her face and smiled. "Of course, she knows me, lass. She never mentioned her soul mate to ya?"

Calling upon all of her strength to not slap his hand away, Haley Rose smiled. "Ennis, please get the gun out of her face. Then we can sit down and talk."

He laughed, looking to the ceiling then back to her. The laugh brought Haley Rose's heart to full chill.

"Like I said, we'll talk. First things first, give me your cell phones, now."

Jen handed hers over to him. Haley Rose reached out, and he gently took hers from her hand, hesitating as he did, adding an almost shy second glance.

In that one touch and second look, she'd sensed something else from Ennis. This crazed man didn't just care for her, good God, he still *loved* her.

Stuffing the phones in his jacket, he pointed to the door.

"Now before anyone else shows up, get your asses out the door and down to the elevator."

He moved the gun closer to Jen's face. "No funny business by either of ya, got it? I'll not hesitate to put a bullet into the wee one there or you, little missy. Do as I say, we'll be fine."

"Don't hurt them. We'll do what ya want," said Haley Rose, keeping her wits as best she could.

"Wise choice, girl. Now get that brat and let's go."

She reached over and lifted Ian's car seat with her right arm and turned toward the door, Jen a step in front of her.

"Easy does it," said Ennis, a strange calmness in his voice.

The four of them moved down the hallway, and to Haley Rose's relief, there was no one between them and the elevator. Ennis Preston would not hesitate to kill again, of that she had no doubt.

Each step was torture. While it was true that no one else was in danger at the moment, what of the three of them?

Just as they reached the elevator doors, a frantic scream interrupted the stillness.

"Well, I guess someone met your dead cop friend," he said, hitting the button that would take them to the parking garage.

The door opened almost immediately, and the four of them were soon in the parking garage. Three stalls over was Manny and Chloe's SUV.

He began to herd them toward the truck. "We're going to take your SUV, and you two are going to ride in the front. Little Ian and I will be keepin' each other company in the rear."

"I think—"

Before Jen could finish her thought, Ennis had her by the hair, pulling her close to his face. "Shuddup. I don't care what you think. Just get your ass in the truck or, I swear, they'll find your damned body right in this spot."

Without so much as an afterthought, Haley Rose reached out and grabbed Ennis's hand. "If ya touch her again, Ennis, I'll not be going another step with ya."

He looked at Haley Rose, then to Jen, then back to Haley Rose.

Slowly, he released Jen and pulled his hand away from her. "I didn't come here to hurt no one, but nothing is going to stop me from what I came here to do. I've waited too long for that."

"Thank you, Ennis."

He pointed to the SUV. "Get in and don't trouble me more."

"We will."

Haley Rose locked Ian in the back in his car seat; he was still sleeping like the world hadn't changed.

She heard Jen click her seat belt and then stole a glance at Ennis. He was watching her. No, more like inhaling her.

"So why are ya doing this, Ennis?"

He responded with a quick frown that evolved into an incredulous articulation.

"Why? You don't know? You haven't figured it out? We have to go home, Haley Rose. We have to go home."

CHAPTER-37

Belle Simmons shifted her feet and leaned against the door frame leading into the interrogation room in the basement of the old building. She was growing accustomed to the musty, dank odor that seemed to ooze from the very foundation itself.

She'd seen a couple of dungeon-like rooms in her time, usually in some rural police station that was far past its prime. But this place went to the top of the class. Maybe it was the spider the size of Wrigley Field that hung from the corner. Or perhaps the scorpion peeking in and out of the crack in the cement flooring, mere feet away. It was funny how she could look at dead bodies and not even think of losing her composure or appetite, but things that crawl and go bump in the night creeped her out.

Well, not really that funny.

While the surroundings were not five-star, the company was.

Through the first three interviews, she and Chloe had sat in the next room, microphone and

PA system working quite well, and listened to Manny and, to some extent, Sophie, talk with potential suspects. Manny treated them as if they were friends attending a church picnic or people he'd met at the local restaurant for dinner. Pleasant conversations. Not grilling them or overt attempts at seeking a confession. Just talking . . . and profiling.

Each body movement, each expression, every intonation while the suspects answered calculated questions had been catalogued either with a pen or filed away in the complex mind that belonged to Manny Williams.

Belle had a few thoughts of her own to go along with first impressions, as did Chloe. And these were good thoughts and impressions, yet she doubted that Manny had missed anything they had to offer. That's why Chloe had decided to go back to the hotel and call her family. She knew the drill.

Sophie's observations would most assuredly complete the picture. Manny and Sophie were a team for the ages. But no one caught everything.

"I can see those wheels turning. It's music to my ears."

She bowed her head, smiled, and then looked up toward the entryway from the stairwell. Manny Williams stood there, head tilted, a mellow, almost contented look on his handsome face.

Handsome didn't really cover it.

Those blue eyes and chiseled chin were riveting enough, but that wasn't all.

Some people are great looking on the outside, yet it was rare to encounter those special folks who glowed from the inside as well. He was a good man. Tortured and carrying some anger, but a good man nonetheless.

"I suppose I was thinking pretty hard. I didn't know it was that loud."

"Sophie says that sometimes. I say use whatever works. We need some magic on this one."

"You don't think the first three are in the magic-making business?" she asked, shifting away from the knee that would forever give her a reason to hurt.

He shook his head as a frown replaced the mellow demeanor. "I don't. They all fit the profile and, if we discount the nervousness, answered the questions reasonably well."

"I made a couple notes on the second man, Gregory Goodhall, after you asked him about the beach."

"You mean if he'd visited any one of them frequently?"

"Yes. Right after he said he'd never gone to the beach and Sophie had asked him why he didn't like women in bikinis," she said.

Manny smiled. "She isn't as subtle as she could be, but the honest reaction in a person's face after being asked a question like that can tell a small tale. After a few small tales, we can start to piece a bigger one."

"That's true, shock factor and all. But I was wondering if he had issues with going to the beach because of his sunburn worries or that he didn't want anyone to see him with just beach clothes."

Manny raised his eyebrows. "That's a good point. We didn't see him walk with any kind of issues, but if he was concentrating, he might have been able to control a problem with his right leg. So you could be right. He agreed to give us a medical background from his doctor, so we'll see what that might tell us."

"The other two?" she asked, studying his face.

"I think not. Chad Parsons, the associate professor, claims he was out of town until last night and the museum's assistant manager, Adrian Vogan, has been researching another dig site near Tulum and has witnesses to that fact. We'll check them out more thoroughly, but neither seems like our guy, at least yet. Their answers were straight. Their body language and micro expressions seemed honest."

Belle felt the pain in her knee remind her that she was putting too much pressure on it and shifted again. Then it was her turn to smile at Manny.

"Yes. My knee hurts and causes me to limp every so often. I'll tell you about it sometime."

"When you're ready. You did a good job of not showing the problem at the airport, so I'm assuming it has something to do with your normal range of motion."

"Yes. And why do I feel like my physical condition is the last thing on your mind?"

"Because it is. Chloe was shot, Alex is trying to find time to have Luke Skywalker's prototype cyborg hand attached, Dean has wardrobe issues, and Sophie, Josh, and I are nut cases. We've all got some issue.

"The thing is, we've got another kidnap victim out there, and I'm trying to sort out the best way to find her before she becomes victim number seven. That's where you come in. You're bright, observant, understand what this gig entails, and we need all of those things. But none of that is your best attribute."

Felling a little uneasy, Belle walked closer to Manny and stood two feet in front of him, arms folded, exposing more of her thoughts than she would have believed possible. People are almost always comfortable with what they know about themselves, but when another begins to dig into that Pandora's Box, shit hits the fan. Manny Williams had dug deep.

"Which is?"

"Look, Belle. The one thing that makes you perfect for this job is that you won't quit. You see what most profilers see, but many stop, consciously or unconsciously, because glimpses into people's minds and motivations scare them. I don't get that from you."

"Go on," she said.

He nodded. "We dance with demons. You, however, aren't going to let that get in the way of doing the right thing. The BAU is nothing more than a group of slightly dysfunctional do-gooders who won't quit. You're only going to add to that persona."

"You got that from two hours of working together?"

Agent Williams shook his head. "No. I got if from about five minutes of working with you. You didn't panic at the airport and saw clearly what to do next. In my experience, that can't be taught."

"So I passed the first test?"

"And lived. Remember what I said about dancing with demons? You don't have your dance card filled yet, but you will."

He glanced at his watch and then motioned to the door. "We'll have time for more of this later, but come join Sophie and me in the room for the next three interviews. You have to earn your paycheck."

She felt her pulse jump. "So training is over?"

"Mostly. Think of the rest as on-the-job education."

"Wow. Talk about government cutbacks."

"That's another conversation entirely. After you."

He motioned for her to enter the IR. She did, and he followed.

She sat down at the eight-foot table and opened the file Manny had slid in front of her. The bright white paper disclosed a list of three men, their pictures, and a brief bio including the circumstances as to how they became permanent residents of Cozumel, even though they were U.S. citizens.

There was nothing unusual about any of them or where they worked except they were all involved in the Mayan culture at different levels and professions. The third man on the list, Jacob Fish, had written a book from his dissertation regarding Mayan sacrificial customs.

That fact was compelling, but she supposed no more than the other's special assets that brought them to this BAU inquisition. Still.

"Anything get your attention?" asked Manny.

"It all does, but the book writer is going to be a good interview, I'd guess."

"I think you're right."

Just then, Sophie plopped down into the third chair.

"Hey, did you miss me?"

"You're hard not to miss, sort of," said Manny.

"Damn. That hurt, Williams, sort of."

"Well, *I* missed you," said Belle.

"Oh. I'm going to like her," said Sophie, flashing a grin.

"Did you talk to Dean and Alex?"

"Yep. They have a couple of things to finish but want to meet right after the last interview. They have some stuff they want to run by us."

"Did they mention what?"

"Something about hanky-panky and body fluids in the back of the car. I cut Dean off right there. TMI is my MO, not his."

Manny frowned, and she found herself following suit. "That could complicate things," she said.

"It could. We'll see. Anything else, Sophie?"

Agent Lee didn't answer, but instead pulled a small object from her purse and placed it on the table. It looked similar to a petrified doughnut.

"What's this?" she asked.

"After I talked to Dean, I stopped by this authentic Mayan/Mexican/Aztec shop and bought this statue thing. Dean collects this stuff. The guy told me it was an authentic Mayan war mace. Just slip a handle on this puppy and bam."

"And why did you bring it here?" asked Manny.

"I want to make sure I didn't get ripped off. These guys know what the hell they're looking at, right?"

"You're going to ask suspects to authenticate your souvenir?"

"Yep. I figure they'll all know."

Then Belle watched Sophie bring out another object, appearing to be identical to the other on the table.

"You bought two?" asked Belle.

"Not exactly. This one is a fake."

"Ahh. Good call. You're going to test the suspects to see what they know," said Belle.

"Smart woman you are."

"I see your point, but they're all experts, right? That shouldn't be much of a test," said Belle.

"True. I don't want to just see what they know, but all of the other stuff it takes to ID one of these things. You know, like *how* they ID them, not just if they can." Sophie leaned back in her chair and looked at Manny. "What do you think, Williams?"

Belle watched as he ran his hand through his hair, closed the folder, and promptly swore.

"Damn it. I should have thought of this sooner."

"You mean this artifact thing?" asked Sophie.

He shook his head. "No. Well, in a manner, I suppose. There is another way to narrow down this search."

CHAPTER-38

"I was hoping to do this another way, in the proper fashion that is demanded, but this will have to do."

He lowered his upper body toward the woman lying on the floor of the abandoned shack near the edge of the forest on San Gervasio's north side.

Her pretty face was quiet, serene even, with the gag draped across her mouth. She hadn't awakened from the last dose of happy gas solution, but she would shortly.

Touching her hair, he wondered if, at any time, she'd suspected that she was to be his diversion from the rest of the reality he'd created. His truly final act of sacrifice. But situations had changed. The police were actually sniffing down a rabbit hole that could possibly be a problem for him.

Possibly.

He knew the authorities would be almost desperate to find him. Too bad the police had not been as diligent those months ago when he'd needed them.

He was keenly aware of chance and variables. Anyone doing what he did for a living knew of those principles. Yet, with his meticulous preparation, he'd narrowed down the effect those circumstances could possibly render.

"To find me, you'll have to be smarter," he whispered.

Leaning closer still, he reveled in her scent. He hadn't intended to linger over her, he simply found himself enjoying being that close. Intimate.

Intimate was such an overused term, yet wasn't that what each of these encounters had been?

Hate, like love, carried its own brand of intimacy, as did life and death.

His smile grew; he knew them all quite well.

Standing, he picked up her legs and dragged her to the other end of the shack, glanced outside, waited, looked again, and then pulled her to the crumbling stoop, the decaying wood giving off another hard-to-forget aroma as he positioned her toward the early afternoon sun.

Soon he'd be away from all of this, but not before this semi-ritual was performed. It would cast more doubt on his true mission.

Reaching into the Velcro pocket of his khaki shorts, he pulled out the ancient ceremonial knife, turning the blade over in his hand, caressing the jade handle. He closed his eyes and repeated his caress. The knife was fine to his touch, and even finer to his purpose. But there was no more time. There were places to be and stories to tell.

Reaching quickly, he cut the tape from her tanned wrists and did the same for her ankles. She would at least be free from the physical bonds when he slit her throat, if not from the cumbersome bonds of the mind and spirit.

Raising the knife to her neck, he hesitated. He then bent over her, trying to feel her breath. She'd been out too long. She should have been—.

The next instant, her head rose up and smashed against his mouth, sending the blade flying and him back on his haunches then completely through the door onto his back, sprites of color pirouetting in his vision. Something warm ran down his chin and onto his shirt, and he struggled to regain his balance and clear the cobwebs. Even before he truly realized he was doing it, his instinct took over, and he reached for the woman . . . and missed. He lunged again, this time finding her hand in the blurred light. He yanked with the strength he had left and felt her reel in his direction. Then the hand was out of his grip. Before he could get to her again, he felt her foot crash into his chest. He yelped with pain, rolling on his side, clutching for air that seemed to be as elusive as his intended victim.

Finally, he was able to gulp at the moist air and rise from the warped floor as quickly as his rubbery legs would allow.

His mind clearing, he jumped through the door onto the stoop, the wood protesting under his feet. He looked to the left. Nothing. He spun to the right, again nothing. His eyes darted to the path that circled the cabin, and he rushed around it.

There was still no sign of her.

Desperation reached for his stomach and clenched tightly as he began running down the path. "No. No. No! This can't be happening." Where the undergrowth began constricting in size, he heard the faint sound of leaves rustling straight ahead of him. He ran as fast as he was able and reached the end of the trail and the beginning of the two-lane dirt track where his SUV remained.

His heart froze as his eyes darted toward the windshield. He wasn't going to find this woman, the last chapter in his triumphant story.

The word on the glass, written in the dust, was simple.

"Gone."

CHAPTER-39

"What are you thinking?" asked Sophie.

Manny had pulled Sophie and Belle from the interview room and collected Josh, Chloe, and Munoz from their vantage point in the two-way mirror cubbyhole. It was tight quarters, and Manny swore he could hear the racing thoughts of each of them as they huddled in the hallway near the fire escape stairwell.

"When we were going through the evidence yesterday to prepare the profile, we saw the misplaced block showing the Mayan god of war—the stone in a place where it wasn't supposed to be."

"I don't remember that," said Josh, grinning.

"Of course not, smartass, you were chilling at home. And you need a breath mint," said Sophie.

"Onions. Sorry. Go on, Manny. I read the report."

"Yes. Go on. I'd like to know where this is going," said Chloe.

"We talked about how out of place it seemed to be. Plus the weapon used could have been ancient. I expect that to be confirmed by Alex and Dean. God knows what else may have been used or worn in this killer's fantasies," said Manny.

"All right, what does that have to do with anything?" asked Sophie.

"When you put those artifacts on the table, Sophie, it occurred to me that I didn't know how they were acquired. Who finds them? Who digs them up? Who catalogues them? We didn't truly talk about who would have access to relics like that."

After a few moments, Belle broke the silence.

"The person who actually located and catalogued the artifact would be the one who might have the most access, right? If that's true, we simply need to find out who that was?"

Manny shook his head. "I don't think it's that simple. Excavation at these sites is usually done in teams. A couple of professors, a few grad students, and enthusiastic civilians who help with the grunt work, if I understand this process correctly."

"Now you've got me confused, again," said Sophie, hands on her hips. "How does the fact that there are, like, a billion people working these sites help narrow down our search parameters? We Asians are pretty damn smart, but I don't get it."

"I think I agree with Sophie," said Josh.

"I can see that," said Manny. "But if we can find out where that block came from, we can find out who was in charge of that dig site. We can then go directly to the woman or man in charge of working that dig."

"And since the professors are the ones who are typically in charge of presenting the findings to museums or whatever, he or she will be able to tell us about the dig and who was working it," said Belle, an air of excitement in her voice.

"That's my thought," said Manny, glancing around the circle of cops. "Any takers that a man in charge of that area is someone on our original profile list?"

CHAPTER-40

Jen Williams hurried into the house and watched as Sampson greeted her in his own special custom. He trotted around the corner and came directly toward her, but once he got to within a foot of her, he stopped, sitting on his haunches, offering her a quizzical look. She dropped to one knee and hugged the bear of a dog, despite her mandated mad dash, tears running from her cheeks into his thick, black fur. He raised a paw and placed it gently on her thigh. She felt the tears start again.

"I don't know what to do, Sam," she whispered.

Ennis Preston had forced Haley Rose to drive directly to her house before taking them to another location. He didn't say where; he simply told Jen, at gunpoint, when they reached the driveway, to be quick. She was to get the items he had listed on the dirty, yellow scratchpad and return within three minutes. If she did not, he'd shoot Ian.

It wouldn't take her long to get what was on the list, she knew that. She simply wondered if she should. Was this madman going to kill them anyway? Should she call the police? Could they get here in time? Would he truly do what he said? She thought about the last question as she rose away from Sampson and headed for the back end of the house.

"Yes. I think he would," she said out loud. She realized she couldn't risk any possible situation when it came to Ian and Haley Rose. Watching her sweet mother die on that living room floor two years ago was more death than she'd ever want to see again. Especially if those deaths were a result of something she'd done, or not done.

Steadying herself, Jen glanced at the list in her hand and flashed into Ian's room. She grabbed ten diapers, pajamas, and two outfits, including his new Detroit Tiger's hoodie, to go into the diaper bag in the car.

Charging into the kitchen, she tore open the freezer and grabbed all the packages of breast milk Chloe had pumped before leaving for Cozumel. It would be enough for a couple of days, if this nightmare lasted that long. And if it didn't? What if he—?

She shook off the next set of thoughts that threatened to cause a breakdown conjured by real fear.

Her dad had always told her in high stress situations like taking final exams, which she hated, not to pile more junk on top of the situation by letting her imagination go crazy. Stick to whatever made getting through those situations easier. Study, take the test, and call it good. Worrying about the results only detracted from what she could control.

I've never taken a test like this one.

Running to the other side of the house, she stopped in Haley Rose's room, grabbed a pair of jeans and a sweatshirt off her dresser, then ran into her room and did the same thing. Ennis Preston had specifically requested they wear jeans and a sweatshirt. She thought she knew why. They'd look more like a family dressed in the same style.

Why did he want them to appear to be a family? She shivered and kept going.

Glancing at the watch on her wrist, the one Preston had forced her to wear before she came into the house, she saw she had fifty-five seconds to get the last items on the list and get back outside.

She frowned, her stomach leaping up her throat another inch. Why did he want those things? How did he even know that Ian had one? And why didn't he ask for Haley Rose's?

Moving to Manny and Chloe's room, she opened Manny's top dresser drawer where he kept family documents. She supposed it made sense because Chloe was from Ireland, but she'd never thought about it.

Preston had.

She found hers quickly and then continued to dig through the stack of papers, desperately hoping that Ian had one.

Nothing.

Misery brushed her cheek as she burrowed around the drawer again.

Still nothing for Ian.

Perspiration began to form on her forehead. She was running out of time, and she knew in her heart of hearts, Preston was going to do what he said.

Peering into the drawer, she saw it. It was pinned against the front of the drawer by the large screw holding the handle in place. She thought she might pee herself with relief.

Closing the dresser drawer, she glanced at the one below it. The one that held the two guns she'd placed on the table one night before. Time stood still as Jen wondered . . . could she get away with putting one in her jacket? She touched the handle, pulled it gently, and then stopped. If she made one mistake, one slow reaction . . .

The image of his crazy eyes danced across her mind. There would be a better way, she prayed.

Maybe there was.

Opening the sliding glass door on her way through the living room so that Sampson could get out, she sprinted out of the family room and through the kitchen, glancing at the watch.

Thirteen seconds.

Bending low, she whispered to Sampson and then headed out the door.

The SUV's engine was still running as she raced around to the passenger seat and pulled on the door.

It wouldn't open.

She looked at Preston and felt her heart freeze. He was shaking his head, moving his finger back and forth, shaming her like some severe schoolmarm.

His crooked-toothed grin took what was left of her emotion.

He then raised his weapon and pointed it at Ian.

CHAPTER-41

"Have you seen this relic before, Professor Emmerson?" asked Manny.

The slightly built, older gentlemen peered at the images Manny had laid out on the table. After a few seconds, he slid closer to the edge of his chair and went from peering at the photos to studying them. He then reached a thin finger out to the third photo on his right and traced the lines of the stone.

"Oh. So interesting to see it in this setting," he said softly.

"So you've seen it before?"

"I suppose I have. Or one like it, I should say."

Professor Blake Emmerson glanced to the other side of the table where Manny sat, his narrow eyes blinking quickly—perhaps a type of benign blepharospasm twitch or a nervous tic triggering the rapid eyelid movement. He seemed to be reading Manny's mind or had recognized the look Manny was unable to hide.

"I have a myoclonic jerk brought on by stress and lack of sleep. Both hazards of my profession.

It effects my eyelids mostly, but there are times when I can't speak well. This meeting has added to the stress segment, Agent."

"I suppose it would and I thank you for your explanation. I assure you that this is only an information session. No stress required."

Emmerson smiled with no humor, his eyes blinking faster. "Easy for you to say, yet I have little choice but to accept your words as truth."

Manny placed his hands on the desk, palms down. "If we truly thought you were a suspect at this juncture, you'd be wearing a different set of clothes and your dinner menu would be decidedly different."

"I hadn't thought that way. At any rate, why are you asking about this piece?"

"We believe it was recently placed in that area of the San Gervasio ruins and not part of the original structure."

"Well, that's obvious. A god of war would certainly not be carved into the mecca of fertility offerings involving the Mayan women. So, your assumption is correct," said the professor.

"Why would someone do that?" asked Manny.

"I don't know."

Emmerson turned his gaze back to the pictures, fingering all three of them in turn. He seemed totally mesmerized by the carving.

Let's find out why.

"Where would that stone have come from, sir?"

More blinking. "I believe the proper term is where *could* this have come from," he answered quietly, not looking in Manny's direction.

The professor shifted ever so slightly, pulled his hand away from the table, and looked at Manny as if it were the first time he noticed his presence. The spell was apparently broken.

Another why.

Emmerson asked, "You're speaking with me alone? Don't you people usually do this in teams or something?"

"Sometimes, when we think the interview might be more intense, so to speak. Is this an issue for you?"

"No. I guess I watch too much television. Besides, you have a two-way mirror room over in that direction, correct?"

"We do . . . to make sure I don't miss anything." Manny leaned over the table. "Professor, could you answer my question? We have some time-sensitive issues here."

He sighed. "Yes, of course. The best that I can. Two dig sites were started on the Yucatan Peninsula about three years ago. We, several of my colleagues along with Mexico's government, believed that both sites were relatively unscathed by human interaction because they were both in deeply secluded areas."

"Is that important?"

"Yes. It means the area's artifacts would be relatively intact, telling a better story of the history of the Mayan people and culture."

Manny pushed him. "Why is that a big deal?"

The professor's eyes burned and, for the moment, stopped blinking. "Agent, have you not heard of the phrase that a nation who doesn't know its history is bound to repeat it? The Mexican people can learn a great deal from this culture, perhaps leading to a better state of affairs for the current regime."

"You believe that?"

"Of course. This present world is far more interested in gain than living a good life. We've learned nothing from previous civilizations that ran down the path of destruction guided by greed and selfishness."

Manny watched as his eye glanced at the table while one corner of his mouth turned hard, thin. His disgust was obvious.

"I think you're right. But why would you say that?"

Emmerson caught himself as he opened his mouth to speak. Then he offered a small, tight smile. "I suppose that's a conversation for a different setting."

Manny nodded. "Please continue about the dig sites."

"Yes. Yes. At any rate, I was selected to oversee both digs. I chose my staff, and we began work."

"Staff?"

"Yes. I had four grad students, six undergraduates who weren't allowed to touch anything and were assigned to grunt work, and two curators who observed the process and also helped to catalogue the finds. Both are PhDs and work locally with two of our museums."

"I'll need contact information for everyone who worked on the sites please."

"Certainly. I'll have my assistant get that for you. At least what I have."

"What does that mean exactly?"

"It means that students move around and do irresponsible things, like drop out of school and such."

There it was again, that look of almost contempt when talking about his staff.

"Okay, back to the digs. After you gathered your staff . . . then what, Professor?"

"Then, Agent, we spent twelve-hour days, some longer, unearthing what time had hidden from us."

"Sounds like tedious but rewarding work."

"Correct on both fronts."

"So you're telling me this stone came from one of those digs?"

His eyes narrowed as he looked at the photos again, then back to Manny. "I'm not sure. I'll have to look at our inventory list."

Rising, Manny stepped around the table and sat on the corner, hands folded. The good professor wasn't telling him everything.

"Professor Emmerson, there is another life at stake here. This killer has kidnapped another victim and unless we unwind this bastard's motives and identify him, more blood will spill. We've contacted you and five others with similar backgrounds because you have knowledge of the Mayan culture that reflects this man's reality."

"I understand your situation but—"

Manny slammed the table with his open hand, causing the unsuspecting professor to jump, eyes darting in Manny's direction.

"Do you know why I do this job, professor? It's because I can read people like an open book. You're not telling me what the hell I need to know. That makes me pissy."

He moved inches from Emmerson's face.

"So I'll ask again. Did this stone come from one of your digs?"

"I . . . I don't know. We uncovered a similar stone five months ago. It's in our facility at the college, but it's not the same one. These pictures shouldn't exist."

"What does that mean?"

Emmerson grabbed the bottle of water from the table, steadied his hands, turned the cap, and took a long draw.

"The Mayans sometimes created identical objects to offer in certain types of celebrations and worship. They believed two were better. Not uncommon in other cultures as well. Like two crosses in a church, for instance. When we found the stone located at the university, we soon realized that this stone must have had a match. That would have been a real find."

"Why?"

"The one we possess is the second created stone and not as well conceived as the original.

Not to mention, the first one would traditionally have been placed near an area where the priests would have stored more valuable relics."

"Like knives or daggers inlaid with precious stones?"

The professor shot him a look. "And much more. How did you know that?"

"I read a lot. Go on."

"Even though it should have been in the same approximate area, we never located the first stone of the pair."

"You're telling me this is the second stone?" said Manny picking up one of the pictures.

"Yes. But it shouldn't be in anyone's possession unless . . ."

"Unless one of your staff found it and removed it without your knowledge?"

"Yes. I'm afraid that's correct," said the professor, bowing his head.

"Why would one of your people take this one?"

Manny stood straight up and knew what the professor was going to say before he said it. No wonder the reoccurring look of disgust showed when he talked of his staff.

"Money, Agent Williams. Money."

CHAPTER-42

Ramon Alvarez leaned against his cab and inhaled a deep draw from his cigarette. A moment later, he released the breath along with the spiraling wisp of smoke. It had been one of those days. What did the Americans call it? A pisser?

He had four fares that went right with good tips, three customers who didn't bother to tip him even though he'd managed to bring up the fact that he had three young children at home, and one woman who had no money after he'd taken her completely across town.

He released another trail of smoke.

He'd covered her fare, even though it cost him half of his tip money. His mother had taught him to respect his elders and he knew some older folks, even in this day and age, still had trouble finding enough to eat and pay their bills. In a way, it had been his fault. He'd promised himself not to pick up older folks anymore because they stiffed him more than one would imagine.

"Another lesson my friend," he said to himself.

After taking three more drains from his cancer stick, he reached into his shirt pocket and lit another. It would probably be his last of the day.

He couldn't smoke at home, and the cab company had advised him that customers didn't like a smoke-filled cab, so he had to stop or work somewhere else.

There is much crap to deal with these days.

So here he was outside of his car, standing by the roadside in a lonely stretch of gravel road between San Gervasio and his home in San Miguel, taking time with his smokes because it was one of the only locales in his life where no one would disturb him, unless you count the bugs and the iguanas. But even they stayed away when the smoke began to roll.

Reaching into the running cab, he turned the music up. The sweet sounds from the Mexican mariachi channel filtered through the window. He began to tap his feet. That was something else he was forced to endure: American music. It was okay once in a while, but on days when the cruise ships came in, he'd learned that no one wanted to hear good Mexican music for long.

There were no Americans in the cab now.

Reaching back inside the car, he flipped the volume knob and the music grew louder. This was his time—to hell with all of those rules.

The next song began to blare, and he felt his feet move past tapping. Placing the cigarette in the corner of his mouth, he began to dance in the gravel. Left. Right. Then a foot shuffle that, in his eyes, would have helped him to win it all on *Dancing with the Stars Mexico*.

After another gyrating journey toward the back of the car, he stopped, bent over at the waist, and tried to catch his breath, his lungs on fire.

Maybe his wife was right. Maybe he better quit smoking.

"Ramon, you can't even walk to the store without stopping for deep breaths," she'd say.

"You're *loco*," he'd answer.

Perhaps he was the *loco* one.

Standing upright, he removed the smoke from his lips, turned it slowly in his fingers, then dropped it on the road, grinding out the remaining embers.

That was it. He was never going to light another. Listening to his boss or his wife rag on him to quit was one thing, but when he couldn't dance to his favorite music . . . well, that was an entirely different story. He never went to college, but he wasn't an idiot.

Raising both hands in the air, he tilted his head to the blue sky. "I win. Today I—"

The hand that seemed to come out of nowhere, clutching his arm, not only stopped his mouth, but almost stopped his heart.

Spinning, he grabbed the hand and tore it from his arm. He'd already formed a fist with the other and was ready to swing with all he had.

The sight of his would-be attacker put all of the wild motion spawned by his mind and body into full halt.

The thirty-something woman was blood-streaked from numerous cuts on her legs and arms. There was a gash on her forehead, and her nose was dripping red. Her shorts and tank top were tattered, and she must have endured a hundred mosquito attacks.

She began to fall. Without thinking, he reached out and pulled her to him.

"Help me. Please. He's coming. He's coming," she whispered.

The sound of her raspy plea brought him out of the frightened part of his state of mind.

Helping her to the rear door, he opened it with one hand and then placed her in the back, where she promptly sprawled the full length of the rear seat, mumbling a soft thank you over and over.

Ramon dove into the front seat, shifted into drive, and began to drive like the devil himself was hot on his trail.

Maybe he was.

Three minutes later, he approached the next intersection—a four-way stop famous for its blindside accidents because overgrowth from the jungle blocked the view from three corners.

Glancing back at his passenger, who seemed to have calmed, he looked into the rearview mirror and saw nothing. Reluctantly, he downshifted and rolled to a stop. Looking to the left, then back to the right, there was nothing. The SUV pulling up opposite him had come from the direction of San Miguel and not from behind him.

He let out a breath, put his foot on the clutch, and shifted into first gear. He'd been wrong about the devil chasing him. Maybe today wasn't a total loss after all. Helping a woman in distress was a good trump card.

Ramon Alvarez never reached second gear. Two bullets ripped through his windshield, one lodging in his throat, another in his forehead.

He didn't see the SUV ram his tiny car. Nor did he see the man with the slight limp exit the vehicle and fire three more times directly into the back seat. Nor did he smell the gasoline as the killer soaked the inside of the cab and tossed in a burning matchbook.

Nor did he hear the laugh that proved the devil had indeed been chasing them.

CHAPTER-43

Slamming her hand against the window of the SUV, Jen Williams yelled, "I've got the stuff. I'm here for God's sake. Don't do that. Not Ian. Not Ian."

Ennis Preston tilted his head in her direction, and she watched the insane grin crawl over his face as he waited, staring. After what seemed like an eternity, he broke eye contact, looked back to Ian, over to Haley Rose, and then slowly raised his hand, pointing for her to get into the front seat.

She had never climbed into a car faster, her heart racing. But not just with fear and relief. Anger had begun to creep into her emotions. What right did this crazy piece of junk have to do what he was doing? She knew that answer: none. But guns talked.

"Don't cut it that close again, lass. Old Ennis was a wondering if ya had decided to call the police or something stupid like that."

"I thought about it, but it wasn't worth taking the chance," Jen said, unable to stymie the chill in her voice.

"Smart choice. There would have been a lot of blood."

He pointed to Haley Rose, who was staring in his direction. "Get this car in motion, sweet Haley Rose."

Jen watched as she shifted the vehicle into reverse, but didn't take her foot from the brake. As she turned toward Preston, her granny face was wearing a look Jen had seen only one time previously.

Haley Rose Franson was beyond pissed.

"If ya point that gun at either one of these babies again, you'll have to use it before I rip the heart out of your chest," she hissed. "Whatever you're thinking has nothing to do with them, and I won't stand for it."

Preston entertained a quick, confused frown. Jen could see he was absorbing what Haley Rose had said, and it wasn't what he wanted to hear. She felt her pulse quicken at a higher pace because the crazy man in the back of the SUV began to act like a crazy man.

His free hand began to bounce erratically on his knee as his eyes darted between the outside and Haley Rose's determined expression. Jen could swear the very air in the vehicle turned to ice as this man wrestled with a demon that her granny may have awakened.

His sudden, loud laugh caused her to jump and scared Ian. Her baby brother began to cry. Preston laughed louder. Then, moving like some kind of jungle cat, he had Haley Rose by the hair, yanking her almost over the seat.

"You won't stand for it? You bitch. I love ya with all I have. Focus on ya for the years I was locked up because ya were my hope, for God's sake. I sent letters that always came back to me. But I just knew there was a reason that made a wee bit of sense. Not that ya wanted no part of me. That wasn't possible.

"After I finally found ya, I break rules and get illegal paperwork that lets me come to good old America so we can be together. I do all of that for us, and ya talk to me like that."

Ian cranked it up louder. Preston hardly noticed.

"These babies *are* part of this because they're a part of their granny. Don't threaten me again, woman. I'll be takin' us all on a ride to the other side if ya do. I've missed you for these thirty years, and if ya won't give us a chance, finding out if we can be together on the other side has a certain appeal. Are we clear?"

"We are Ennis. Perfectly."

He released her hair.

"Good."

He pointed to Jen. "Get back here and shut this kid up. Leave the door open and wait until I get in the front before ya take my place."

Without hesitating, Jen got out of the car and opened the back door.

The seating change took only a few seconds, and then they were on the road, heading out of the neighborhood to a destination of Preston's choice.

Taking Ian out of his seat, Jen rocked him and talked to him like she always did when they were this close. The scent of his hair helped her to relax as he began to calm as well. She loved her granny's bravery and how she was trying to protect them, but it had almost backfired on them. Hadn't it?

Or had it? She was back here with Ian and away from Preston's focus. Maybe that's what Haley Rose had wanted, but why?

The small voice in her head that her dad and mom had always told her to trust was telling her to be ready.

She would try.

Ian snuggled closer, and she held him tighter as the SUV made one last turn. They were on the main artery heading toward the west side of town.

As the landscape changed, Jen Williams couldn't help wondering if she'd ever see her home again.

CHAPTER-44

Another meeting. Taking place in a stuffy, hot, antiquated conference room to boot.

The sharing of information was the life blood of any investigation, and Manny was aware of how important that communication was. This meeting junk could get old, however, especially when his mind was wandering to wherever Chloe was at the moment.

She had gone back to the hotel to call home to get an update on Ian. Something he hadn't done since last evening. A full twenty hours. He wished he were with Chloe. He was almost jealous that his wife would hear Jen's voice and he wouldn't. If she were lucky, a laugh from his son would make her entire day.

Shifting in his chair, he rearranged the files and two stacks of reports as they waited for Munoz's arrival.

He knew his children were fine. Haley Rose would ensure that. What could go wrong?

"Are you ready for this?" asked Sophie, sitting on his left.

"Yeah. I am. Just thinking about my kids and not being able to talk with them right now."

"Hey. When this meeting is done, nothing wrong with stealing a few minutes to make another call, right?" she said.

"You're right. I promised Jen I wouldn't bug the heck out of them, but I might have to break that promise."

"She'll get it. She might sound a little cranked, but she'll get it."

Josh touched his arm. "Sophie's right."

"I'm going to find out."

"So I've got to ask . . . what do you make of the claim that one of Emmerson's staff was stealing artifacts?"

"I've had time to think on that. What if this killer had been planning his spree all those months ago? But I want to wait for Munoz's research before I go there, okay?"

"Fair enough," said Josh.

Just then Munoz hurried into the room with two local officers, who sat at the opposite side of the table from Manny and the rest of the BAU. Munoz walked over to Manny.

The inspector was always calm and collected, not in a hurry. This time, he seemed almost excited as he sat another stack of files in front of Manny.

"There is one for each of you. It seems we have some coincidences to discuss, and you could be on to something, Agent Williams, with what you asked me to locate."

"That sounds promising. Let's get to it."

Manny handed files down each side of where he sat and opened the one in front of him, then thought better of it and shut the green file folder. "Wait. Let's start this from the beginning. It might drive you crazy, but we have to do it this way so we don't miss anything."

"I understand, but Agent Williams, these findings are important and need to be discussed," said Munoz.

"I agree, but I haven't heard what Alex and Dean have found, and that could be essential in taking the next step."

Munoz stared at Manny then ran his gaze over the rest of the BAU, stopping at Belle.

She glanced at Manny, who nodded at her. She said, "Inspector. The reason many crimes aren't solved is because somewhere in the process someone jumps to conclusions. One little tiny piece of information could change everything, and we need to make sure that doesn't happen here."

"What she said," added Sophie.

"I assure you, what's in these files is not jumping to conclusions."

"I believe you, but everything is important," said Manny.

Throwing up his hands, Munoz sighed. "As you wish. Let's hurry."

"Alex and Dean?" said Manny.

"We took a second look at the life raft and really didn't find much more than the first crew. The salt water and heat on the rubber service did a good job of destroying most of the micro-evidence. We did find a few hairs and another one of those damn feathers tucked under the end seat. There were some prints that probably belonged to the victims. I'm waiting for the IAFIS reports to confirm. Other than that, the boat probably won't help much," said Alex.

"We then processed the car, and even though we didn't have everything available to work with that we usually have, it gave us a few things," said Dean, stroking his beard. "We found more hairs, more fibers from the trunk as well as from the front seat—and a discarded toothpick. We're hoping some of that evidence might get us some info on the man who drove the Lexus back to the hotel. We'll see."

Alex stood, stretching his back. "We also determined that there was sexual activity in the back seat of the car. We're awaiting DNA results from the U.S., but it doesn't take a genius to see that Aaron Rathburn was fooling around in the vehicle. We're sure it was him because the nature of the tests can tell us if activity is fairly recent. Since the Rathburns were on their third week at the resort, the male contribution to the mix most probably was his."

"Say you're right . . . who was the woman involved?" asked Josh.

"Could it be the dead woman in the raft?" asked Manny.

"Yeah, good guess. You got there faster than Dean and I did," said Alex. "It makes sense with how Manny was talking about the killer displaying them together for a reason. Again, we're waiting for the analysis to come back from Quantico. We did, however, try to compare fingerprints of the victims with a few smudges that we found in the car the old-fashioned way."

Dean clarified, "We used a magnifying glass to evaluate them. Unfortunately, without much luck. We'll have to wait for the science to talk to us."

"Anything else?" asked Manny.

"No, not really. The cheap jewelry around the first four victims' necks could be purchased at several stores and stands on the island, so nothing unique there. The feather we found at a couple of the crime scenes matched, but again, a dime a dozen in Cozumel," said Alex.

"That was more information than we had," said Josh. "Maybe it will help with determining the motivation of this killer."

"We still have questions about the public display of those two bodies," said Sophie. "Connected or not, what the hell was he thinking?"

Manny shook his head. "I don't know, but it's a big deviation from his first four murders."

He turned toward an impatient Munoz. If the inspector had what Manny thought he had, this case could take an entirely new direction.

"Let's see what you came up with, Inspector."

"Agreed. We dug into Professor Emmerson's background, and he seems impeccable in how he handles his professional life. So I don't believe he is involved."

"Involved? In the murders?" asked Sophie, sitting straighter.

"Not the murders. After Emmerson gave us the names of people who had worked the digs, I had the inspector get some other information while we checked the background of these people," said Manny.

"Like what?" asked Sophie.

"Before we discuss that, I'd like to point out something we discovered about three of Emmerson's staff," said Munoz.

The room became quiet in anticipation.

"Wait. Let me guess," said Belle. "They were victims?"

"Close. Two of them were. A third died at one of the sites about six months ago. She was cataloguing some items and died from an allergic reaction to scorpion stings, according to the coroner's report."

"What? Why didn't Emmerson say something about the two murdered staffers?" asked Sophie.

"He probably didn't know about their murders. Both people had changed their names from the time they worked for him. Emmerson wouldn't have known that. Which makes perfect sense with the rest of the information we discovered at Agent Williams' request.

"Which is?" asked Josh.

Munoz exhaled. "It seems that my island has a very robust black market involving stolen Mayan artifacts."

CHAPTER-45

Chloe pushed the red button on her iPhone and dialed Haley Rose for the third time. The result was the same. Her mum's voice encouraged the caller to leave a message, and then the annoying beep that accompanied the request made it official.

"Hey, Mum, call me. Thanks."

Chloe then laid the phone on the glass table, trying to wipe the frustration away.

"Everything all right?" asked Barb.

"Yes, I guess. They're probably shopping again. Mum also has a tendency to let her phone die. Jen was to make sure that didn't happen while we were gone."

Barb took another sip from her margarita, crossed her legs, and adjusted her sunglasses.

"Did you call Jen? That girl would never let her phone go dead. It's her lifeline."

"No. Not yet. I don't want to be a total alarmist here. I'll give Mum some time." Chloe looked out over the beach from their perch at the outside bar in back of the resort.

"Hey, I've never been a mom, but I understand. I've been married to Alex, and that's almost the same thing," said Barb, smiling.

Chloe laughed. "I imagine it is. Men are much like children. Their toys cost more, and they have more hair, even if it's on their backs, and other . . . things, but mostly the same."

"Well said."

"So if you don't mind me asking, how come ya had no children?"

"That's no real secret. We simply couldn't get pregnant. It was a little of him and a little of me. We checked out the fertility route, and that really wasn't for us. We discussed adoption, but in the end, we decided no, at least so far. I'm pushing forty, though, and seeing little Ian is a serious reason to reconsider. Alex thinks so too."

"That's great. Some lucky kid could get you two for parents."

"That just might happen." Barb stole a quick look at Chloe. "So is it tough? Being a mom?"

"It's wonderful. It's like falling in love every day without the drama, ya know? Well, except for the diaper part."

"Oh, that works for me. Even the diapers."

They laughed.

"Do ya have another question?"

Barb exhaled. "I do. Why aren't you with Manny and the others? They could use you."

"Maybe. I've seen a thing or two. But Manny is always so far ahead with the profiling part that I didn't see the point, especially with the new girl, Belle. She's very bright and eager to get to it."

"You're not so eager?"

The ocean breeze gently pushed Chloe's hair away from her face as she reflected over the last year. Joining the Lansing Police Department had been good. Losing Gavin and Mike in Las Vegas had been hell, then Ian was born and the scale tipped in the other direction again. Ups and down in life were the norm. Yet . . .

"I guess I'm not. Manny thinks there's only so much of the negative parts of life that we can bear. Then the mind or body simply won't handle more. I think the man is on to something."

"That man of yours is special."

Chloe's phone rang, and she almost jumped to answer it. She looked at the number and frowned. She didn't recognize the number, and then she did. Her stomach dropped as her mind immediately ran wild.

"This is Chloe Williams."

"Hello, Detective. This is Detective Frank Wymer with the LPD."

"Yes Frank, I got that. Is there something wrong?"

"I'm not sure. When was the last time you heard from your mother or step-daughter?"

CHAPTER-46

"Define robust," said Manny.

"According to the files I received from my offices in Mexico City, perhaps thirty to fifty million American dollars per year. And that is probably conservative. Cozumel as well as the mainland has seen more thefts and robberies involving the Mayan and Aztec ruins over the last several years. We had a small task force assigned to stop it. They were fairly successful, but it was simply impossible to guard the dozens of sites throughout Mexico. Eventually, after a few months, the task force was disbanded, and the locals were on their own."

"Why?" asked Josh.

"The government simply doesn't have the money to protect all of our people's needs, Agent Corner. Our resources are focused on saving lives."

"Were there any big players arrested in this game?" asked Manny.

Munoz shook his head. "A few underlings, two or three museum officials, but these people are very bright and have far more resources than we do."

"Wow. Who knew?" said Sophie.

"A better question is why this is important to this case?" asked Josh.

Manny ran his hand through his hair. "I'm not totally sure yet, but I don't think the killer is as motivated by his psychosis or his dedication to the Mayan way as he wants us to believe."

"I'd call killing six people and kidnapping another pretty psychotic," said Sophie.

"I don't think that's what Manny means," said Belle. "This guy is covering up his real reasons for killing. Is that right, Manny?"

At times, when someone says out loud what you've been thinking, it somehow validates, or invalidates, the offbeat thoughts running around in your head. This was one of those times.

"That's right. I think this man has been hiding behind a mountain of red herrings."

"I need to hear this," said Alex. "And don't make my head hurt, okay?"

"I'll try. Listen. The first four killings were personal, obviously. He killed them in a private area and left them. There was no hint of sexual activity with any of them, and that speaks volumes as to his motivation. He wanted these people dead, seemingly enjoyed doing it, but had no desire to desecrate the bodies sexually. In my line of thinking, that makes him a vengeful man and brands these killings a revenge state of affairs."

"Revenge for what?" asked Sophie.

"I don't know, but I think we're getting closer. Sophie's real relic and the fake one got me to thinking about how the store owner actually came by the authentic piece."

Munoz answered. "We did check him out, and his claim that he found it before it became illegal to sell them without a full disclosure of how the artifact was acquired seems correct. There are dozens of stores and merchants on the island that have done the same. They were, as you say, grandfathered in."

"What does full disclosure mean?" asked Belle.

"The Mexican government has determined that there are thousands of minor artifacts that can be sold without affecting the history of our people and the Mayan influence on our culture. The more rare and special finds are analyzed by men like Professor Emmerson and assigned to museums and put on traveling displays throughout the world," said Munoz.

"For a price, yes?" asked Manny.

"Yes. Much like the Egyptians have done. And if I might add, like you Americans have allowed in Las Vegas with historical objects taken from the *Titanic*," Munoz answered with a trace of a wry smile.

"Touché. At any rate, that's why I wanted the black market information. I checked eBay and a couple of other online sources and found some Mayan pieces there, but none were truly expensive and not altogether rare. And certainly nothing like the stone carving we saw or the second one the university is studying," said Manny.

"You said you wouldn't make my brain throb. What does that mean?" said Alex.

"It means that people all over the planet have unusual tastes for rare, exotic objects and can afford them. We know from our work in the U.S. that where there is a will, a network can be built to market and sell anything, including women and children. I think that's what is happening here with our artifacts."

"But how does that relate to the murders in this theory of yours?" asked Sophie. "And get to the point. I'm getting hungry, and I haven't had a margarita in my hand since last night."

Manny glanced at Munoz then over to Belle. The light in her eyes and the quick twitch around her mouth told him she was getting the picture, no matter how bizarre it would sound. This woman was indeed going to be an asset.

"Say these people who died in this spree were connected in another way. I mean let's look at what each of them did for a living," said Belle, tapping the files.

"Samuel Rozen owned several businesses on the island, but if you look at his travel history, according to this paperwork, he was out of Mexico ten to twelve times a year and almost always in the same foreign location at the same time of the year. Dubai. Africa. England. Germany. The list goes on. It could be business related, but he has no known holdings that Munoz's folks could find in those countries. So why was he there?"

"Go on," said Josh.

"Two of the victims worked in the same building that housed Rozen's main office, not counting his bodyguard, who was probably collateral damage to get to Rozen. According to their salaries, bank accounts, and spending habits, both of those ladies had the ability to print money or had another source of income—a big one that the Mexican government knew nothing of. One other thing. Both of those women had worked for Emmerson at the dig site."

"Shit. Really?" said Alex.

"I'm afraid so. Their AKAs were discovered by a combination of a background search from one of the FBI's databases and from the Mexican government's tax records," said Manny.

"The fourth victim, the man found at the second sacrificial altar, ran an accounting firm. Based on a search of his travel history, he was also out of Cozumel several times a year," said Belle.

"And it was at the same time as Rozen, right?" said Sophie, her eyes scanning Manny's face.

Good girl. The light was on.

"Yes. Different flights and times of day, but always in the same cities at the same time," said Manny.

"That brings us to Aaron Rathburn and the woman he was with when he was murdered."

Manny glanced down at his notes and then shut the file. He wouldn't need them.

"Remember when I talked to Penny Rathburn? She said that her husband loved to collect jaguars. She said it reminded him of his cats in the UK. What she didn't know, I suspect, was that he was dropping thousands of pounds and euros on rare, illegal Mayan sculptures."

"You know that how?" asked Dean.

"Let's just say, after we found his body, we had probable cause to search his accommodations while his wife was undergoing a room change and found this," said Munoz.

With that, he reached into his pocket and produced a four-inch emerald jaguar enclosed in a clear plastic evidence bag. Manny had seen it before, yet it was just as mesmerizing the second time. The jade color was faded in a few places and one ear was missing, but even a layman like himself could see the value.

"This piece was discovered in the room's safe, covered in a thin film of oil and dirt to make it look like something other than it is. The curator at *The Museo de Isla Cozumel* says it is authentic and was probably recovered near Tulum on the mainland. She claims it is worth between fifty and one hundred thousand U.S. dollars for the gemstone alone," Manny added, "Not accounting for any historical significance."

"And Emmerson's people were working at Tulum as well," said Josh, looking up from his file.

"So we have a black market sale of this relic, and a few circumstantial situations involving people who changed their names, and an accountant who may have been keeping illegal books or, at the very least, helping Rozen hide money from items he was selling, maybe," said Josh. "Where's the knockout punch here?"

Reaching for one more file folder from one of his staff, Munoz tossed it on the table.

"I fear these people were not as smart as they believed. The phone records from the first five victims make for interesting reading, once we finally received them. While there were some clever attempts to hide identities by purchasing pay-as-you-go phones in different countries and in Mexico, they failed to consider tower locations. You are all aware of how close communications can be traced to tower usage. Each of the first five victims had been in contact with a minimum of three of the others. In the end, it is enough to link them all together."

The room took a collective breath. Manny thought it good. New air brought new perspective.

Sophie broke the silence. "You said five victims. What about the woman found with Rathburn and our missing number seven?"

Munoz shook his head. "We don't know yet. The female with the Brit was a local, but doesn't appear to have anything to do with this black-market ring. She worked at a local coffee shop and modeled on the side. We're still digging, however. And as far as we can tell, the still-missing woman, number seven, is employed with a pharmacy five blocks over and has no apparent connection either. Again, we're still checking."

Belle stood, flexed her knee, and then lifted a sheet of white paper from the wooden table, holding it tight in her hand.

"So this killer wipes out five people, and Rozen's bodyguard, associated with this black-market group. He had to be well organized and knew exactly what he was doing. I'd say it took months to put everything in place the way he wanted. He probably also made lists of things to remember and monitored habits of the victims so he knew when and where to strike. If he truly does have some kind of physical condition, then that makes him even more dangerous because he was determined in spite of any handicap."

"All true," said Manny.

"But with all of that, we still don't know *why* he killed these people," said Belle.

"Like, what's his motivation?" asked Sophie, batting her eyes.

"Smartass," said Alex.

"Hey, don't be talking about my ass, Dough Boy."

"Yeah. That's not a problem. Is that fake too?"

"I don't know. Is that gut for real?"

Belle snickered and Dean followed suit.

"Later you two," said Manny.

"Just a little comic relief to change the mood," said Sophie, smiling.

Mission accomplished, thought Manny. Sometimes this girl was brilliant. Getting off the subject for a moment always brought a certain freshness to discussions like this. He suspected they would need it.

"Theories on why he killed?" Manny asked.

"How about the obvious? He hated the artifacts leaving the country and wanted to preserve the Mayan history on Cozumel?" asked Josh.

"That would explain the sacrificial side of his killings. He wanted to remain true to the culture and protect it at the same time," said Belle.

"The thing is how would he know about the illegal sales? It's not like they put out a sign," said Alex.

"We haven't talked about this yet, but did we get back all of the other background checks of the people who worked the sites?" asked Sophie. "Obviously, those people are suspects."

Shaking his head, Munoz answered. "We didn't bring it up sooner because they seemed to be irrelevant. As with the first six people you profiled, none of these people panned out as true suspects. Two were victims. The curators both check out. One is female; the other has a heart condition that barely allows him the energy to get to work and return to his home. Three of the undergrad students are working archeological finds in different parts of the world. Three others are in grad school in the U.S. and Mexico City. His PhD candidates are also not of interest. Oddly enough, they married each other and moved to Washington, D.C. One is teaching at Georgetown University, the other works at the Smithsonian. Of course, we still have a few things to verify, like passport and travel records for these people, but none of them look like our killer."

"Damn it. Now what? We're sure of our profile, right?" asked Sophie.

"We are. I'd swear by it. We're obviously missing something, however. Not to mention trying to decipher what role these last two women are playing in the killer's world," said Manny.

"You make the big bucks. What do you think?" asked Sophie. She turned to Josh. "He does make big bucks, right?"

"Hell yes. He ain't cheap. Manny?"

Rubbing his face with both hands, Manny offered a tired smile. "You both need a drink. Wait, maybe all of us need one."

He turned to Josh. "What about this line of thinking? If you were this type of killer and trying to cover your real purpose, and assuming you weren't a psycho spree killer in the true sense . . . what else would motivate you?"

"Well, firstly, I'd like not to be caught, buying into your line of thinking, so I'd think that through?" said Belle. "Again, assuming I wasn't a true sociopath."

"I'd want to be as far away as west is from east then. So maybe I'm not an actual expert on Mayan sacrifice rituals in the true academia sense," said

Dean. "With the Internet these days, one could become fairly versed in just about any arena."

"Hey. Not bad, handsome. I'll thank you later," said Sophie, winking. "Umm. Okay. Going along with that, just brainstorming here. Maybe he's done research on what spree killers really do too."

"And maybe he doesn't have a true limp," said Alex.

Manny shook his head. "That's a ton of ifs, and we could be overthinking the hell out of this. Say we're not, however. We need to examine one thing at a time. I still believe he's educated, but that can take on a few faces. Perhaps he needed something to change his focus, and ours. You know, something that has truly piqued his interest versus what he's trained to do. His methods are still those of a scientist, in my mind. I'll give you that he wants us to think differently, but there is no denying his methodology. Also—"

The door sprung open and one of San Miguel's finest entered, running straight to Munoz. He handed him a note and waited.

The inspector read the writing on the white paper and sighed, crushing the paper in his hand.

"We have located the latest kidnapped woman."

Manny felt the chill run down his spine.

"And?"

Munoz's eyes became glossy as he fought his emotion. Inhaling while drawing himself to his full height, he moved toward the door, speaking to

Manny and the rest of the BAU without looking back.

"Come with me."

CHAPTER-47

Chloe rose from her chair, knocking over her drink but hardly noticing.

"What does that mean, Frank? Is there trouble? And don't ya lie to me, man."

The large detective's hesitation did little for her confidence and encouraged the fluttering in her chest to new heights.

"Calm down, Chloe. It's probably nothing. Jen's friend Stacie Wells was involved in a carjacking."

"What? Is she all right?"

Barb got up and stood beside Chloe, eyes wide with concern as she stood next to her friend.

Frank said, "She's fine. She's going home today."

"What's that got to do with Jen or Mum or Ian?"

"I'll make this short. It seems that Jen got a good look at the jacker, because he drove by your house a few hours after taking Stacie's car. Haley Rose took Jen to the hospital to see Stacie, with

Ian of course, and together they did a composite of the perp, and it's on the wire."

Her nerves began to untangle, somewhat.

"That sounds like routine, but why didn't Mum call us?"

"You know they didn't want to bother you with something if it wasn't serious, and this wasn't . . . until a few hours ago."

The worry factor bounced high again. She felt like a damn yoyo.

"Go on."

"Stacie was in a private room with an even more private waiting area. We didn't find him for twenty to thirty minutes after it happened, and then it took us another hour or so to put together what may have happened."

"Find who?"

"I'm sorry, Chloe, there's no other way to say this. The cop assigned to investigate the carjacking was found in the private waiting area with a bullet in his head."

"Good God, man. Right in the hospital?"

"Yes. We have no idea of any motivation. In fact, it's probably not related to Stacie and her family at all."

"Again, what's this got to do with my family?"

"We're not totally sure it does. Haley Rose, Jen, and Ian were the last ones in the room, as far as we know. Since the hospital doesn't have security cameras, we don't know when they left or when the shooter might have entered the room. Listen. This probably has nothing to do with

Stacie and Jen. This guy made some enemies, so we're looking into everything."

"So they could have been long gone, before the killer entered the hospital, or—"

"Left with the killer? Not likely, but we have to ask, right? One other possibility is that Haley Rose shot the cop for being a dick, which he was. We tossed that one out."

"I think that's a safe bet. Stacie or none of the nurses heard anything at all?" asked Chloe, already preparing to call Manny and then get back to Lansing.

"Not a thing. No one saw or noticed anyone coming or going. It's actually kind of strange, but then again, people walk around with their heads up their asses or glued to their damn smartphones and wouldn't notice an alien invasion. Okay, rant is over. You didn't answer my question."

Glancing at Barb, Chloe answered, staying as calm as she dared. "I've been trying to call Mum for twenty minutes or so. I've left messages. Damn it. This isn't funny. I'm going to call Manny, and we'll—"

Chloe's phone vibrated and then rang with the Lady Antebellum song Jen had set up as her personal ringtone on both hers and Manny's phones.

"Frank. Hold on. Jen's calling."

"Jen. Are you all right? Are Ian and Mum okay? Where are you? What's going on?"

"Ahh. Well, which question should I answer first?"

If this was what it was like when your kids didn't call home when they were supposed to, she wasn't letting Ian out of the house until he was twenty-one—and no driver's license, ever. Yet, she hadn't heard too many sounds in her life that had brought her more instantaneous relief.

Thank God.

"All of them."

"Okay. We're, like, at the mall shopping. Granny's phone died, but she thought we should call because you and dad were probably worrying about stuff. We're all fine. Why wouldn't we be?"

"Well. I couldn't reach Mum and . . . you're right, why wouldn't you be?"

"You sound a little upset. Is everything all right with you?" asked Jen, her voice calm, even.

Chloe frowned. Then let it go. Jen was usually high energy on the phone, but she probably could, just like her daddy, tell Chloe's emotional state and was keeping things low key.

"I got a call from Frank Wymer, the Lansing detective that works with me, and there was an incident at the hospital where Stacie is staying."

"You know about Stacie, huh? That so sucks. That guy must be a real ass. An incident? Like what?"

Trying to decide whether she wanted to worry Jen and Haley Rose or wait to talk to Manny first was the hardest decision she'd had to make in weeks.

Barb seemed to know what was going on and slowly shook her head.

But Chloe thought differently, instinctively.

"Someone was attacked in the hospital near where you all were visiting, and Frank was wondering if you three were okay. And if you saw anything that could help them."

"No, we didn't see anything weird other than the hair of the girl who was working behind the counter at the food court. Talk about a mess," said Jen.

More relief. Jen was joking around.

"Can I talk to Mum and Ian, maybe, if he's awake?"

"Just as I was dialing, Ian had one of those diaper explosion things, you know? So Granny took him into the restroom. I can have her call later, okay?"

"That will work. Make sure she charges that phone, and don't let her forget. Thanks for calling Jen. I love you."

"No problem. Love you too, and tell Dad I love him and to call when he gets the chance. Bye."

Jen's phone cut out, and Chloe took her phone from her ear.

"What was that?" asked Barb.

"A misunderstanding."

Chloe touched another button on her phone and found Frank's call.

"Hey, Frank. That was Jen, and they're fine."

Silence.

"Frank?"

There was a snort and Wymer answered, his mouth obviously had just been full of something. "Sorry, Chloe. I took time to eat lunch."

"In one minute?"

"I'm good. So everything's peachy?"

"Yes. Jen said they were at the mall shopping."

"Then I won't bother you anymore. Enjoy yourself."

"Thanks, Frank, I will."

She hung up thinking about the last thing Frank had said.

Only Chloe wasn't at all sure she was going to enjoy herself. Jen's call had eased her tension, but what if Frank was wrong? What if someone was stalking her family?

Looking at her screen for a long moment, she finally scrolled down to Manny's number and hit the call button.

****

Preston snatched the phone from Jen's hand and then sat her down on the hotel's horribly smelling bed.

"Ya did good, girly. I almost believed ya myself. Good thing too. If you'd made a mistake, BANG, no more little brother."

"You're such a creep. You get off on scaring us? You're going to get yours. Karma, you know?" hissed Jen.

Without any hesitation, he backhanded her. She felt the blood flow inside her mouth as teeth and flesh collided and her head snapped backward.

"You should be scared, and don't talk to me about karma, you little shit. I got some saved up, don't ya know. Now turn around."

She did as he asked, not caring for another swat. Her anger burned deeper as she twisted and held out her hands. She envisioned them around his throat.

He worked quickly and then, with one last yank, drew her ropes tighter than before.

She winced but refused to call out.

"What are going to do with us?"

"You'll find out soon enough. But for now, I want ya to stop talking while I visit your granny and brother. There ain't much room in that bathroom, so they'll be needing to stretch."

Titling his head, he leaned toward her. His eyes were wide and as cold as anything she'd encountered in her life.

"I don't owe ya nothin', lass. I'm here for one reason. Remember that if ya get the urge to be brave."

With that, Ennis Preston ambled toward the locked bathroom.

CHAPTER-48

Standing on the side of the small, two-lane dirt road, Manny looked toward the fading sun, slowly shaking his head. No one had seen it all, although he believed he'd come extremely close months ago with the body staged as a mummy in that Las Vegas hotel room.

The semi-charred remains of the taxi entombing the two victims was just one more reminder of what people were inexplicably capable of doing to each other.

The killer had shot both victims multiple times. While what was left of the man and woman was far from pretty, the fire was extinguished before scorching the car entirely, leaving enough of each person to positively identify them. He wasn't sure of the relationship of the driver and the seventh victim, but it was probably a case of being in the wrong place at the wrong time for the driver. Chalk up victims seven and eight to what seemed to be a never-ending stream of bodies caused by an out-of-control fantasy.

Damn it.

If he could only figure out this sick bastard.

Exhaling, he sent the guilt packing. This wasn't his fault, no matter what the inner demons wanted to convey. He wasn't the killer here.

"This is nuts, Manny. I don't get this at all," said Sophie.

She'd moved up beside him, along with Belle. He hadn't really noticed until she had spoken.

"That's two of us," said Belle. "And it'll be awhile before I get the images of the inside of that car out of my mind."

"Make it three of us," he said. "Good luck with that, Belle. Good luck."

The faint smile appeared and disappeared on her striking face. She'd figured that out in quick fashion.

"More wine and soft music will help. At any rate, this scene reeks of desperation. These killings are way off the beaten path with his *modus operandi*," said Belle.

"I agree with both of those assessments. The question is what transpired for him to go that route?"

"Because he's a psycho bitch that's out of control?" said Sophie.

"There's that," said Manny.

"Dean and Alex are going over the car, along with Munoz's folks, so maybe that will tell us something. I have my own thoughts, however," said Belle, reaching down to rub her knee.

"Fire away," he said.

"Okay, hear me out. Maybe, somehow, when the killer wasn't paying attention or thought she was incapacitated, she got away from him. This taxi driver, being a Good Samaritan, just happened along to pick her up. The killer couldn't have her getting into town, so he had to take them both out, you know?"

Manny nodded. "Great deduction. I was thinking that the driver was probably in the wrong place at the right time, so that makes sense. If you tie in the scrapes and scratches on the part of her body that wasn't scorched, a reckless jaunt through this island's underbrush adds up."

"So explain the bullet holes in the windshield," said Sophie. "Wait, never mind. The killer obviously shot through it, but what I mean is . . . how did the unsub know the seventh victim was in the back seat?"

"I'm not sure, Sophie. I'd hate to think it was a lucky guess because the roads are pretty secluded at this time of night. Maybe he saw the driver help her in the car and looped around the mile block. Actually, if that happened, it was fairly clever. If I saw a vehicle fling up behind me like a bat out of hell, I'd be pretty desperate to make sure I wasn't caught by the maniac in that vehicle," said Manny.

Belle added, "Someone coming from town would certainly be less disarming. The driver wouldn't even be thinking of that car as a problem. Plus, shooting someone from the front would have been an easier task. You know what else? I said it before, but don't you believe this unsub is becoming bolder or maybe desperate?"

"I do. No matter how secluded this area is, he took a serious risk doing what he did. Putting the bodies in a raft at the beach of the resort was less dicey because he did it under the protection of the night. This was in broad daylight. But maybe he had no choice."

"That sounds right. He could also be trying to, like Sophie said before, wrap this up. To be done. Even if that included a chancy situation."

"Maybe. I just can't get a handle on why he's been so erratic for the last thirty-three hours, other than the desperation angle? Anxiety about what?"

"Getting caught?" said Belle.

"Yes. I suppose that could be it."

Sophie raised one hand and the other followed as she spoke fluently and in total rhythm with the movement of her hands. "Just to eliminate one more thing, there is no way this was random, right? If it'd been arbitrary, then why burn the vehicle? I'm not sure your theories are right on, but you're close. So now what?"

"Good question. You heard Munoz confirm that all of the people working on the two dig sites were accounted for, one way or another. Our profile led us to five dead-ends and another almost worthless set of circumstances, other than an unknown motivation for killing off a Mayan-relic trafficking ring that doesn't, at least so far, amount to any true leads to the killer."

"Do you know how that sounds?" asked Sophie. "It makes it seem like we're going to totally screw up this vacation because we can't solve this case with what we have."

Manny *did* know how it sounded.

So far, since he'd joined the BAU two years prior, they only had two cases he would call unsolved. Both involved circumstances where, like this one, evidence-gathering had been limited by the environment. And motivation had been difficult to establish. Could this be number three?

What am I missing? Where is the key to this thing?

"Sorry for the out-loud thinking. This one just stinks," said Sophie.

Josh, Dean, and Alex arrived, Munoz a step behind, talking on his satellite phone, their faces puzzled. Interesting how Dean and Alex took on the same sort of expressions the longer they worked together.

Alex wiped at his sweating forehead with his prosthetic left hand.

"Well, we might have a couple things to work on. We found traces of tire tracks that could belong to the SUV that rammed this car from the front at about a forty-five-degree angle."

"SUV?" asked Belle.

"Yeah. The tire tread tells us that. Also, there was silver paint transfer from the vehicle to the taxi. We have a database for that as well, so we'll get those pictures shipped to Quantico as soon as we get back into cell phone tower range," said

Josh. "We just have to pray that the SUV wasn't stolen."

"We found a few more pieces of evidence to examine, including a footprint, but we'll need a lab to work from. It could be a long night," added Dean.

"That sucks," said Sophie.

"Working late?" asked Dean.

"No. Well it does, but no cell reception? That's why I'm not getting any Words With Friends notifications," said Sophie, pulling her phone from her purse.

"You play that game?" asked Alex.

"Hell yeah. I never lose."

"Oh, it's on. When we get back to town, I'm going to challenge you. What's your handle?"

"Queen Sophie, peasant. And bring it. I'm going to whip you like a red-headed stepchild."

"She's good," said Dean.

"She'll need to be," answered Alex, crossing his arms.

"Can we work this case first?" asked Josh, shaking his head.

Manny ran his fingers through his hair. "So we can't receive or make calls out here?"

Munoz shook his head. "I'm sorry. There just aren't many places to put towers out here. Mostly because the population is sparse and not worth the money, as of yet, to the cell phone companies. We are Mexico, and this is a small island." The satellite phone was in his hand resting at his thigh. He raised it. "That is why I possess this."

"Who were you talking with?" asked Manny, glancing at his own bar-less phone.

"My office in Mexico City. They confirmed the last segments of information we had on Professor Emmerson's team. None of the people on his team could have been the killer because we firmed up a check of cell phone records with providers. None of Professor Emmerson's team members had contact with the victims on the list for over six months."

Munoz sighed. The inspector looked older than when Manny had met him just two days ago. They all did.

"Unless the evidence Alex and Dean have gathered pans out, we're not in a great position for leads," said Manny.

"We will canvas the roads leading into town in hopes that someone saw the damaged SUV. You all know how that can go, however," said Munoz.

Here they were again.

Manny scanned the circle of talented cops with incredible experience and a degree of technology at their fingertips that could lead them to the killer— but most likely wouldn't. He thought this man was too smart to knowingly use anything that would incriminate himself.

This man understood science. Yet he seemed to be driven by a force Manny couldn't deduce totally. Given the mixed signals of his death spree, Manny wasn't sure the unsub knew what that force was anymore either. Had this killer's mission become somewhat muddied? Was he feeling guilt that he hadn't anticipated?

Some men and women believe their purposes to be noble, like Caleb Corner had in San Juan, but become enchanted with the power of life and death. They then tap into a primordial lust that was better buried.

He again ran his hand through his hair as the warm breeze blew against his face.

That didn't quite fit here, did it? This was different. It was almost like the unsub worried about not finishing what he started. As if he was going to disappoint someone.

He also had a firm grasp on how to—

Wait. Belle had said something that caused him to rethink a sentence Emmerson had said and Munoz unknowingly repeated.

"Inspector," said Manny, grasping his arm.

"He speaks. How was this trance session?" asked Sophie.

"So that was it?" said Belle.

"Oh yeah. I've seen better though."

"Better?"

"Listen up, you two . . . you six," he said. "Inspector, you said no calls for the last six months, right? Did you mean none of these people had really spoken to each other for that length of time? Or did they all talk six months ago? Or something in between?"

Munoz's scowl told him that the inspector was totally puzzled by the questions.

"The report said no contact for six months. I didn't ask for details."

"Please call and get them. I need to know."

Munoz began to dial.

"One more thing. You said two of the murder victims were on Emmerson's staff."

"Yes," he answered, putting the phone to his ear.

"There was a third. The woman who died at the site from scorpion stings, right?"

Munoz nodded.

"I need to know her name."

CHAPTER-49

Confession was good for the soul. He'd heard that. Yet in his life, there had never been a time when he deemed it necessary.

Confessing a sin would entail guilt.

Not the type of superficial culpability one experienced at the hand of someone who believed you purposely caused them pain. Most people were simply unaware of how their actions could affect others. In most cases of hurt feelings and misplaced revenge, there was no real merciless intent. In his experience, for the most part, cruelty was reserved for the wicked.

He never felt wicked. Not like the people he'd sent to hell. They'd placed ill-gotten gain ahead of human life. There was no excuse for that. None.

That had all changed hours ago. When, in his panic, his blind rage, he'd killed an innocent man.

The bitch in the back seat of the cab had been a willing participant in the actions that had separated him from her. She'd gone along with the others, and for what? Money?

She got what she so richly deserved.

He bowed his head, reaching out to touch the stone in front of him.

The driver, who imagined he was helping a woman in need, had died because of it. If the driver had known the truth, he would have left her on that dirt road and lived another day.

That's not what happened. So he'd been forced to kill the driver to finish what he started. As much as he hated the term, the driver had indeed been "collateral damage," and for that, he did carry a certain amount of guilt.

Yet, he'd do it again, because, in the end, justice was painted in many lights. He'd created his own and would live with it. The bigger picture had been satisfied. Was that not more important? His mollified vengeance said so.

So be it.

He raised his head and focused on her serene face.

"I've missed you. I'm glad we could meet one more time."

She continued to stare straight ahead.

"I know you don't approve of everything I've done. Especially with the driver. I confess to you that I'm sorry for that. But separating us was the worst of all sins. I couldn't let anyone involved in that sin escape free. I pray you understand."

More silence.

What had he expected?

For the next few minutes, he simply took in her beauty, hoping to permanently etch her into his mind. He wanted to stay until he died of old age—except all good things had to end. The ever-increasing weight of the cell phone in his pocket was a reminder of that fact.

Reaching into his front pocket, he clutched the phone, anticipating the call that would set up one last meeting before he left Cozumel forever. It would be short and effective, as planned.

Exhaling, he steadied himself. "It is time for me to leave."

The tears moistened his eyes as his words echoed from somewhere inside. Leaving her was akin to hell on earth, but what could he do? There was a season for everything, including difficult goodbyes.

"You will always be part of my heart of hearts. So, my love, until we meet again."

Kneeling, he kissed her face, placed two objects near the foot of the stone, and then slowly walked away.

He reached the tall iron gate, left the cemetery, and dialed the only number this phone had known.

"Yes?"

"It's me. I have something for you. I'll be at the resort in one hour."

"That will be fine. Don't be late."

CHAPTER-50

The ropes were looser than a minute ago. She had to keep trying without drawing attention to herself. The sound of Preston's voice, and her Granny's muffled responses, told her enough. He *was* distracted, and Haley Rose meant to keep him that way.

Jen glanced at her captor again. She didn't seem to be on his radar for the moment. She counted that a blessing. As long as Preston stood in the doorway of the tiny bathroom, his attention focused on Haley Rose and Ian, she was safe to continue her struggle.

Leaning forward helped to get her fingernails between the coarse loops of the knots, but he'd tied them well. Her hurting, cramping fingers and hands verified that. She pressed on between bouts of pain and rest. She could now get her index finger from her right hand through the first loop on her left wrist.

She pulled. Her finger screamed. She pulled again. She stifled the yell.

Breaking her arm once as a kid had been the worst physical pain she'd had to bear, until now.

Catching her breath, she waited for the burn to subside. Yet, she couldn't wait long. Somehow, she knew this was all coming to a head—that Preston was ready to finish whatever he'd begun.

A tiny ripple of fear reared its ugly head, dancing into the middle of her thoughts.

Who do you think you are, little missy? You're going to die here. It's your fate. You're just a kid. You can't stop it. Can you?

"We'll see," she whispered, renewing her efforts.

Another hard pull and she had two fingers under the bindings on her wrist. Her fingers cramped again, not responding to her mind's commands. Jen had no choice but to wait.

She looked up to where Preston stood. His position had changed. He was now half in and half out of the dingy bathroom. He'd grown silent and so had Haley Rose. It had grown so quiet that she heard Ian make one of those soft sounds he made when he was tired or hungry.

In an unexpected flash, the silence was shattered. Preston began to yell.

"Give him to me, darling. Now."

"No," said Haley Rose.

The accompanying sound of hand on face reverberated into the room. Jen's stomach turned upside down.

The sound was almost worse than seeing it.

Preston emerged from the room carrying Ian. He seemed to not see Jen as he placed Ian roughly on the other bed, then disappeared back into the bathroom.

"Don't worry, Ian. I'm here," she said softly. Her little brother heard her and offered a big grin. She thought she might cry.

Jen began working the ropes again.

A moment later, Preston came out, dragging Haley Rose by the collar. There was fresh blood on her face, trickling down from her lips and mouth. Her eyes were closed, and she wasn't offering any resistance to Preston.

"What did you do?"

"Don't you pay no mind, lass, or you'll be getting the same," he answered. Then he bent over her granny, running his hand over her face.

Jen shivered.

His voice had taken on a different quality. A different crazy. His actions were not comforting either.

Desperation clouded her mind, and then helped cleared it.

Scanning the room, she looked for any solution that might present itself as a way out of this nightmare. After the second desperate go 'round, she found it sitting on the ancient, beaten dresser.

It seemed to laugh at her, taunting her very soul. Telling her she wasn't strong enough.

One more look at Ian and Haley Rose said she had to try.

Tugging with all her remaining strength, she felt the rope give, and then, wonders among wonders, her left hand was abruptly free.

CHAPTER-51

Manny watched Inspector Munoz as he spoke through the satellite phone in his native language. He was running the gamut of human emotions and expressions as the conversation grew more intense. The dialog caused Manny to believe they'd struck a vein, if not a gold mine, with their line of thinking.

He waited, leaning against the blue and white police van that had brought them out to the isolated crime scene. Sophie and Belle flanked him while Josh, Dean, and Alex stood a few feet away, trying to get cell signals. If one simply looked at their collective actions, you could draw a conclusion that they were wandering in the dark, searching for a light by raising their magic light boxes to the heavens.

He shook his head. He'd just gone through the same fruitless exercise trying to reach Chloe. She was probably starting to worry, but they should be back to the resort in an hour or so. And, if he was right, with the number one suspect in these murders unmasked.

Sophie elbowed him. "Oh hell, do you see that? You didn't tell me there were freaking Godzillas out here." Sophie pointed to the other side of the road at the dark-green lizard perched halfway up a small tree.

"It's an iguana, Soph. They're harmless," said Manny.

Dean moved to her side, and she took his hand. "Tastes like chicken, I hear," he said.

"Oh, that's just gross. I am never eating something like that," said Belle.

"Never say never. You might have to someday," said Alex, grinning.

"Like hell. I'll just get skinnier. Is that right, Manny? People eat them?" asked Sophie.

Manny was about to answer her when he heard Munoz sign off.

They moved into a circle and waited for the inspector to speak. They didn't have to wait long.

"It seems you have made an interesting observation, Agent Williams," said Munoz, placing the phone on the hood of the van.

"How so?"

"The young lady who died at the dig site near Chankanaab National Park six months ago from the scorpion sting was one Diane Kelter. She worked for Professor Emmerson, to be sure, and was apparently very gifted and one of his favorites, according to the investigation records. She was very driven and worked long hours and late nights, so no one was around to assist her when she was stung."

"Interesting that he didn't mention her," said Manny.

"It is. Perhaps he'll need to be consulted again."

"Why?"

"It could be nothing, but it appears that they spoke often and at all hours of the day and night just before she died."

"That wouldn't be unusual, given she was a grad student at a career-making dig," said Belle.

"I agree. Still, I think we need to find out why he didn't mention her," said Munoz.

"What else?" asked Manny.

Munoz nodded. "Yes. Yes. After her death, there were a few calls, but it appears that most of the communication to wrap up the dig site was handled by email and text. Once again, nothing unusual about all of that, based on the reports."

"Keep going. You have a troubled face," said Manny.

Munoz exhaled. "I do, my friend. We are going to reopen the investigation into her death."

Manny stood up. "Why?"

"Three reasons. Apparently she was stung several times, yet in the follow-up interviews, the staff claims there were no scorpions in or near the dig area. The professor himself had made sure of it. We also are unable to find any toxicology reports. Even Mexico requires reports in cases such as these."

"So her death could be a homicide?" asked Sophie.

"Let us simply say for now that we need more information. But it could be murder."

"Sounds like that would be wise," said Manny.

It didn't take a profiler to see where this could be going.

"What are the other two reasons?" he asked.

"It has to do with her husband, Andrew Kelter, who had insisted that there was something wrong with her accident, that she was murdered. The local police chalked it up to his grief and ignored him as long as they could."

"What does that mean?" asked Josh.

"Three weeks after her death, Andrew was arrested for not complying with the chief of police's order to stop harassing the officers in charge of the incident. While in jail, he had an accident and broke his right leg in two places," said Munoz.

"Shit. Really?" said Sophie. "So he probably has a minor limp."

"Makes sense. Those broken legs can take a while to heal," said Belle.

"Do you have a description of this Andrew Kelter?" asked Manny, feeling the excitement build.

"He, of course, matches your profile physically and educationally. Andrew Kelter fits your physical description. Also, he was not studying Mayan culture; instead, he was gaining his PhD in marine biology."

Bingo. Manny knew in a flash that Andrew Kelter was the killer and why.

"This man was out for revenge and that's why he killed these people," said Manny.

"Why? Because he thought his wife was murdered?" asked Belle.

"That's my guess," said Manny. "As for why she was killed, I'd say it had something to do with finding out that some of her colleagues were involved with that black market ring. She probably threatened to expose them."

"Let's pick him up," said Sophie. "He's got to be the one."

"Yes. I believe he might be. I've sent two squad cars to his last known address. They will call me when he is in custody. But that isn't the end of it."

"Why not?" asked Belle.

The inspector pulled at his earlobe, his mind working furiously.

"The third reason you're reopening the investigation . . . does it have to do with the murdered wife's parents?" asked Manny.

"It does, Agent. Her mother and father had moved to Cozumel from England when she was two, to teach grammar school. After becoming Mexican citizens, they stayed until she was ten. About that time, her mother died from a boating accident. She and her father then returned to London, where he eventually remarried."

Manny shook his head at the *oh shit* moment. "Damn it. Let me guess, you sent another car to the Casa Palms to pick up her stepmother."

Nodding, Munoz offered a tiny smile. "Very good, Agent. Yes, we have. Diane Kelter's father was Aaron Rathburn."

CHAPTER-52

After ten minutes in the van, racing back to San Miguel, Manny heard his phone's ringtone go off. They'd finally reached cell-tower haven.

He'd missed three calls from Chloe and two text messages. There was a brief spike in his already heightened anxiety, wondering why she was trying to reach him that often within two hours.

Pushing the call button, he stared out the windshield waiting for her to answer. It took one ring.

"Manny? Where are you, for crying out loud?"

"We're on our way back from another crime scene. We've got him though. It's complicated, but it appears he killed these folks because they were maybe involved in the death of his wife. Munoz's people are on the way to pick him up."

"What? Well, that's good news. Who is he?"

"Like I said, it's complicated, and I'll explain everything when we get there. We think that woman, Penny Rathburn, might be the last person on his to-do list."

"That nice lady?"

Manny thought back to their conversation when he'd first arrived. "She is a nice woman. The locals are on their way to take her into protective custody."

"Good to know."

"Listen. If you see her, call security and let them handle things. She could be in danger, and there's no reason for you or Barb to get involved, okay?"

"No worries from us."

"So why were you calling? You've got me revved up."

Chloe explained her conversation with Frank, including the hijacking of Stacie's car, and then Jen's subsequent call that defused the whole missing situation.

Manny didn't care for how either state of affairs had unfolded.

"Has Haley Rose called like you asked?" said Manny.

"Not yet. Should I be more concerned? Or less? Am I just acting like an overprotecting mom?"

"How did Jen sound?"

"You mean was she nervous or out of character? I don't think so. She even joked about some girl's hair at the food court. Then she said for you to call her when you got time. Why would you ask that?"

His scowl went deep. "Jen joked about someone's hair? I've never heard her do that. She's not the type who makes fun of people, other than me. Then she said to call her? I don't remember the last time she wanted me to call her, because I already do that too often, according to her."

Alarm was creeping into Chloe's voice. "Again, Manny, is that something I should be worried about?"

"I don't know. Probably not. We'll be at the resort in five minutes or so. I'm going to call her. Why don't you call Frank and have him drop by the house, then give your mom a shout? That will make us both feel better."

"I will. I love you, and see you soon."

"I love you too."

She hung up.

He touched his phone to his cheek, thinking about what Chloe had said. Jen wanted him to call? That didn't fit. Was it her way of saying she was in trouble and needed his help? Or a case of 'absence makes the heart grow fonder'? Jen's and Ian's faces raced into his mind, and he suddenly felt heartsick. He needed to be with them, to see them, to make sure things were as they should be.

What could truly be wrong?

You are a little on the paranoid side, aren't you, Williams?

Yet . . .

"Trouble?" asked Sophie.

"I don't think so. One of Jen's friends was carjacked and sent to the hospital, and Jen may have seen the guy. Then a cop was killed at the hospital where Haley Rose, Jen, and Ian had gone to visit the friend. Chloe has talked to her since all of that came down, but I'm going to check with Jen to make sure everything's okay."

"Damn. Really? What the hell is this world coming to? We can't even do a vacation without having trouble on both ends."

"You know us and vacations," said Manny.

"Chloe talked to her? Are you being overprotective?" asked Josh.

"Yep."

Manny dialed Jen's number. After five rings, it went to voicemail. He hung up and repeated the process two more times.

The van made the turn down the service street and accelerated toward the resort at the end of the secluded drive. He tried again and threw up his hands in frustration. This time he left a message.

"No luck?" asked Sophie.

He shook his head.

"She's probably trying clothes on or something," said Alex.

"Maybe."

Squeezing the phone in his hand, he decided to call again. Same result.

As he jerked the phone away from his ear, he looked out the window and saw it.

"Stop the van, now!"

"We will—"

"I said stop the damn truck."

The driver slammed on the brakes, sending every loose object, and everyone inside, pitching forward.

"What's wrong with you?" asked Sophie.

Pointing toward a stand of trees near the south end of the resort's long driveway, Manny unfastened his seat belt then threw open his door.

"That silver SUV has a smashed front end."

CHAPTER-53

Never in her life had Jen felt what she did when her hand burst free from Preston's knot. The rush of untainted hope was such a stark contrast to the fear and anger she'd experienced over the last few hours that she had to focus to truly believe it was real.

Calmly, she looked toward Preston. He was still leaning over Haley Rose, trying to wake her.

"C'mon, darlin'. You've been hit harder. Ya need to wake up to see what's comin'."

There it was again. That quality in his voice that offered an insight to just how far south Preston had gone.

Keeping her eye on him, her heart pounding so loudly that she thought he might hear it, Jen slowly removed the rope from her left wrist then slipped her right hand through the loop.

Now what? Was she ready to try what she'd only seen done in the movies?

No. She wasn't. But she had been painted into a corner and had to do what was necessary, as her dad would say. She was beginning to grasp what that meant.

Holy God in heaven, she missed that man at this moment. If she got out of this alive, she was never going to let him out of her embrace. Never.

She found Ian's face. He was still looking at her. The wide grin had disappeared but he wasn't crying, yet. He would be soon, she guessed. He was ready to eat, and she could tell by the pungent odor that his diaper was past the ripe stage. She doubted Preston had noticed because, frankly, he smelled worse.

Trying to steady her nerves, she closed her eyes and breathed slower, deeper. Calling upon her training on the track team was easy; making it work was another thing entirely.

"Stop touching me, Ennis. I don't need ya over me like that."

Haley Rose was back. She sounded weaker, but there was no mistaking the fire in her granny. Jen fought the quick onset of tears. No matter what happened, she was proud of Haley Rose Franson. She was as tough as they came.

The more she thought about it, the more strength she found in the extraordinary idea of that toughness.

"I'll touch you whenever I want. You used to like my touch, now didn't ya?"

"Yeah. I used to like your kissing too. But that was before ya went bonkers and killed that young man."

Preston's wide eyes darted left and right, then froze, making him look like some reject from a Marty Feldman movie. He was close to being totally gone. He grabbed Haley Rose by the hair again, his voice rising. "I did that for us. I loved ya. I didn't want no man a touchin' ya. You was mine, Haley Rose. No one else's. Then you left me to rot in that prison. Never came to see me. Never wrote."

"What did ya expect? What ya did was terrible and scary. I didn't want to be anywhere near ya," said Haley Rose, keeping her voice calm.

His voice grew louder still. "I expected ya to honor me for protectin' ya from men like him. But I can see now that you was never my woman, not truly. It took comin' here to figure that one out. You're just like the rest of 'em."

"What does that mean, Ennis?"

"It means I made a mistake, and now I have to clean up after myself. I can't let you go, Haley Rose."

"Why not?" She reached a hand toward his cheek and caressed it. Preston's eyes closed, his expression one of pure ecstasy. "We didn't do ya no harm and won't say anything."

His dark eyes bolted open. He raised his hand again then stopped short of hitting Haley Rose.

She didn't flinch.

"Ahh, but ya did do me harm. Ya broke my heart. Now you're gonna pay. Old Ennis ain't had much say on things over the last thirty years, but none of ya are getting out of here alive. I can't take the chance."

"No, Ennis. At least let the children go. They didn't do anything."

He laughed. "Maybe not, darlin', but the pain you'll be a feelin' when I cut them to pieces will be that karma shit your granddaughter so smartly brought up. You killed me inside. Now it'll be your turn."

Preston stood, looking at Jen. "You'll be next, smartass girl. I want you to feel a little of this too."

"My dad will hunt you down. You're a dead man."

"Ahh. So I hear. The FBI's Great Manny Williams. That may be true, lass, but that ain't gonna do you no good now, is it?"

Pulling the long blade from his boot, he laughed again then turned away, reaching for Ian.

Haley Rose screamed.

Jen sprang from the bed, seizing the Smith and Wesson .38 from the dresser. As she swung around, Preston's expression exploded into pure rage.

"Stop. I'll shoot. Don't think I won't," she demanded.

"I'll be killin' ya now, girly," he roared, stepping at her.

She pulled the trigger . . . and nothing happened. In her haste, she forgot to check the safety.

Preston lunged with the determination of a man on a mission. She ducked to her left, hearing the knife create a menacing swoosh that barely missed her head. Strands of hair left her scalp.

Feeling for the safety, she stepped closer to the door, just out of reach of another wild swipe of the long blade.

"Damn ya. Killin' ya is going to be more special than a second ago," he snarled.

Gathering himself, he started toward her again and then stumbled, thanks to a well-placed foot on Haley Rose's part.

Hitting the wall in an awkward angle, his shoulder took the brunt of the fall. Preston yelped then swore as he rose from the floor.

He stood breathing hard, looking at Haley Rose, then back to Jen. "You're both dead. Then the wee one."

If there had been any decency left in this man, it had left the building. The madman had taken a full dose of insane.

"Put it down. I really will shoot," said Jen, feeling calm in a way she hadn't anticipated.

"Ya think it easy to kill a man, girly? We're done here."

With that, he came charging toward Jen, knife raised high.

The revolver exploded in her hand, then again, then again. Three times bullets ripped into his chest, the last one sending him to his knees, a look of unadulterated confusion etched on his face.

Ennis Preston then tumbled face first to the floor, inches from her feet.

Dropping the gun, she crawled over the bed, picked up her crying baby brother, held him tight, and began to rock him.

CHAPTER-54

"And you are positive this is the right vehicle?" whispered Josh.

He caught up with Manny just as they reached the last small grouping of trees to the left of the SUV. They knelt low.

"I am now. See the yellow paint on the bumper and lower fender? The cab was yellow," Manny whispered. His mind raced with hope. Could this really be this easy? Had they caught such a break? They were about to find out.

"Okay. Then let's do this the right way," whispered Josh. "You hear me?"

Manny caught the look in Josh's eyes and realized he was right. They had the manpower. They had a restricted area with minimal danger to the rest of the public.

"I hear you loud and clear, but we need to move now."

By then, the rest of the BAU, Munoz, and four of the locals had arrived.

Ten to one looked like good odds to him.

"I didn't know why you had stopped, Agents, but now I see," said Munoz, the perspiration flowing from his temples.

"How do we want to do this?" asked Sophie.

Josh took control, something Manny loved to see. Josh's gift wasn't profiling so much as understanding how operations like this worked.

"Listen, the tinted windows and the dusk will make it impossible to tell if he's inside, so we do it my way, got it?" Josh's voice was firm.

The collective nods told Manny everyone was listening loud and clear.

"First, turn off your cell phones. No surprise calls here."

"Good thinking, Agent," said Munoz.

Josh gave them a moment to do just that.

"Inspector, you and your people need to swing around the back and cover each corner. It will give you better sight angles in the event you have to use your weapons."

"Yes. More good thinking."

"Sophie and Alex. I want you to align yourselves with the passenger side of the SUV, no closer than twenty-five feet. If he's in there, he might try to leave on that side of the vehicle."

"Aye, aye, Captain," said Sophie. "Don't worry, Dough Boy. I'll watch over your ass."

"Thanks, I think," said Alex.

"Manny and Belle, take the driver's side angle, over by that red-flowered bush. That way we'll have a good look on each side of the truck."

"We've got that," said Manny.

"And like Sophie said, I've got your ass . . . er, back." She grinned.

"Also good to know," he said, returning her smile.

"Dean and I are going to stay here and ask him to politely exit the vehicle. Dean will watch my back, in the event he's coming from behind us for whatever reason. Are we clear?"

"I can do that," said Dean.

"Listen. He has a gun and will use it. Don't be stupid," said Josh.

"When you start talking, and if he's in there, and if he's going to shoot, you'll be the object of his affections," said Manny.

"I know that. But he'll need to roll down a window or come out through that sun roof. If you see that happening, don't wait. Take him out." Josh exhaled. "Okay. Dean and I will have you covered while you get to your positions. Now hit it."

There was a flurry of motion as eight cops went to their appointed positions while Dean and Josh held their guns high, eyeing the SUV.

Belle and Manny reached the bougainvillea bush and waited. From there, they could see everyone except Sophie and Alex, but Manny knew it wouldn't take long for them to reach their position.

His heart pounded in anticipation.

"I hate these dark-tinted windows. I can't see anything, even this close. Belle, watch the door. I'll keep my eye on Josh," said Manny softly.

"I don't like it either. Nothing we can do, and . . . I will."

The seconds seemed like hours as Manny awaited Josh's signal. He wanted this one to be over. More than that, he wanted everyone safe. The last face-off in Vegas hadn't ended to anyone's liking.

Finally, Josh raised his hand. Then he stepped closer to the last tree in the line.

Before he could speak, a gunshot exploded from inside the SUV.

The startling, unexpected roar sent them into protection mode as eight cops sought better cover.

"What the hell was that?" asked Belle, breathing hard as she slunk closer to the base of the bush.

"Suicide?" asked Belle.

Manny frowned. "Or murder."

"What? Why murder?"

"We know that at least one person is inside. Maybe there are two—"

He didn't finish his statement as the driver's door opened and a familiar figure exited the vehicle.

Penny Rathburn brushed at her red sundress, dropped to her knees, and began to cry, the thirty-eight still in her hand.

Manny rushed to her, grabbed the gun, and slid it along the asphalt away from the SUV. "Penny. What happened?"

"Agent Williams. I . . . I . . . look inside," she said barely loud enough to hear.

He stood, turning to get a full view. A man he assumed to be Andrew Kelter lay sprawled in an unnatural position against the passenger-side door. He'd been shot in the face, removing his cheek and a section of his eye.

"Damn. That did some damage," said Sophie, coming up beside Manny.

There was no humor in her voice, only the truth they'd all come to expect dealing with a world like this one.

"Not as much as he did," Manny said.

He took one last look as Munoz's people began to redirect local traffic away from the SUV.

Once again, murder had only brought more death, closing the circle it had begun. His frustration grew because he knew someday, maybe even tomorrow, they'd be called to help close another circle.

Would the beat from hell ever stop?

CHAPTER-55

Bursting through the front door of their home, Chloe at his heels, Manny hurried into the living room and through the arched doorway.

Jen sat on the sofa, Haley Rose on one side, Big Frank Wymer on the other. Ian was fast asleep in his crib a few feet away.

His daughter's eyes met his. There was a brief smile, then she was in his arms.

"You okay, baby?"

She nodded, tears rolling from her face as she buried deeper into his shoulder.

He held tight as the rest of the world disappeared.

The flight home had been the closest thing to hell since he'd lost Louise. In some ways, worse. No one wanted to hear that their daughter, their eighteen-year-old daughter, had to shoot a man to save her life and the life of her family.

No one.

Manny knew what it felt like, more than once, to take a life.

No matter the justification. No matter the circumstances. It was unnatural for most people to take another life. The act of killing another was something that never left one's soul.

True to their word, the FBI's pilots made sure the minor damage to the jet had been repaired quickly so there was no delay leaving Cozumel. Manny was more grateful for that than he could have imagined back then, especially now that he was here for Jen.

After Penny Rathburn had been placed into custody, the BAU went back to the resort, greeted by Chloe and Barb.

The look on his wife's face had been heart-stopping.

She'd quickly explained that Frank Wymer and the LPD had picked up Jen, Ian, and Haley Rose from the motel room and had taken them home. He said there had been a shooting, the family was fine, and the police were still sorting out the details . . . but it might be good if they got home as soon as possible.

Manny stroked his daughter's hair, telling her it was all right. But would it be? Could it be?

Jen and he had talked three different times on the way home. Chloe had spoken with her as well. She seemed to be his normal Jen . . . until she broke into tears after a few minutes of hearing their voices.

Each time the phone went dead, his heart followed suit.

"I'm okay, Dad. I couldn't let him do what he was going to do. I did what you taught me to do. I . . . I did what needed to be done."

The calm in her voice was reassuring, yet the underlying confusion and pain also had a voice.

"It's a good thing you did, Jen. If you hadn't, we'd be out two kids and a granny, and I don't think I could take that. You did the right thing. Thank you for being strong enough. I love you."

She pressed tighter still. He held on, fighting his own emotion. He'd cry later for her innocence lost, irretrievable.

Eventually, Jen pulled away, wiping at the tears, holding her dad at arm's length.

"Thanks, Dad. I hurt inside. Shooting him was the second worst thing in my life. But I'd do it again, you know? I'd do it again."

"I do know, sweetheart. And if you had to do it a hundred times again, it'd be worth it. We have to protect our own," he said softly.

She reached up and kissed him again. "Well, I'm tired, and I'm going to bed. We can talk some more tomorrow, okay?"

"Sounds like a good idea. We can talk whenever you want, Jen. No rush."

After hugging Haley Rose and kissing Ian on the cheek, she embraced Chloe for a long moment and then headed down the hall toward her room.

He watched as she stopped, turned, and smiled his way. "I don't think I'm going to put this on my babysitting resume, you know?"

He smiled back, then she disappeared into her room.

"Tough kid," said Frank. "You should be proud."

"You have no idea," said Haley Rose, her eyes moistening. "She reacted with perfect poise, and if she hadn't, you'd be making funeral arrangements for us all."

Rising, she stood between Manny and Chloe, touching them both on the arm. "It was my fault. I hadn't given Ennis Preston a second thought in years. I had no idea he'd go this far off the deep end. I should have paid more attention. I'm so sorry, Manny and Chloe. My heart is broken for her and both of you."

"It's not your fault. I know what you're feeling. I understand the guilt. The thing is, you can't control or figure out how everyone on this messed-up planet is going to act. How would you know he was going to do what he did?"

"I should have checked on him. I knew he'd be out in thirty years. I just didn't think of him."

"Mum, you didn't know. He was crazy; like Manny said, you can't control that," said Chloe, her own green eyes glistening.

Haley Rose stared at her feet then looked at them. "Thank you both. You're wonderful people, if I say so myself. I suppose you're right . . . about folks, I mean. I simply seem to be unable to judge them so well. First Preston, then the Good Doctor, then Gavin, not to mention Chloe's father."

"Bad luck, Mum. That's all."

After entertaining a strange, almost haunting look, she gave both of them a quick peck on the cheek. "Bad luck, huh? Perhaps. At any rate, I believe Jen is right about needing some sleep. I'll be heading that way myself."

Then, as if each step were slowed by the weight of the world, she trudged to her room, leaving Manny wondering how much more Haley Rose could bear. Hopefully, sleep would give them all a better take on the day's events come morning.

"She's resilient, Manny, but what she went through is the limit of what she can bear," said Chloe softly.

"You're right, she's tough. She gets no blame from us, and that'll go a long way in helping her resolve her guilt."

"Should I go talk to her? Tell her that?"

"I think she knows. I guess the question is, if you were her, would you want to talk or sleep?"

Tilting her head, Chloe stared down the hall and then glanced up at Manny. "I'd want to sleep. Too much talk can make it worse."

Ian made a sound, and Chloe was quick to pick him up, pressing him close, soothing their son like only mothers can.

"Do you two want to do this now? It's almost one a.m., and I'm sure you're beat yourselves," said Frank, sliding to the edge of the sofa.

"I'd like to hear what happened," said Chloe. "I'm wired anyway."

"Then let's get some coffee and talk," said Manny.

"Great. Do you have donuts or cookies too? I'm hungry," said Frank.

"I think I can scare something up," said Chloe. She handed Ian to Manny and went into the kitchen.

Ian was warm, comfortable, and that baby scent was strong and alive. Just like his son. He felt his gratitude stick in his throat as he thought how brave his daughter had been. Because of that tough-minded teen, their family was intact.

Could a bigger blessing exist?

Chloe came back into the room, sat down a tray of coffee and soft, chocolate-chip cookies, then took Ian away from Manny, smiling as she did.

"My turn, Dad."

Frank leaned in toward the treats. "Thanks for the snack, Chloe."

"So how did this all come about?" asked Manny.

Frank went into the detail of everything involving Ennis Preston's crime spree in the last two days, ending in his death.

"The Irish officials had no reason to worry about him leaving the country; he wasn't deemed any kind of threat after he was released. He fooled them by getting counterfeit documents to get to the U.S. and set his warped plan in motion."

"Just exactly what was that plan?" asked Manny.

Frank shoved another cookie into his mouth, then raised a finger to notify Manny and Chloe that he would continue momentarily.

"According to Jen and Haley Rose, he was going to take Chloe's mom home with him, but she rejected his advances, so to speak. He went off the deep end, and Jen had to put him down." The big detective frowned. "Jen *put a man down*. That's sort of hard to say. I remember her when she turned ten, you know?"

"I do know, Frank. I do," answered Manny.

Reaching into his pocket, Frank tossed two passports on the coffee table. "I think maybe he was thinking about taking one or both of your kids back to Ireland too. Maybe starting his own version of a family, right?"

Manny felt his veins grow cold as he stared at the blue booklets. It was hard for him to comprehend what kind of hell that would have been.

He finally exhaled. "You're right. Insane doesn't cover this one."

"That's what I've been saying. Anyway, when we got there, Jen and Haley Rose were hugging each other, Ian in the middle, and Preston was unresponsive. Good riddance, I say." Grabbing another cookie, he held it high while he spoke. "After Chloe and I talked on the phone, we took them out of the room, put them in my car, and then brought them here. I took statements, and we waited for you to get home."

"Our department shrink showed up too, right?" asked Chloe.

"Yep. Standard operating procedure, but neither wanted to talk to her. Maybe they will later. Or maybe you two will be all they need."

"Let's hope. Anything else?" asked Manny.

He shook his head, downing the cookie then brushing at the crumbs on his slacks. "Not really. I mean, you got the report." Frank scratched his throat, then shrugged. "You know, I do have to say this. I'm glad you took her to the range and taught her to shoot, Manny. She grouped those shots so close together that she might have stopped a rhino."

"What does that mean?"

"It means this guys was nuts. You know the kind that almost seem like they're on PCP or something? If she hadn't kept it together . . . well, we might be having a different conversation."

More mixed emotions rattled Manny's soul. He'd taught Jen to protect herself, praying she'd never have to use that training. Then she did, and his view of teaching her to kill, if necessary, didn't seem so noble. But he knew that when they were at the range.

Life was as much about survival as anything else. She'd survived.

"Well, I'm leaving. If anything else comes up or you need me, you know how to reach me,"

"Thank you, Frank," said Manny, shaking his hand. "We will."

The detective bent low, gave Chloe an awkward hug, and then headed for the front door. Walking him to the entrance, Manny shook his hand again. Frank drove away, leaving Manny feeling grateful for good cops. Reaching for the lock on the outside door, he clicked the tumbler just as one of the FBI's black SUVs pulled into the driveway.

Sophie jumped out of the driver's door, followed by Alex Downs from the front passenger side.

"You busy or anything?" asked Sophie, walking up to the cement stoop.

"I'm tired and it's been a hell of a day, but come on in."

"No, this won't take too long," said Alex.

"Your call."

Reaching to the light switch, Manny turned on the second outside lamp and sat down on the cool cement of the step. "What's on your mind?" he asked.

"I know you know, but I'm sorry Jen and you had to go through that shit. I want to hug her and tell her it's all right too," said Sophie, sitting down beside him.

Sitting on his left, Alex nodded. "Me too. We want her to know that we're here for her in case she doesn't want to talk to her old man."

Manny smiled. "Good to know you've both got my back."

"Sooo?" asked Sophie.

"She's strong, and she knows she had no choice. She gets it. It's just not easy to deal with, at least not yet. Like we suspected when we were talking about this on the jet ride home."

"Good. Just tell her we want to see her tomorrow, if she's willing," said Alex.

"I will. By the way, where is everyone else?"

Sophie rolled her eyes, scooting closer to Manny. "It's not that warm out here. Anyway, Dean and Josh are chicken shits and went to bed at our house. They said we should leave you alone. I said they didn't know what the hell they were talking about."

"Belle didn't think you'd need her, yet. I love that girl. She's going to fit well, but I think she was a little uncomfortable being in the middle of all of this. She checked into the hotel, and said she'd meet us tomorrow to wrap up Cozumel."

"Oh yeah. Cozumel," said Manny.

"Some getaway that wasn't," said Alex.

"No BS on that. Next time, Williams, I'm NOT going on vacation with you. You don't have a damned clue what those puppies are supposed to be like," said Sophie.

"No argument from me on that one."

"Munoz called Josh and then sent him his Mexican Government Report. Penny Rathburn is doing well but gave a full statement. She said Andrew Kelter wanted to talk about something and called her to meet. Apparently they'd gotten close after Andrew's wife, Diane—Penny's stepdaughter—died at the dig."

"How close?" asked Manny.

"Real close. I'll tell you more in a minute. Anyway, she says Andrew told her about Aaron's involvement with the black market scam and the killing of his daughter Diane, from his first marriage, by a couple of thugs hired by the black market ring. Andrew went crazy when he figured out she'd been murdered and eventually contacted Penny about what he'd found out," said Alex.

"Is that why they met at the resort?" asked Manny.

"Not exactly. Like Alex said, we'll get to that," said Sophie. "Anyway Penny told Andrew that she didn't believe him. That her husband wasn't a thief and certainly wouldn't have killed his own flesh and blood. Andrew had insisted he was right and, on top of that, told her that her husband was cheating on her as well. He then said something to the effect that he had taken care of the people responsible for killing Diane. When Andrew confessed to Penny that he'd killed the others, including the woman in the raft who was having an affair with Aaron Rathburn, she became angry and grabbed the gun he had laying on the dashboard. They fought, and the gun went off," said Sophie.

"That was it?" asked Manny. "Did Munoz believe her?"

"Not quite. The report was a little inconsistent, but who's going to argue with her?" said Alex.

Manny shook his head. "How sick can people get? Kill your own daughter for money? So, Penny didn't know about his dealings?"

"Hey, like Sophie says, it's almost always about money or sex," said Alex.

"Andrew found out that Diane's father was involved in her death?" asked Manny. "That would explain the psychotic episode."

"Your guess that he wanted revenge was spot on," said Sophie.

"We've seen stranger things. Andrew may have even thought of killing Aaron as another step toward ending his pain, not just taking out Diane's killers. No more family, no more attachment," said Manny.

"Yeah, Munoz mentioned something like that in the report," said Sophie.

"I do have one more question. Did you get the DNA report back from the lab?"

"From Rathburn's Lexus that we processed at the resort?" asked Alex.

"Yes."

"We did. We got a surprise. It wasn't Aaron's DNA; instead, it was Penny's and an unknown male."

"He's not unknown anymore, right?" asked Manny.

"Right again," said Alex.

"She was having sex with Andrew Kelter, our killer, wasn't she?"

"Yep, right out of some *True Love Confession* kind of magazine," said Sophie. "That makes even *me* want to puke."

"Just when I think I can't be surprised anymore," said Manny.

"I heard that. Munoz got her to admit to the affair—sort of. She said it wasn't what it seemed. She justified it by saying she was comforting him," said Sophie.

"So by putting Aaron Rathburn and his play-time woman on public display, Andrew had accomplished two things. One, payback for Diane's murder. Two, public mortification for Rathburn at being found like that," said Manny.

"Looks that way," said Sophie.

"In the end, this was about money and a murder, and not a spree killer carried away by his own fantasy," said Alex.

"It was, but there's something else. An ingredient that made most of this possible," said Manny.

"Yeah? What?" asked Sophie.

"Grief. An unbearable loss that takes on a life of its own and takes away any sense of wrong or right can be more powerful than life itself," he said quietly.

Images of Louise's smiling face waltzed across his mind, then vanished in the light that Chloe, Ian, and Jen represented. She'd always be his first love and, in a way, a part of this family. But he'd learned to carry on and to find happiness. Not everyone was as fortunate. He understood the pain that Andrew Kelter must have experienced.

"I don't think I want to find that one out any too soon," said Alex.

"Me either," said Sophie.

She kissed Manny on the cheek, telling him with a simple gesture that she understood he'd already run that race.

Standing, she tugged at Alex's arm. "Well, I've got to get Dough Boy home to Barb, and I can't wait to crawl in bed with Dean. He might even get lucky."

"For once, you might be on to something. And don't call me Dough Boy."

Manny's friends left the driveway. He waved, began to stand, then didn't. Instead he scanned the heavens.

The spring stars showed bright in the Michigan sky, and for the first time in three days, everything was quiet. He knew it wouldn't stay that way forever. That wasn't how his world worked. But for now, he'd count his blessings and thank God for what he had.

This case in Cozumel had been born out of deception, manipulation, greed, and a husband's love and loss. Ennis Preston had been another form of evil incarnate and had left a mark, but the Williams family would get through it together. They always had.

In the end, the positive side of life's equation had rallied and won because people rose up and did the right thing. Who knew for sure . . . maybe they'd even had a little Heavenly help.

Rising, Manny Williams gave the incredible sky one last, long gaze before going back inside his home to hold his son.

Thank you for reading Caribbean Fire! I know you have choices out there, and I'm forever grateful that you chose Manny, the gang, and me.

As always, if you want to talk to me, so to speak, email me at rickmurcer@gmail.com. And visit my website at www.rickmurcer.com.

God Bless,

Rick Murcer

Books by Rick Murcer

Manny Williams Thrillers
Caribbean Moon
Deceitful Moon
Emerald Moon
Caribbean Ran
Carolina Rain
Vegas Rain
Caribbean Fire

Ellen Harper Thrillers
Drop Dead Perfect

Short Stores
The Light House
Capital Murder
413
Herbs Home Run
Manny Blue and Black Max
The Killing Sands

For your enjoyment, the first two
unedited chapters of

SEER

Chapter-1

I never saw them coming. Not the roaring, out
of control tractor-trailer, the indescribable fear
and pain, and most assuredly, not the inexplicable
"gift" the accident would lavish on my previously
benign senses.

Perhaps lavish is a somewhat paradoxical term
because it means to expend without limit, and my
senses certainly have limits, or at least the "gift"
seems to. Those limitations unquestionably could
be my lack of understanding and leery
unwillingness, and not the function of the

bestowed gift. I'm pretty new at this seeing thing and what it brings to the proverbial table.

And I'm scared of it.

No, that's not quite right. Petrified works. As in, pee-my-pants, get-the-spider-off-from-my-face-there's-a-freaking-snake-the-length-of-U.S. 75-in-my-commode, terror. Yeah, that fits.

I'd never thought of myself as someone afraid of much. Then again, seeing what I've seen over the last few weeks has changed that. It would change you too.

But I'm getting a head of myself. Let me bring you up to moment in the best way that a man with my unlikely background is able. I'll hurry, but I don't have much time.

None of us do.

My name is Gabe Stark. Actually, my parents named me Gabriel Andrew Stark, nice initials, eh? There isn't anything particularly special about me, at least in laymen terms, until the accident changed my perception of that could entail.

I can sing a little and I have a knack for keeping most folks relatively calm. That comes in handy in my line of work. People who possess unusual athletic talent, incredible musical ability, or grand wealth seem to fulfill the criteria that special implies these days, and for that, I am grateful.

We, our society needs all of them, well almost all of them. I don't watch Miley Cyrus or Tiny Tim videos any longer.

I suppose you could argue the merits of special, yet I perceive the term as subjective and elusive to quantify as "chocolate ice cream tastes better than vanilla," or my "dad is tougher than your dad? It's difficult to beat chocolate anything, however.

Anyway, one week after my forty-third birthday, I began my jaunt of six miles to our country home. I left around 6:30 from my job as a bill collector at the Caring Collection Agency, geared up to engage one of the sudden, blinding December snowstorms that so often attack our quaint little town of North Star along Northern Michigan's west coast.

Sometimes these storms bring a sense of excitement to the community, suffusing the good cheer of the season and an old-fashioned Christmas theme into a more memorable Christmas experience. I suppose for some, it did exactly that. In retrospect, *I* wish it had been eighty degrees that evening.

As for my place of employment, I know what you're thinking; Caring Collection Agency? What hogwash! The name of our company may very well contain as diametrically opposed ideas as any in the English language. Kind of like signing up for one of those all of the pasta and candy diets that guarantee you'll lose five pounds a week. Or too much baseball. Or too many books. None of those ideas compute. However, we are as real as our company name implies. We *do* care, but more about that later.

There were two weeks remaining until glorious Christmas morning and I was contemplating what final gifts would be appropriate for my wife of twenty-one years, Kara, and our chocolate Lab, Apollo.

We hadn't been able to conceive children over the years, not enough fish swimming upstream, so the dog, and a boat load of orphans in the local orphanage, were the fortunate recipient of our generous affections. The spoiled, oversized K-9 seemed to realize that fact better than the children in the home and played it to the hilt.

While we both love kids, we never really considered adoption because we always thought that God would provide us a child when the time was right. We had been wrong and now, in our middle-aged minds, we were well past prime child-rearing energy. And kids take energy, right?

As the dancing, wind-driven snowflakes bounced from my windshield like an endless swarm of pallid insects, I cranked up the stereo and began to bellow out *The Christmas Song,* accompanying the incomparable Nat King Cole, (who really didn't need my assistance, but hey, it was Christmas and I was in a charitable mood.) After a few bars, I looked into the rearview mirror and noticed the halogen lights of the vehicle behind me vacillating in a manner that often accompanies lack of control. Not a terribly encouraging trait on icy, snow-swept roads at fifty miles-per-hour.

I kept my intense vigil as the vehicle grew closer and consequently larger, much larger, moving precariously closer to my red 2000 Ford Taurus, almost blinding me in the process.

It was obviously a much bigger means of transportation than mine, and the fearful little feeling one acquires when panic replaces tension began rising up from somewhere south of my throat. I would later find out that it was a Chevy Tahoe being guided, or not guided, as the case proved out, by a teenage driver who was trying to impress his companions with his newly-discovered ability to drive in winter weather. Did I say I love kids?

Backing off the accelerator in hopes that the driver of vehicle behind me would realize the error of their way and slow down accordingly was my first mistake.

The unit appeared to pick up speed and now was literally inches from my bumper and eminent disaster for one, or both, of us. I considered tapping the brakes in that situation, but it could have done more harm than good. Moreover, what was wrong with the driver, was he blind?

Nat was still crooning while I queried through my options traveling an icy two-lane with a moronic driver behind the wheel of a large SUV fixing to become my car's proctologist and maybe mine in the process.

Those options were few.

My perspiration was now beginning to out-perform the holiday air freshener hanging from the mirror, odorizing the interior of my car with refreshing evergreen and tantalizing candy cane, with good reason; I only had about a mile before we reached the busy, major intersection drawing Hwy. 62 and Hwy. 85 together.

The traffic light at this particular junction was notoriously slow to turn and, in this weather, the hue of the light meant much less than the velocity of oncoming traffic. San Francisco driving had nothing on the likes of rural Michigan traffic or its drivers. Right of way was more like a suggestion.

I glanced to my left, eyes wider than a cartoon character, and could see a stream of headlights in the north- bound lane and to my right ranged a ten to twelve-foot drainage ditch with steep banks and tall snow banks cascading into an intimidating "V". That's when the first recoil between bumper and trunk jolted me to the next level of terror. I guess that wouldn't be terror, it would be terror two?

"Oh God," I croaked.

I guess I was hoping my pathetic plea, reeking of carnal desperation, would send an instant army of God's angels to rescue me from whatever unpleasantries destiny seemed to have ordained for me.

Don't laugh, one can hope. I was hoping my derriere off.

The next glimpse was of my wavy red hair in the rearview mirror and wondered if it would still be attached to my scalp when this was over. Or, even if my head would be, you know, would still be connected.

I wasn't overly optimistic.

The Taurus progressed into its horrifying, control less spin with my hands virtually squeezing the steering wheel into gray synthetic pulp. In the vernacular of my co-worker, Abbey Manis, I was pretty much bent over two ways from Sunday.

According to some, experts I suppose, time slows to an inexplicable creep in situations like this. I've read that it was the brains way of helping the body to survive. Apparently my brain was tired of the rest of me because a slowing of my environment was the last thing I experienced. In fact, if things had moved any faster, I would have passed out.

I'd always pretty good at keeping my limited wits in tight situations so my brain reminded me to do all of the things we were taught in the infamous drivers training course required of every high school student. I tapped the brakes, turned into the spin, swore like a sailor, and begged for the car to listen to my voice, blah, blah, blah. Nothing worked.

It became increasingly apparent that I needed an unanticipated miracle to avoid boatloads of pain...or worse. I then rushed to the most universal of defaults in times like these, I prayed like a man being ominously strapped into a Texas electric chair.

As if by some divine cue, or just sheer crappy driving by one or both of us, I received my answer almost immediately, in the form of another bone jarring thump to the Taurus's rear, compliments, of course, of the large car traversing amazingly close to my slow-spinning vehicle.

Immediately after the spontaneous slam to the right quarter panel, Old Red straightened out and the spinning segment of my road adventure was complete. I was entirely grateful. Spinning and I don't get along.

I am one of those folks that can spontaneously puke by just helping some little tike stay steady for a couple revolutions on the playground's merry-go-round. Motion sickness and I have deep-rooted love and hate relationship. I hate to puke and it loves to make me.

In any event, I barely had time to blurt out the breath I had been jealously hoarding (one never knows when the opportunity to take another may present itself and I was taking no chances) and to focus wide eyes through the snowy windshield.

I didn't care for what was next on my dance card.

This nightmare was spiraling into just that, a nightmare. I was no longer traveling along the intended route the engineer had designed for this shimmering, ice-covered asphalt ribbon. I was, instead, streaking out of control toward the twelve-foot trench that doubled as a drainage ditch, and perhaps, in this fastidious instance, a frigid underwater deathtrap.

I find it amazing how one's sense of positive thinking evolves into a disciple of Murphy's Law under circumstances such as these. I, wanting not to offend the masses concerning that paradigm, knew without a fraction of misplaced doubt, death was waiting with open arms for me. Of course, I would first have to go through the horrific act of striking the embankment and watch, in even more pointed, horrific, slow motion, as I sank slowly to the bottom of the frigid, watery trench.

Old Gabe could already feel my body temperature dropping twenty degrees. I suddenly wondered what my underwear would feel like in that environment.

Hey, think about it.

I then did what every able-bodied, macho man on the planet would resort to and covered my face, screamed like a terrified school girl, and waited for death's scythe to harvest yet another soul.

Chapter-2

IN THE PAST, WHEN I HEARD PEOPLE SPEAK OF THEIR LIVES PASSING IN front of their eyes, in perilous situations like my current predicament, I paid it little credence and passed it off as an urban legend or some old, less quantitative, wives tale.

I hate being on a roll because I was wrong again, dead wrong.

In the instant before impact, I saw much.

Hurts I had administered, wrongs I had perpetuated involving people I had never really met or, at the very least, forgotten. Intentional or not, I felt what those poor souls had felt.

My humiliation and shame involving certain contexts were driven even deeper with the knowledge of selfish desires and ambitions that really had no defined purpose, other than to fulfill some self-centered impulse. Like, for instance, the incident with the peacock feathers and my grandfather's tractor. (There will *not* be more information forthcoming on that little episode.) Even if I survive what's coming.

There were good things, too. Wonderful things.

Meeting Kara had been the very best thing to happen to me. Her undaunted support and influence had coursed through my adult life with remarkable consistency.

I saw her enchanting, beryl-green eyes gazing at me with such love that it had startled me, again. That expression, that unexplainable gaze impressed even more intently my nearly complete lack of understanding of why a woman with her undeniable physical beauty, (she is hot) and unmatched gentleness could have been drawn to someone as ordinary as me.

I heard once that we should never question the destinies that lure loving soul mates to one another, no matter what that looks like to the rest of the world. I haven't. Okay, maybe once, or three thousand times.

Or in other terms; don't knock it.

Strangely, there also appeared, in this instantaneous reflection of my rather unremarkable existence, a very young, wonderful face accompanied by one much older; almost ancient.

They were both people I knew I'd never met, but each held a countenance that radiated such eccentric familiarity, that they both caused my heart to jump.

Not the heart that pumps blood, that one was surely jumping enough already, but the one that is purely undefinable emotion. We all have it. We all covet more of it, and we all spend time denying it, at least to ourselves.

Yet, as my immediate circumstances would dictate, I really had no time to dwell on these unusual visualizations, as it were, because precipitously my stream of life-experiences and back-visions were abruptly interrupted by the loathsome collision I'd been anticipating.

The impact was . . . brilliant.

My head slammed forward at the same time my airbag deployed, countering the forward momentum of my somewhat prodigious noggin. I'm not great at physics, but even I knew this was going to hurt. Yep, it did.

I'm no boxer, but I felt like Mike Tyson had decided I was an IRS agent and began to rearrange my face. It wasn't just my pretty cheek bones either.

I heard popping and cracking as my vertebrae spoke, debating whether to put me in a wheelchair, end my life, or just make some spine wrenching chiropractor the happiest person in the fine village of North Star. I had vaguely wondered if my insurance policy included clauses that cover prolonged ventures into the realm of natural healing, or would I be calling myself from the collection agency, demanding payment for unpaid treatments? Bizarre deliberations, I admit, but, as they say . . . well, who really cares what the hell they say?

That's what was going on in the old thought process, for whatever reason.

With my head firmly encased within a nitrogen-filled nylon bag pressing entirely too fiercely, intimately sharing its somewhat putrid chemical odor on my face, I felt the car side wind after the head-on kiss, strike the bank, and rise up on the two passenger-side tires like a cartoon scene from Speed Racer. (Isn't it wondrous how he and Jeff Gordon could be twins?)

There it remained, balanced for what seemed like an eternity. I wondered what was taking so long and why fate was teasing me like this way.

By then, there had almost no question that I was already paralyzed from the neck down anyway so let's just get this debacle over with. But fate, as it turned out, had other plans and the car dropped, as gently and ceremoniously as possible, back to all fours, crunching snow and ice while completing its unlikely journey to stability.

I took a few seconds to evaluate what had just happened. Good God, I was alive. I hadn't gone down the Valley of Ice. In fact, I hadn't even hung on the precipice of the sinister ice hell just feet away.

Maybe my desperate pleading to a God I didn't know had worked. Or maybe my Irish luck had finally worked for once. Either way, air bag and all, I knew I was a live.

Elation over that truth hardly covered the significance of that unexpected gift.

A moment later, I made the hardest decision I had ever made to date, well, other than evoking all my will not too wet myself. I decided to get out of Old Red, but that meant I'd have to move my left leg, something quadriplegic's couldn't accomplish.

I gathered every ounce of intestinal fortitude, and then gave it my best shot and—nothing happened.

My mind ran berserk with thoughts regarding the difficulty, or lack of, with moving one's leg. After all, I had been doing it a hell of a long time, right? Unless, of course, one has lost all sense of motor control and is destined to become dependent on wheelchairs, church ladies, and Meals-On-Wheels.

Not relishing the thought of Kara leaving me and being forced to beg for food, I gathered my remaining courage and attempted to wiggle my right toes and...they frittered around my size ten wingtip. I had hope.

Bravery coursed through my veins like an illegal drug and I attempted, successfully, to move my arms and hands. Everything was working except for my left leg. Three out of four ain't bad.

One can't imagine the feeling of pure relief that moment rendered. I felt warm tears gather, and then I manned-up and sent them packing, nearly.

By now the pallid airbag had deflated at a rapid pace, allowing my eyes access to the real world, and more importantly, more sweet air rushed to my lungs.

Reaching out my left hand with new-found confidence, I dialed the dome light to on and could immediately see the reason my left leg hadn't responded to my effort. The emergency brake foot pedal had dropped down against my leg, pinning it fast against the inside firewall. It had apparently come loose from the fabulous assembling that American-made autos are known to perform.

Gingerly, and with less pain than I had anticipated, I reached the foot pedal's steel linkage and pulled. It gradually, as I exerted increased effort, moved to the right, just enough, to allow my calf well-earned freedom. I rubbed the pinched area and immediately thought that Thor would have been proud of my exhibition involving super-human strength. On the other hand, he probably wouldn't have rubbed his calf with half the enthusiasm I had.

I took a moment to be thankful to a God Who may or may not be real there for keeping me safe. I learned a long time ago to cover as many bases as possible. There was no mistaken that I was here and lucky it was so. This little incident had had the potential to be something other than just a well-embellished story to entertain my friends with for the next few months. Far more

With everything working well enough, I decided that my blood pressure had dropped to an acceptable level and it was now time to survey the damage rendered to my long-time faithful Big Red. I pulled the door handle, heard the hinges creak like some trap door scene in a grade "B" horror flick, and stop at about half its full range.

"Crap," I muttered.

Always something, have you noticed?

I sighed, retrieved black leather, fur-lined gloves (necessary apparel during the frozen winters of Michigan) from the floor and began the ordeal of squeezing my one-hundred and ninety-pound frame through the opening. I keep myself in fairly good shape so it wasn't going to be too daunting of a task. Don't get me wrong, at forty-three, I had no offers to model naked, (well, there was that one incident at the office Christmas party a couple of years back. I refused on the grounds that the security cameras were still very much functional), but I could still get around a softball field pretty well.

As I exited the car, the snow still fell and was swirling gently, although not as intently as a few minutes, I prior glanced around and observed slow-moving headlights shining from both directions, and for a moment, those lights caught the splendor of huge, dancing flakes reflecting against the evening's darkened background. Dazzling. Interesting the beauty one can observe in even the most stressful of situations. Then again, my stress was over. I'd made it.

Tiptoeing with ice-induced caution toward the front of the vehicle. I could see that the hood, bumper, and engine were tangled and now were somewhat related to an accordion. It was a minor miracle the door opened at all. Perchance it would have been better, for me, if it hadn't. I guess, from my point of view, the jury is still out on that one.

Cursing in my house had been a no-no. I didn't care at that moment. I cursed. Well, mayhap. I don't know, is "oh, horse balls" cursing?

My deceased mom, bless her heart, had infused into her three children the principle of "if you can't say something nice, shut up" so growing up there weren't many idle words floating around the Stark homestead. I didn't think even she would mind, given my current state of affairs. I know that because I heard her say the same thing when my father had come home with two new Lab puppies one Christmas. She also had said something to him about not getting close to her for a month. I figured out what that meant a little later in life.

I'm fairly new to the whole cell phone culture so it took a moment for me to realize I didn't need to flag down a vehicle, instead I could just pull the little flip toy, (I had one that reminded me of an original Star Trek communicator), out of my coat pocket and call 911. I reached in, pulled the black and silver phone out, flipped it open with Kirk-like flair, and straightaway dropped it into ten inches of cold, wet snow. I didn't have Abbey Mani's flair or talent for double cursing. I gave it a shot anyway.

Twisting toward the general direction the phone had done a three and one-half gainer; I spotted the severely muted blue light throbbing just beneath a bank of white.

Realizing I could still get home for hot chocolate and some trumped up explanation to Kara that I need special treatment tonight, I bent to retrieve the accursed thing, as any reasonable person would. That was my second mistake.

As I rummaged through the snow, I swiftly realized that my world was becoming ever so much brighter. Like football-field flood lights all being switched on simultaneously.

I stood straight up and began to gyrate toward the perceived source of that light. Before I completed that turn, the night was shattered by the heart-stopping scream of dual air horns speaking to my ears from a location entirely too close to exist as a good thing.

By reflex, I cupped my ears and turned just in time to see the jackknifed semi-tractor skidding directly toward me.

There was simply no time to move or even scream, and oddly, no time to see my life flash before me for the second time in a ten minute stretch. Not even sufficient time for an attempt at a triple curse as I watched helplessly as fifty Thousand pounds of steel and glass slammed into me. The impact drove me into Big Red with as much resistance as ten-ounce rag doll and with all of the authority the runaway vehicle could muster. I felt everything, and then nothing.

As I think back, just before my world succumbed to the dark, I wondered how Kara and Apollo would take this.

Then *I* was over.